PRAISE FOR *RED THREAD OF FATE*

"I couldn't put this book down. A masterful story of sorrow, secrets, and unexpected romance. Ms. Butler writes with humor, compassion, and honesty. Simply wonderful. I can't wait for more from this gifted author."

—Kristan Higgins, *New York Times* bestselling author of *Pack Up the Moon*

"Lyn Liao Butler does it again! I was anticipating Butler's second book after devouring *The Tiger Mom's Tale*, and *Red Thread of Fate* did not disappoint! With a poignant tale and beautiful prose, Butler once again whisks us onto a powerful journey of loss, sorrow, but ultimately a journey of quiet strength."

—Jesse Q. Sutanto, critically acclaimed author of *Dial A for Aunties*

"Lyn Liao Butler is quickly becoming a go-to author for heartfelt, complex stories. *Red Thread of Fate* has everything—family secrets, mystery, identity. The rare blend of suspense and humor makes this story hard to put down. I can't wait to read what Butler writes next!"

—Saumya Dave, author of *What a Happy Family*

"A heartfelt contemplation on the course of our lives—what is fate, what is the result of the choices we make—coupled with a central mystery that will keep you reading late into the night. It seems Lyn Liao Butler's fate is to entertain with absorbing stories and compelling characters that linger long after the final page."

—Steven Rowley, *New York Times* bestselling author of *The Guncle*

PRAISE FOR *THE TIGER MOM'S TALE*

"*The Tiger Mom's Tale* is a heartfelt, delightful read. Lyn Liao Butler's story of Taiwanese and American identity had me turning pages and laughing (and drooling over the delicious descriptions of food)."
    —Charles Yu, author of *Interior Chinatown*, winner of the 2020 National Book Award

"Unembellished and forthright, *The Tiger Mom's Tale* is a touching story that illuminates intricacies of race, ethnicity, traditions, and stereotypes . . . Filled with potential book club discussion topics and perfect for fans of YA novels by Jenny Han, *The Tiger Mom's Tale* will unleash timely dialogue about identity, family secrets, and cultural divides."
    —*BookPage*

"Sharp and humorous, *The Tiger Mom's Tale* is a scenic debut novel with a cast of complicated characters sure to bring laughter and discussion to your next book club. I can't wait to read what Lyn Liao Butler writes next!"
    —Tif Marcelo, *USA Today* bestselling author of *The Key to Happily Ever After*

"An absolutely absorbing story . . . *The Tiger Mom's Tale* grabbed me from page one and never let me go. I highly recommend this book to fiction readers, especially those who like plucky, get-back-up-again female leads, stories set in New York City, and those with settings on less familiar terrain."
    —Fresh Fiction

"Filled with mouthwatering descriptions of food, a messy family, and a bit of mystery, this is a heartwarming story of one woman's search for her place in the world."

—Bust.com

SOMEONE
ELSE'S
LIFE

OTHER TITLES BY LYN LIAO BUTLER

SOMEONE

ELSE'S

LIFE

A Thriller

LYN LIAO BUTLER

THOMAS & MERCER

Text copyright © 2023 by Lyn Liao Butler
All rights reserved.

Published by Thomas & Mercer, Seattle

www.apub.com

Amazon, the Amazon logo, and Thomas & Mercer are trademarks of Amazon.com, Inc., or its affiliates.

ISBN-13: 9781662501081
ISBN-10: 1662501080

Cover design by Ploy Siripant

Printed in the United States of America

For Jim, my Fireman

1

Laptop ANNIE file

My life has been a nightmare for years, with one bad thing happening after another. And I've let it happen, struggling to keep my head up. But I'm finally ready to take back control of my real life. In case something happens to me, I'm documenting it all here for you, so that you understand why I'm doing this when you find it.

This is for my son, to make sure he's taken care of and finally living the life he was born to. I'm his mother. I feel in my soul that what I've planned is the best thing for him. I know some people will think I'm wrong, but I know I'll convince you that I'm right. My son deserves to know my love, to know me. I don't want him to be afraid of me. I want him to trust me, so that he realizes who his mommy is. That I love him so much. I really do.

But the darkness still pulls at me, trying to drown me. I have to stay alive, not give in to it. Stay strong and focused so that everything goes as planned. Because it's finally time that something good happens to me and to him. It's our turn.

I thought everything would fall into place once I got to Kauai but it hasn't. Bad things are still trying to drag me down but I'm not going to let them anymore. I don't really know what I'm doing, but I know you are the key. You are the one who can give me what I need. For the first time in years, I have a clear goal and I will fight with all my might to reach that goal. It's what any good mother would do for her son.

2

The moment Annie Lin opened the door of the ohana, she wanted to slam it shut again. Their neighbor Kalani Pang waved at her from across the street with as much enthusiasm as a teenage cheerleader.

"Annie! Aloha!" Kalani's booming voice wafted across the warm air toward Annie, along with the fragrance of the plumeria flowers that dotted Annie's father's property. He'd been letting Annie and her family stay in the guest cottage behind the main house since they'd moved to Kauai from New York after the new year.

Annie closed her eyes briefly, taking a breath to brace herself. It wasn't even ten in the morning yet, and she was still groggy from a restless night. She opened her eyes and turned to run back inside (manners be damned), only to slam into her son and husband on their way out.

"Mommy, what're you doing?" Finn asked, squinting up at her in the bright sunlight. He hugged his bear, Hot Chocolate, close to him. He never went anywhere without it, not since that August day almost six months ago.

Annie didn't answer and glanced over her shoulder. She stifled a groan when she saw Kalani crossing the street toward them. Their neighbor's chipper energy was soul-sucking, and Annie's soul was already as hollow as a GI tract after a colonoscopy. (Thank goodness she still had a few years at forty-two for one of those.) Add a hangover and she'd much rather have opened the door to find a serial killer, to be honest.

"You want to go grab a coffee?" Kalani asked when she'd made it to their side. She pouted her full lips into a smile. "You've been living here for over a month and we still haven't gotten together." The sunlight bounced off Kalani's shiny black hair so that the waves flowing to her low back rippled like lava down an active volcano.

"I can't. I'm on my way to volunteer at the shelter." Glad for a legitimate excuse, Annie raised her hands to her own dull black hair, which she'd wound up into a messy bun.

"Your wife's too busy for me," Kalani said to Brody, who was watching their exchange with an amused smile.

"Oh, I'm . . ." Annie started to say but stopped when Kalani burst into laughter.

"I'm just kidding." Kalani's hair swayed as she laughed. "But seriously, we need to get together soon. Our kids might get married one day." She beamed at Finn. "Want to come over when Leila gets home from preschool?"

Finn had gone over to play with Kalani's three-year-old daughter a few times without Annie. In another life, she would have enjoyed getting to know Kalani while their kids played. But now there was no way she could handle the social niceties needed to engage with the woman during a playdate. She would rather go an entire year without alcohol. Wait, no, she wouldn't. She'd need the wine.

"Can't," Finn said. "Daddy's taking me to . . ." He broke off and glanced at Brody, his forehead creased and bottom lip caught between his teeth. He carried too much burden for a little boy who had just turned four. Annie's heart broke a little and she reached out, but Brody had already laid a hand on Finn's shoulder and drawn him close.

The smile that Kalani flashed at them was as bright as the yellow hibiscus and colorful bird-of-paradise flowers that lined the walkway from the lanai to the driveway. "Okay, well, then have a great day, all of you." She pointed at Annie, who froze. "And we'll catch up soon. You can't avoid me forever."

With another tinkling laugh, she turned and practically glided down the driveway. Annie watched Kalani cross the street to her house hidden behind a line of swaying palm trees. "Busted," she muttered under her breath.

Brody chuckled as Finn wandered away, talking to his bear. "You still haven't gotten together with her?" He gave Annie a questioning look as he locked the door of the ohana.

"She's one of those enthusiastic types. Way too cheerful." Annie looked away, not wanting to see the disappointment in his eyes.

Brody heaved a sigh and turned to her. "You don't like her just 'cause she's cheerful?" He crossed his arms over his broad chest, causing her eyes to focus on his sternum. It had once been her favorite place to lay her head. When was the last time she'd done that?

"We have nothing in common." Annie gave a shrug and looked down, noticing a small box sitting by the front door. Where had that come from? She didn't remember seeing it before.

"You did once." Brody's voice softened. "You used to be like her. Friendly and . . ."

Annie wrinkled her nose when he trailed off. "And now I'm just a grumpy old potato? I think I'm a fucking blast of sunshine, thank you very much."

Brody's mouth twitched, and then he gave in and laughed, reaching out to draw her into a hug. "You sure are my fucking blast of sunshine." He leaned down to kiss her on the top of her head, and Annie relaxed into him.

She'd missed this. The closeness they'd once had, when she couldn't wait to hug and kiss him. She'd destroyed all that the past few years with her grumpiness and sour moods. She needed to try harder with both Brody and Finn. Moving to paradise was supposed to be a new beginning, their chance to make things better again. Kauai had always made her heart happy in the past, and she was determined to absorb the Aloha spirit, even if it killed her.

"It'd be nice for you to make some friends here. Maybe even get a job." Brody's voice rumbled in his chest, and Annie pulled away.

"Who'd have me? I'm a failure. A washed-up ex-dancer who lost her company and studio." She turned and focused her eyes on Finn, who was walking around the backyard.

"You're not a failure." Brody's voice was firm and she melted, just a little. Her husband had stood by her these last few years while Annie had dealt with one blow after another. He had the patience of a saint. If the roles were reversed, Annie wasn't sure she would have been as understanding as he'd been with her.

She turned and met Brody's eyes. "I know it's been almost four years. I'm trying, okay?" She pursed her lips, fighting the tears that threatened.

Brody reach out and brushed a thumb under her eye, catching the lone tear that fell. But before he could say anything, Finn shouted at them, "We're going to be late, Daddy."

Annie gave her husband a tremulous smile. "You'd better go."

They shared a look, and then both glanced at the main house, where Annie's father lived with Annie's younger sister, Sam, and Sam's six-year-old daughter, Cameron. Annie's father didn't believe in therapy, and his Taiwanese family did not speak of mental health issues. Annie and Brody had an unspoken agreement not to let her father know that Finn was seeing someone after the incident back in New York.

"Finn still won't talk about it." Brody dropped his voice. "He's almost emotionless when he talks to the therapist. Like . . . he's not there. The only time he seems upset by what happened is at night. The nightmares."

Even though she knew her father couldn't hear them from inside the house, she lowered her voice too.

"But he likes the therapist?" Guilt twisted in Annie's gut that she'd never taken Finn to an appointment. Years of growing up in her Asian family had made her resistant to therapy.

Annie had been born in Taiwan. Her First Auntie, her father's oldest sister, was always going on about how smart her kids were, how they weren't weak and didn't bring shame on her, unlike—and here she always dropped her voice to a whisper, as if talking about something dirty—Fourth Auntie's daughter, who'd been hospitalized after attempting suicide. Annie's mom had been born on Oahu and was more progressive, but she wasn't around anymore.

Brody nodded as Finn came running back to them.

Finn slipped his hand into Brody's and tugged, gazing at his father with trust. "Let's go. You said we could have shaved ice after."

Watching them together, Annie couldn't deny a stab of jealousy at their bond. She reached out and took Finn's other hand, wanting to be a part of their circle. Finn held her hand tightly but wouldn't meet her eyes. This was their relationship. Damaged, just like Annie's heart had been ever since her dog, Lili, and her mother had died four years ago, just a few months apart. Why couldn't she be easy and comfortable around Finn, the way Brody was? Finn was her son too, yet so often, she didn't know how to make him happy.

Brody picked Finn up, breaking Annie's connection to him, and tossed him in the air. "You're getting too heavy for this." He groaned as Finn giggled in delight, clutching his bear. Brody turned to Annie. "We'll see you later? Maybe do something special?"

Annie nodded, puzzled about what he meant by "special," and then on impulse, she stood on her tiptoes—Brody was six one to her five two—and planted a kiss on his lips.

When he responded, she leaned into him, thinking how much she'd missed this, until Finn screeched, "Ew, stop kissing Mommy. We have to go."

Annie and Brody broke apart and laughed.

They were about to leave when she suddenly remembered the box by the door. She gestured to it. "Hey, did you put that there?"

"No," Brody said. "I thought you did. You went into the carport last night and came back with a few boxes. You said you were going to finally unpack."

Annie rubbed her forehead as she struggled to remember. Had she stumbled out to the storage area last night? What else had she done that she didn't remember today?

Not wanting him to see her concern, she put a smile on her face and waved as he and Finn got into his car and drove away. Then she crouched down and opened the box. Her forehead furrowed as she pulled out a filthy purple and white gardening glove. Turning it over in her hand, she was just wondering why anyone would keep a dirty glove when she realized what she was holding. She found its mate in the box and pulled one onto her hand, not at all surprised when it fit her like a . . . well, glove.

Annie sat heavily on the ground. This had been her favorite pair of gardening gloves but had disappeared a while ago at their lake house in New York. She'd had a habit of taking them off when she worked in the flower garden at the front of the house and then having to hunt them down. Until one day, when she couldn't find them anywhere. What were they doing here?

Taking the glove off, Annie looked in the box again. She pulled out a small blue Paw Patrol shirt of Finn's that she'd also thought they'd lost. Her hands shaking, she reached in and found a stuffed pink pig with one ear chewed to pieces and stuffing coming from a hole in its side. Lili's toy. She dropped it on the ground next to Finn's shirt as a shiver went down her spine. She looked in the box again and found the lake bumper magnet that used to be on her car in New York. She'd thought it had fallen off, but here it was, in Kauai.

How had these things gotten here? She had absolutely no recollection of finding these missing items and bringing them to Kauai.

Dropping everything back in the box, she quickly stood, her breath catching. She was fine. There had to be a good explanation. But she didn't have time to think about it. She was already late for the shelter. She walked down the driveway, pausing to look down their street, which was on the banks of the Wailua River, before getting into her car.

A flash of white at the end of the dead-end street caught her eyes. It was a car doing a three-point turn. As she watched the car turn right, a sense of déjà vu washed over her—she'd done this before, watched a white car drive away. But where? And when? She rubbed at the goose bumps that had sprung up on her arms and darted to her car, slamming the door with more force than was necessary. Putting her forehead down on the steering wheel, she closed her eyes. What was happening to her mind?

3

Annie opened the washing machine at the Kauai Humane Society and threw in some soiled towels and bedding. After adding soap and bleach, she started the machine and then took clean towels out of the dryers, folding and placing them on the shelves behind her. Laundry done for now, she headed back to the kennels.

Dogs of all sizes and colors came running up to their doors as she passed, some wagging their tails, some barking and jumping for attention. She greeted each one until she stopped in front of the one who'd stolen her heart. Frito, the saddest-looking dog she'd ever seen.

"Want to go in the play yard?"

The black terrier mix didn't respond from his position on the ground, but Pickles, the pit bull mix around the corner, barked and started whining.

Annie laughed and called to Pickles, "I already took you out today. Next time, okay?"

She unlatched the door to Frito's kennel and slipped inside, shutting it firmly behind her. "Hey, buddy," she said in a soft voice. "You still depressed?" She crouched down next to him and slowly reached out a hand. When he didn't flinch or move, she laid it on his back and started petting him. He was a year old and had come in as an owner surrender last week. Pollie, the volunteer coordinator, had told her he hadn't perked up at all.

"I get it. I really do. Come on—you're going out whether you like it or not. This kennel is too depressing." Annie held out the harness in her hand and slipped it over his head.

Once in the play yard, the medium-size dog sniffed the grass and did his business. Then he stood so still that she bent down to make sure he was breathing. She took his head between her hands and looked into his eyes, startled by the depth of sadness she saw in them.

"Oh, Frito. It's okay. Why don't we sit in the shade? It's so hot today." She pulled her red volunteer T-shirt away from her sticky body as she led him to the bench in the play yard.

He surprised her by jumping up next to her. Even though he didn't look at Annie, she was happy when he leaned into her side ever so slightly.

She put an arm around him. "I know how you feel. My life sucks too." She glanced down, amused that she was carrying on a one-sided conversation with a depressed dog. Talk about hitting bottom.

"I had a dog once, a mini dachshund named Lili. She was a smooth black and tan. I got her when I was single and living in New York City. We did everything together. She was my constant companion." Was it her imagination, or was Frito leaning closer?

"I miss her so much." Annie wrapped both arms around Frito and hugged him close. He didn't move, but he didn't resist her either. "I know Brody's been wanting a dog again. But I just couldn't." She looked into his eyes. "First Lili, then my mom, both gone the same year. Then my dance company and studio. I think a part of me died that year." Frito stared at her as if hypnotized. Annie lowered her voice. "My panic attacks are back. And I think I'm doing things I don't remember."

Frito didn't break eye contact. Annie released a shaky breath. "Don't tell anyone, but I have to take antianxiety medication. And sleeping pills sometimes. I feel as if I'm losing my mind, like I'm going to lose it at any moment."

She was amazed at the rush of relief she felt at saying this out loud. She refused to talk to a therapist, but staring into this dog's soft brown eyes, she realized how tightly wound she'd been ever since Finn's life had been threatened. There were days when life passed in a blur, the medication making her fuzzy. But without the pills, when those attacks hit, she was convinced she was dying.

Suddenly, a loud shriek split the air, making her jump. Frito sprang off the bench, his attention turned to the noise.

"Come on," Annie said, wiping the sweat from her brow. "Let's see what's going on."

They walked back in to find a couple, along with their young daughter, standing in front of Pickles's kennel. Pollie was telling them about the Shelter Dogs on Field Trips program, which allowed visitors to check a dog out for the day, giving the dogs a chance to spend the day outside the shelter. There was always the hope that they would find their forever family while on a field trip, but at least it gave the dogs a chance to be socialized and exercised.

The little girl, who looked to be about six, was jumping up and down as Pickles studied her, his head cocked to the side. "I want to take this dog out."

Pollie laughed and called to one of the animal-care technicians, "Can you get Pickles ready for a field trip?" She turned back to the family and brought her hands together in a gesture of thanks. "Mahalo for taking him out. I'll bring you up front to get the paperwork done and get your bag with treats, water, a towel, and poop bags."

While Pollie took care of the family, Annie put Frito back in his kennel from the outside. The kennels opened from both ends, so people could see the dogs from inside or out. He collapsed on the floor like a sad-orphaned seal and her heart tugged. She sat on the cold cement floor of the kennel and he walked over, leaning his weight against her.

They stayed like that until Pollie came back. She looked at them from the door on the outside. "Aw, he likes you. That's the first time I've seen him respond to anyone."

Annie rubbed Frito's back. "I think we get each other."

Pollie grinned. "Maybe you should take him home. As a Valentine's gift."

"Oh shit." Annie slapped her forehead. "Is today Valentine's Day?"

"Um, yeah." Pollie snickered. "Did you forget? You're married, right?"

"Not for long," Annie muttered under her breath, causing Pollie to grin. "Shit, shit, shit." So that was what Brody had meant earlier about something "special."

"Why don't you adopt Frito? Best present ever." Pollie looked pleased with herself.

Annie's eyes widened. "You know what? That's actually a great idea." She stared at Frito, and could have sworn his ears perked up. Was it possible this dog was the answer to pulling herself out of the fog she'd been living in?

"I was just kidding." Pollie's laughter died and she gaped at Annie.

Annie and Frito looked at each other, and she knew she was taking him home. "I'm adopting Frito. What do I have to do?"

"Wait, you're serious? Don't you want to discuss it with your husband first?" Pollie stared at Annie, her mouth open. Her hands pulled at the end of her ponytail.

"No. It will be his Valentine's surprise." Annie knew this was the right decision.

"You just have to fill out an application if you're serious."

"I am." Annie stood and brushed off her shorts. "Can I take him home today?"

"Yes." Pollie gave her a hard look. "If you're sure?"

"I am. Let's go fill out the application." Annie let herself out of the kennel and headed to the front with Pollie trailing after her. Brody would be glad, and Finn would have a friend. Frito would have a family, and maybe he would fill that hole in her heart and she wouldn't have to self-medicate with pills and wine to go to sleep at night.

◆ ◆ ◆

While Brody and Finn had been happy about the dog, Frito had ruined the dinner Brody had brought home for Valentine's Day by getting into the container of Korean kalbi short ribs. Then he'd chewed up Brody's favorite Mets cap and one of his flip-flops. She'd taken him out of the house this morning before he could chew anything else and make Brody change his mind about adopting a dog. They were now on Kealia Beach, watching the surfers and enjoying the strong breeze that made Annie's hair dance, cooling her off.

After walking up and down the beach dodging waves for half an hour, they stopped and she sat on a fallen tree branch. Annie watched the waves crash against the shore before the water ebbed back out to the ocean. Her toes dug into the sand, and she took in a lungful of the sweet, humid air. Something about Kauai always filled her with renewed energy. She was hoping some of that energy would hit her soon.

She rubbed Frito on the head and realized he was still covered in the red dirt that was so prevalent in Kauai. She'd have to give him a bath later. But she could see what a healthy coat he had, as black as the marley dance floor she'd had in her studio.

"That's it!" She sat up straight. "Marley. I think that's a good name for you." He never responded to Frito, and Brody and Finn had agreed they should change his name.

The very tip of his tail moved. Was that a wag? She'd never seen him wag his tail.

Encouraged, she said again, "Marley?"

And again, his tail moved, the whole thing this time. Then he licked her face.

"Oh, Marley." She hugged him, and joy burst through her body. Everything would be okay. She had a dog to love again. "Let's go give you a bath, Marley."

There was a spring in her step as they walked back to the car. After securing Marley in the back seat, she got behind the wheel and pulled out of her spot. Driving slowly toward the exit, she hummed to the music on the radio, suddenly filled with an optimism she hadn't had in a while. Maybe she'd go house hunting with Finn tomorrow while Brody was at work. And look to get Finn into a preschool.

From the corner of her eye, she caught a glimpse of something black bearing down on her. She slammed on the brakes, her hand automatically hitting the horn, but it was too late. An SUV that was pulling out of its parking spot backed into Annie's side of the car. It screeched to a halt, and then the driver pulled the car forward.

Annie sat still for a moment. Then she got out, after looking back to make sure Marley was okay. She walked over to the driver of the other car, who had gotten out as well.

"Hey, you backed into my car." That was all Annie managed to get out before the older woman began screaming.

"I did not! I stopped before I hit your car. This is a brand-new car. It has a sensor that tells me there's a car behind me, and I stopped before I hit you."

Taken aback by the woman's attitude, Annie let her voice rise. "You hit my car. I felt it." The woman continued to yell out denials, and Annie threw up her hands. "You hit me. Stop yelling."

The woman pointed. "There's not a dent on your car. *I didn't hit you.*"

Annie inspected her car and had to admit there was no dent. But the simple fact of the matter was the woman had hit her, and instead of apologizing and discussing it like a rational human being, she was screaming at Annie like a banshee. Annie's blood began to boil. "You didn't hit it hard enough to make a dent, but you did run into me."

"You're crazy. I didn't. Move your car. *Now.* I need to leave." The woman waved her arms in the air, her face red and her mouth drawn down in an ugly snarl.

"I'm not the one who's crazy." Annie took a deep breath. She couldn't do this. She couldn't engage with someone who wasn't rational. She could either call the police and waste a lot of time filing a report, or she could walk away before she lost it.

She turned without another word. Biting her lip hard, Annie got back into her car. She pulled away and turned left out of the lot. But she made it only a few minutes before her nose prickled. Knowing she needed to pull over, she stopped at the first safe place, in front of the Saint Catherine Cemetery, and gave in to her tears.

Why was the world so intent on tearing her down? Just when she was feeling optimistic, feeling great about rescuing a dog, that ugly incident had to happen. She was shaken by the woman screaming at her when the woman had clearly hit her. And why was she getting so upset? The old Annie would have laughed it off, knowing the woman was completely irrational. But this new Annie took everything so personally it was as if the woman had physically attacked her.

Her breath quickened, and she felt that tingling sensation in her fingers and knew a panic attack was starting. She grabbed for her purse and pulled out her Xanax bottle, gripping it tightly as she tried to control her breathing. She'd been prescribed the antianxiety meds the year her life fell apart and she'd had her first panic attack in the subway. The attacks had lessened over the years, but when Finn's life had been in danger last summer, they'd returned with a vengeance. Now she always had the bottle with her, as if the act of carrying the pills would ward off those moments of panic when her heart felt like it would stop beating. No, she wouldn't go to therapy, but yes, she would rely on pharmaceuticals. Because a panic attack was a physical thing, and the drugs did wonders to keep her body from failing her.

As her heart raced, her vision tunneled, and she could no longer breathe. Frantically, she yanked open the door, desperate for air. When her body finally responded and she could breathe again, she flopped back against her seat. Tears dripped from her eyes, but the panic attack had her in its throes and she couldn't even reach up to brush them away. She stayed like that for what felt like hours, battling her terror and the feeling she was dying. She knew she should take at least a half of a Xanax, but she couldn't move.

A wet nose nudged her neck. Marley was straining against his seat belt so he could reach into the front seat. He gazed at her steadily until she was finally able to move. She twisted back to put her arms around his head and kissed him as her heart rate slowed. They stayed like that, listening to the traffic whizzing by, until she was calm again.

Then Annie took a deep breath and screamed as loud as she could. Marley didn't move, didn't flinch from the sound. Her grip on him tightened. She had to get it together. She had to.

4

Annie studied Finn, who was playing with his cars on the floor. They'd just come home from looking at two possible houses with a real estate agent, who'd kept calling her Mrs. Devlin. Annie hadn't changed her last name when she got married but hadn't bothered to correct the agent.

She rubbed the side of her head. After the scene with the screaming woman yesterday, she'd popped half a Xanax before driving home and then, as soon as she got to the ohana, a whole one. And she'd taken a sleeping pill when two glasses of wine hadn't made her sleepy. Which was why she'd woken up this morning in a fuzzy blur, something that was becoming all too common lately.

Brody was at work, and it was just the two of them. Maybe if they did something fun together, Finn would stop looking at her with those worried eyes.

"Do you want to go to the beach?"

"Yes!" Finn's face lit up, and for a moment, Annie glowed from the inside. She could do this. She could make her son love her as much as he loved his father.

They changed into their bathing suits and then drove down to Lydgate Beach Park, less than five minutes away. As they walked over the expanse of grass from the car to the beach, some of the chickens that roamed freely all over Kauai followed them. Finn ran next to a mother with three little chicks, and Annie smiled at his delight.

She found a spot for them on the sand, and while she spread the blanket and opened the beach chairs, Finn finally tore himself away from the chicks. He grabbed his pail and shovel and ran to the water's edge, only about twenty yards away. Annie kept an eye on him as she sat back in her chair, feeling the sun warm her skin and her hair catch the wind. For a second, she closed her eyes, letting the sounds of the ocean wash over her. This was why they had come to Hawaii.

When she opened them again and didn't see Finn, she shot up straight in the chair. Her heart pounded, and it was just like that day in August: the disorientation, the sweaty palms, and the panic in her body that spread like poison in her veins. Even all these months later, the same feeling of dread made her fingers tingle, her vision darken, as she frantically searched for Finn and called out his name.

Just as she was about to surrender to the darkness, her eyes finally found her son's familiar form huddled near one of the rock walls. She let out a huge breath but remained rooted to the spot, her hair now blowing wildly around her face. She wanted nothing more than to rush forward and scoop Finn up in her arms, reassuring herself that he was fine. But the panic attack made her immobile.

Would she ever get over this fear of something happening to Finn on her watch? Brody had never once hinted at blaming her, but she knew he must. How did other mothers do it? Look at that woman over there, reading a book and not paying attention to her daughter, who was sitting waist-deep in the water. Granted, the water was calm, since the enclosed ponds created by two rock walls provided a safe haven from the ocean waves, perfect for kids. But anything could happen, and yet the mother just continued reading as if she didn't have a care in the world.

When she could finally move again, Annie stood up. "Do you want help building a sandcastle?" she shouted to Finn as he came running back to her.

Finn halted, squinting in her direction, and shook his head. They looked at each other for a moment, and she wondered again why being with him was such hard work. She loved her son so much, but she was so awkward with him.

He broke eye contact and walked over to a little girl wading in the water with her father. The children started digging in the sand, and Annie sank back down in her chair. Just then, her phone rang, blaring the theme song from *Three's Company*.

It was her father. His gruff voice came over the phone: "Annie-ah? You out?" He always spoke in Taiwanese to his daughters.

"I'm at the beach." She tucked her hair behind her ears.

"We need eggs."

Annie waited, but that was all he said. She sighed. Why was it so hard for him to talk to her? Had she inherited this inability to talk to Finn from him? "I'll pick some up on the way home."

"Good." A moment of silence, and then he said, "I'll make herbal chicken for you tonight. You don't look good." And then he hung up without waiting for an answer.

Annie grimaced. She hated the herbal chicken, heavy with cooking wine, that her father thought was the cure-all for everything. She stared at her phone and wondered how it was that her younger sister, Sam, could carry on whole conversations with him, yet he couldn't even say goodbye to her. But Sam had always been Baba's girl. Just like their older sister, Jeannie, was Mama's girl. Which left Annie in the middle, no one's girl.

Annie looked up as Finn ran toward her, kicking up sand.

"Where's your new friend going?" she asked him, gesturing toward the girl walking away from the beach with her father.

"She had to go to the bathroom. But we're going to build a sand-castle when she gets back. She said I could use her big bucket for now." He pointed to a pile of beach toys near them on the sand.

"That sounds like fun." Annie gazed at him, marveling again that she and Brody had made such a perfect little boy.

He beamed at her, and her heart gave a leap. "Thanks for coming to the beach with me, Mommy." He reached out and wrapped his little arms around her neck, and she pulled him in, breathing in the smell of his neck—salt, suntan lotion, and sunbaked little boy.

He pulled away and ran for the big bucket before she could say anything. Annie watched him run past the woman to her left, who was sitting on a blanket with her face shielded by a large floppy hat. Annie put one hand on her heart. Coming to Kauai had been the right decision. Even though Finn still had nightmares, maybe the sunshine and ocean waves would help him, like she hoped they would her.

Annie was so deep in her own thoughts that she didn't see what happened next. But suddenly, the woman with the floppy hat let out a shout and sprang up off her blanket.

"Watch it!" she yelled so loudly that Finn froze in his tracks. The woman brushed angrily at the sand clinging to her body. "Look what you did."

Annie ran to them. "What happened?"

"I didn't do anything." Finn stared up at her, his face blank as he reached for Annie's hand.

The woman turned and locked eyes with Annie from beneath her hat. And even though Annie couldn't really see her face, something niggled in her mind. A memory appeared briefly and then disappeared like loose sand through a sieve. Before she could figure out what was making her senses stand at attention, the woman looked away, stuffed her things into a large tote, and without another word stalked toward the vast expanse of grass that led to the villas of a hotel behind the beach. Annie stared after her, her mind racing.

Finn tugged on her hand. "Mommy? My tummy hurts."

"What?" Annie looked down at him, confused. He'd been fine just a minute ago.

He placed a hand on his stomach. "It feels funny." His forehead was scrunched.

"What's the matter?" Annie placed a hand on his forehead, although she had no idea what she was checking for. It just seemed like a motherly thing to do.

Finn started to answer, but the little girl he'd been playing with called out to him from the water's edge. He looked at her and then up at Annie, his indecision clear.

Annie stooped down in front of him. "Do you have to throw up? Poop?"

He bit his lip and shook his head. The little girl was now calling Finn's name. His face cleared and he said, "I'm fine now. I'm going to go play."

"You're sure?" Annie stood, her forehead crinkling.

Finn nodded and then ran to the water. She watched him for a moment, then turned to walk back to her chair. But something shiny in the sand caught her eye. She reached down and picked up a bracelet, sparkly black and silver beads strung on elastic with a fake rhinestone turtle charm, much like the ones they sold in all the ABC stores around Hawaii. She twirled it in her hand, remembering a similar bracelet Brody had given her when she gave birth to Finn. They'd always joked that Annie didn't like jewelry—she'd rather have the cheap bracelets and necklaces from those tourist-oriented stores than real diamonds and fancy jewelry. Brody had bought a bracelet just like this one on their last trip to Kauai and given it to her in the hospital. She'd loved it, wearing it every day until, one day, it disappeared. She hadn't thought about it in years. But this one looked just like the one she'd lost, down to the turtle charm.

Pocketing the bracelet out of sentimentality, she walked to her chair. Sinking down, she looked back in the direction the woman, no longer in view, had gone. Annie searched her mind, trying to place her. Why did she look so familiar? And why had she run away when she saw Annie?

5

When she and Finn got back from the beach after picking up eggs, her father was waiting in the driveway, looking up at the sky. Annie studied him as they got out of the car. Living in Kauai agreed with him. He was tanned, his body wiry from working in the garden and all the outdoor activities he did with Sam and Cam. He was in his seventies but easily looked to be in his early sixties. She only wished she knew how to talk to him.

"Storm coming. Tomorrow, I think." He untangled himself from Finn, who had wrapped his sandy body around his grandfather as soon as he got out of the car.

Annie looked up and realized he was right. The sky had darkened, when just a while ago, it had been sunny and bright at the beach. But she'd realized Kauai in February was like this: you never knew when it would rain. It would suddenly hit, and just as suddenly, the rain would disappear and the sun shine again.

"Nothing new." Annie shrugged.

"This different. Big storm. I feel it." There was a frown on his face.

Annie dismissed his warning, but the next day, she realized he was right. It had started raining about an hour after lunch and was steadily coming down harder, pinging against the ohana's roof. There was something ominous in the air, a gloomy feeling that made her uneasy. She paced inside the ohana, unsettled and restless.

The rain suddenly increased, pattering down so hard that it made her jump. She almost dropped the wineglass in her hand and had to use her other hand to steady it. Taking a sip of the wine to calm her heart, she yelped when the doorbell suddenly rang.

Chiding herself for being so jumpy, she placed the glass on the breakfast bar and went to the door. As soon as she opened it, she knew she shouldn't have answered. She'd watched too many episodes of *Criminal Minds* in the past, where the unsuspecting homeowner opens the door to an innocent-looking person holding a wounded animal, and then bam! The homeowner is dead. But this was Kauai, the sleepy Garden Island, for heaven's sake. Nothing bad happens in paradise, right? It was just her imagination in overdrive.

Besides, the woman standing at the door of the ohana didn't look like a criminal. She had shoulder-length dark red hair and was soaking wet. She blinked to get the rain out of her piercing green eyes and pushed her damp curls away from her face as the rain pelted down behind her.

"Can I help you?" Annie's voice came out with a tremor, and she clenched her hands together. She was home alone. Brody had gone to work at Lihue Airport, and Finn was at the main house with her father, Sam, and Cam.

"I'm so sorry to bother you. But my car died down the road and it's raining so hard? Is there any way I can come in until the rain lets up a bit?" The strange woman's sentences all ended on an up note, as if she were unsure of her words.

Annie stared, indecisive, unable to stop the gruesome scenes from *Criminal Minds* flashing through her mind. She could no longer watch the crime shows she'd loved, not since what had happened to Finn. Marley stood faithfully at her side, and she drew comfort from his presence. Was this the serial killer she'd wanted to see instead of a smiling

Kalani the other day? Was she getting her wish and this was finally when things ended for her? She wasn't sure whether she was relieved or scared. And that made her question her mental state.

The roar of the storm was making it hard for Annie to concentrate. The woman seemed harmless enough, but something was off. Annie's face scrunched up as she studied her. It was as if she knew her somehow. But that couldn't be. Yet something fluttered in her stomach as she eyed the woman up and down. She was the same height as Annie but probably at least ten years younger, and looked like someone Annie could be friends with. But why had she come to the ohana in the back, and not the main house? Annie rubbed her hands over the goose bumps on her arms.

The woman seemed to read her mind. "I went to the big house, but there was loud music playing and I don't think they heard the doorbell. I saw lights on here so thought I would try."

She paused, and Annie remembered that Sam had said they were going to have a dance party when she called before inviting Finn over. Cam was home early from school because of the storm, which was supposed to be as bad as her father had predicted yesterday. The wind howled and the rain blew into the ohana, soaking Annie and Marley. She knew she had to let the woman in. She couldn't send her back out in this. Could she?

Seeing Annie's hesitation, the other woman spoke again. "I'm sorry, I'll go. I shouldn't have bothered you."

She turned to leave, rain dripping down her face. She looked so defeated with her shoulders hunched forward and her head hanging down that Annie's heart won out over her head.

"It's okay; come in." Annie opened the door wider, hoping she wasn't going to live to regret this. If this were a TV show, she could imagine people yelling at her, "Don't let her in! Are you stupid? You're falling into her trap!" But this was real life and not a crime show.

The woman walked into the ohana, dripping water everywhere. The moment she stepped foot inside, Marley suddenly growled deep in his throat.

"Marley. What's the matter?" Annie reached out to stroke his head.

The woman halted and didn't move. Marley continued to growl, a deep rumbling in his chest.

"Stop that. Be nice." Annie ran her hand down his body and Marley quieted. The woman took off her shoes and shrugged out of her soaked windbreaker. "I'll take that for you." Annie hung the jacket on the wall hooks by the door.

The woman stepped forward and reached a hand out to Marley. The hair on his back rose as he sniffed it. As he took a careful step back, the rumbling in his chest resumed.

"He's just being protective of me," Annie said. At least, she hoped he was. She was still getting to know him and wondered whether this was how he greeted new people. "Let me get you a towel so you can dry off." She crossed to the small closet next to the bathroom, took a bright blue towel off a shelf, and held it out to the woman. "The bathroom is right here."

The ohana was really one big square, with the tiny kitchen to the left of the front door and the bedroom and bathroom to the right. The main area made up both the living and dining rooms, with a small alcove in the back, where they had placed a twin mattress on the floor for Finn.

With a smile of thanks, the woman took the towel and disappeared into the bathroom. Annie took another towel and dried herself off, before rubbing it over Marley. He shook himself when she was done and shot her a look, making her laugh. He'd stood still when she'd given him a bath outside the other day, but had stared at her with mournful eyes, as if wondering why she was putting him through this indignity. He had that same look right now.

Annie hung the towel next to the woman's wet windbreaker and walked into the kitchen. She picked up the wineglass from where she'd abandoned it on the breakfast bar when the doorbell rang and took a sip of the cabernet sauvignon. She'd been happy to have time to herself this afternoon, with Brody at work and Finn entertained in the main house. She'd vowed to stop drinking so much, but the minute Finn had been out the door with Sam, her hands had reached for the bottle of wine as if they had a mind of their own. And before she knew it, the bottle was open. She couldn't waste it, could she? She'd just have one glass. Plus, she'd had a good time with Brody and Finn earlier, so this was a celebration of sorts. Right?

She leaned against the counter and thought of the morning as she waited for the woman. She and Finn had driven down to Lihue to have breakfast with Brody at Noka Grill overlooking Kalapaki Beach before he had to go to work. She'd hoped to have a nice family moment sitting at the rooftop deck, looking down at her favorite beach on Kauai. And eventually, they did. But first, somehow, they'd ended up sniping at each other in front of Finn over french toast made with Hawaiian sweet bread for Brody, Spam fried rice for Annie, and loco moco for Finn.

It was her fault, of course. Brody had only commented on the darkening sky and how maybe he shouldn't have asked her to drive down with the storm approaching. And instead of taking it for what it was, a man concerned about his wife and child, she'd been offended, thinking Brody was saying that she didn't know how to keep their son safe. She'd caught herself in midsentence, noting how shrill her voice was and wondering what had happened to them. Why couldn't they have a simple conversation without her turning it into World War III? What kind of example was she setting for her son, who was looking back and forth between them, his brows furrowed?

Brody had caught her eyes, and as if sensing her thoughts, he'd reached out and taken one of her hands in his, giving it a squeeze. The feel of his big palm holding hers grounded her, and the harsh words died on her tongue as a wave of shame washed over her. Brody had squeezed her hand again, and she'd looked up to see him wagging his eyebrows at her, making her laugh.

Brody had laughed too, a happy, booming sound that Annie hadn't known she'd missed until she heard it again. She smiled now, thinking about it as the bathroom door opened. She swung her head to watch as the woman came out and stood awkwardly by the couch.

"I hung the towel in the bathroom." The woman gestured behind her. "Is that okay?"

"Of course." Annie pushed away from the counter. "Can I get you something warm to drink? Coffee or tea?" She gestured to the bottle of cabernet sauvignon she'd opened. "Or a glass of wine? I know it's only three o'clock, but it seems appropriate, given the storm and being alone." Oh shit, maybe she shouldn't have mentioned she was alone. How stupid could she be? "I mean, all my family are just over there, but . . . you know what I mean."

"Tea would be nice." The woman eyed Marley until Annie gestured to the two stools at the breakfast bar. The woman made her way slowly to them and perched on the edge of one, looking ill at ease. Either she was a great actress, or she really was harmless, just someone stuck in the storm needing refuge. "Thank you for letting me intrude on you like this. My name is Serena."

"I'm Annie." She put the kettle on the stove and turned to look at Serena. "Do you need to call anyone? Your husband maybe?"

"I'm not married." Something sparked in Serena's eyes, but it was gone so fast Annie wondered if she had imagined it. "It's just me. I don't have family on the island."

"Oh." Annie couldn't help but feel sorry for the woman. As much as she didn't want to spend an afternoon with her family, she was glad they were there if she needed them for anything. "What can I do? Maybe you can call the insurance company and they can send someone out to get you and the car?"

Serena made a face. "It's a rental. I tried calling the company, but I couldn't get through. I was just going to wait in the car, but it's raining so hard I guess I got a little scared." She gave a self-deprecating shrug. "I'll call them again in a bit."

"Are you a tourist?"

Serena shook her head. "Not really, but . . . I don't have a car yet. I'm looking for one."

"Oh." Annie's brows knitted, not sure what that meant. "Well, you're welcome to wait out the storm here if you want." She kept a pleasant expression on her face, but inside, she cursed herself. *Shit, did I just offer for her to stay here? Why, why, why? I was looking forward to a quiet afternoon by myself.*

"Thank you so much." Serena shot her a grateful look.

Something flashed in Annie's memory again. "Do I know you?" Annie cocked her head to the side as she studied Serena. She was pretty sure she didn't know her, but there was something familiar about her, like seeing a celebrity in real life. Maybe she'd seen her on TV? Was she an actress or something?

Serena tilted her head. "I don't think so. We've never met." Her right eye twitched and she winced, almost as if she were in pain.

"Are you okay?" Annie asked.

"Yes." Serena shifted on her stool as Annie looked at her.

At that moment, the kettle whistled, and Annie moved to pour the water into the blue-and-white china teapot she'd inherited from her mom. It had a built-in filter so she could fill the pot directly with tea leaves without having to use a bag. She brought the teapot and teacups to the breakfast bar and then reached for her phone to text Brody. It suddenly occurred to her that it would be a good idea to let someone know she had a visitor in case her overactive imagination was right.

Hey. A woman is here in the ohana with me. Said car broke down and storm scared her. I invited her to stay here until it gets better out.

Brody answered right away.

I can't believe you let a stranger in the house.

A: I know. But it was raining so hard. And I felt bad. Finn isn't here. He's with my father and Sam.
B: Do you feel funny about it? Maybe you should go to the main house.
A: No.

Annie decided not to tell Brody that she *did* feel slightly funny. It was probably just her paranoia. She didn't want to worry him for no reason.

B: Ok, well, keep me posted.
A: Will do.

Annie looked up from her phone to catch Serena staring at her. "Sorry, I'm being rude. That was my husband." She tucked her phone into the back pocket of her shorts and looked at her guest. Could she be called a guest if Annie didn't know her and hadn't expected her to show up on her doorstep?

"Must be nice to have someone care about you so much." There was a wistful look on Serena's face.

"Yeah, I guess." Annie shrugged, not wanting to explain how complicated her relationship with Brody was right now. "You mentioned you don't have any family here. But you live here? By yourself?" She was still pondering Serena's response that she wasn't really a tourist. She checked the tea and, deciding it was steeped enough, poured it into one of the cups, which she held out to Serena. Then she poured a cup for herself, looking at the glass of wine longingly. She'd feel funny drinking wine when her guest was having tea.

"Um, yes. I live here." Serena wrapped both hands around her cup and brought it to her face. She closed her eyes and breathed in the smell of the Taiwanese mountain tea that Annie's family always stocked up on whenever they visited Taiwan. "This smells amazing. I knew you'd have good tea."

"Thanks." Annie was about to ask her how long she'd been on Kauai, but then she paused. "What do you mean, you knew I'd have good tea?"

"Oh." Serena's eyes popped open, and red spots appeared on her cheeks. "I meant, um . . . not being racial at all. Just that you're Chinese, so you'd know good tea. Sorry." She cleared her throat and took a quick sip, almost blanching as the hot tea burned down her throat. "Not being stereotypical or anything."

"It's okay." Annie frowned as she regarded Serena, wondering whether she was being genuine. And how did she know Annie was Chinese (actually half-Chinese/Hawaiian and half-Taiwanese)? Most people just said "Asian" because they couldn't tell if Annie was Chinese, Japanese, or what. Annie had always thought she had a universal Asian face. Serena returned her look with a steady gaze until Annie looked away first.

There was a pause as they both sipped their tea. This was getting really awkward. She'd looked forward to having time to herself, maybe reading a good book. And now her peaceful afternoon of solitude and wine was ruined. But she would have felt bad not inviting Serena in when the weather was so bad outside. That would have been uncharitable of her. She'd probably be hit by lightning or something for thinking this, but she hoped the storm didn't last too long and that Serena would soon be on her way.

As if to undermine her wishes, the wind suddenly howled, whipping branches against the house and making the loud pounding of the rain even more ominous. Annie was glad to be inside, safe and sound. She hoped Brody was staying dry at the airport.

Serena spoke up, breaking into Annie's thoughts. "How long have you been here?"

"You mean Kauai? What makes you think I haven't lived here all my life?"

"Oh, I mean . . . I don't know." Serena blushed again.

"Sorry." Annie caught herself and realized she was being rude. Seriously. She really had lost all her social filters. But something about Serena was making her nerve endings stand up, like someone had sent a shock of electricity through her body. "You're right—we moved here over a month ago. So we're pretty new to the area."

Serena smiled and Annie was surprised at how it transformed her face. She went from an ordinary-looking woman to one with a luminous face, her eyes lighting up. Serena opened her mouth, but before she could say anything, a loud crack of thunder shook the room and she let out a scream instead.

Annie placed a hand at her heart and walked to the window next to the front door. Wow, that was loud. It rarely thundered in Kauai, so to hear it now, so loud and near, sent her heart racing. She peered out the window. This storm was *bad*. She could see the way the palm trees were whipping in the wind, leaning to one side as if fighting off the storm. Her father had been right to worry. How was Brody going to get home from work?

Annie's phone dinged in her pocket, and she took it out to read a text from Brody.

B: Everything okay?

A: Yes. You?

B: I'm good. People are saying they think the storm is going to be really bad.

A: It already is really bad. Maybe you should come home early.

B: I'll try. I'll let you know.

32

Annie's head snapped up when something crashed outside. She looked out the window again. The rain was coming down so hard that she could barely see anything. But she squinted and saw a large branch had fallen in the backyard. Her heart sank. As much as she wanted to be alone, there was no way she could let Serena go back outside in this. It looked like she was stuck with company for the time being.

6

Annie walked back to the kitchen counter and picked up the open bottle of wine. With a storm so bad out, who could blame her for needing a drink? "You want a glass?" She gestured to Serena with the bottle.

"I'm okay with tea. Maybe later." Serena still had her hands wrapped around her teacup.

"I guess you're stuck here for the time being." Annie looked longingly at the bottle. She needed a drink, bad. Screw it. It was her house, after all. If she wanted to drink in the afternoon, she was going to drink, invited intruder and all. She put the bottle back down and reached for her wineglass. Taking a healthy swallow, she dared Serena to comment.

But Serena wasn't even looking at her. She was staring out at the storm, as if mesmerized by the sheets of rain falling outside.

Annie's phone dinged, and she put the wineglass down to look at it.

B: What's the woman's name, in case I need to tell the detectives later?

A: Oh, right. Good idea. We should be careful. Her name is Serena.

B: What's her last name?

A: No clue.

B: Ask her. So that we have a full name. Just in case.

A: Don't scare me.

B: I'm not trying to.

"Is that your husband again?"

Annie looked up when she heard Serena's voice. "Yes, sorry. He's just checking up on me."

"That's nice." A longing look played across Serena's face. "Don't mind me. Go ahead and text him."

"Thanks." Annie looked back down at the phone.

A: It feels rude to ask her last name right now. I'll ask her later. We're having tea.

Well, Serena was having tea. Annie didn't say that she'd switched to wine.

B: Be sure not to wash her cup. We can use it to get her DNA later to ID her.

A: Hardy har har. You're so funny.

B: I'm not trying to be funny. And hardy har har? Who says that anymore?

A: ☺

B: Maybe you should let her know you've contacted someone from the outside in case she's planning on robbing us blind.

A: We don't have anything of value to rob. And besides, she knows I'm texting with you. She's sitting right in front of me. Be right back. I feel rude just sitting here texting. I should probably turn on the news.

B: Ok. Talk soon. I'm here.

Annie looked up from her phone to find Serena studying her.

"Where's your husband now?" The woman tilted her head to the side. "At work?"

"Yes. He works at the Lihue airport. I don't know how he's going to be able to get home tonight." Annie worried her bottom lip with her teeth. "I hope they don't close down Kuhio Highway." She walked to the coffee table and picked up the TV remote. "We should probably keep an eye on the news."

Serena swiveled on her stool so that she could see the TV. "I hope your husband can get home safely. You guys look like you have a wonderful relationship."

Annie was absorbed in finding a channel that had the weather on, so it took a moment for her brain to catch up to Serena's words. When it did, she turned sharply toward Serena. "What do you mean, we look like we have a wonderful relationship? When have you ever seen us together?" She narrowed her eyes. "I thought you said we've never met?"

"We haven't." Serena's eyes widened. "I just meant . . ." She broke off and gestured toward the wedding photo Brody had unpacked and placed on the side table next to the couch. "From your picture . . . I, um. And the way he texts to check up on you. It just sounds like you have a wonderful relationship. That's all I meant."

"Oh. Sorry. Didn't mean to jump down your throat." Annie relaxed her death grip on the remote, not realizing she'd been clutching it so tightly until she eased off.

As if to prove Serena's point, Annie's phone dinged again.

B: All good?

A: Yes. But something about her bothers me. I feel like I know her, but I can't place her.

Annie looked up from her phone, but Serena was absorbed in watching the news and not paying attention to her. Still, it made her feel funny to be texting about someone when they were sitting right there with her. She looked down when Brody responded.

B: Wait, what? You're serious?

A: Yeah. It's just a feeling I have. Can't put my finger on it.

B: How would you know her? From Kauai?

A: Maybe? I don't know. I asked her if we knew each other and she said no.

B: That's not good. Do you feel unsafe?

A: No. At least I don't think so.

B: I can't believe you let a stranger into the house, given your past obsession with Criminal Minds and true crime shows. And what happened at the lake.

A: She doesn't look like a murderer.

B: Murderers never look like a murderer. You're the one who's always told me that.

A: Yeah, yeah. Use my words against me.

She looked up when the meteorologist came on and started talking about the storm. In silence, they listened to her, and Annie's heart sank when she heard phrases like "rare severe thunderstorms," "wind gusts up to sixty-five miles per hour," "flash floods," and "road closures due to coastal flooding." She even warned of possible evacuation for parts of Kauai. This didn't sound good. Especially because they lived right on the Wailua River.

"This is bad." Serena's voice echoed Annie's feeling of dread. "I thought Kauai was supposed to be paradise. I wasn't expecting storms like this."

"This isn't normal. My family has been vacationing here for years, and my father and sister moved here almost four years ago. This is pretty rare, as the news is saying." Annie left the TV on but lowered the volume and made her way back to the kitchen. "But wait, didn't you say you live here?" Had she said that?

"I envy you." The longing in Serena's voice distracted Annie from the fact that Serena hadn't answered her.

"You envy me?" Annie couldn't keep the surprise out of her voice. "Why?"

Serena's shoulders jerked up and then dropped. "You seem like you have the perfect life."

"Ha!" Annie snorted. "Far from it."

"You do." Serena leaned forward, her face an earnest mask. "You and your husband look so perfect together, and you have a son and a dog too."

Annie was about to take a sip from her glass but then stopped. "How do you know I have a son?" Marley was here with them, but Annie was pretty sure she hadn't mentioned a son.

Serena pointed to a picture of Finn by the TV. "Isn't he yours?"

"Oh, right. Yes, that's Finn." Annie took a gulp of her wine.

"Finn." Serena turned the name over on her tongue, almost as if she were savoring it. "Where is he?"

"He's at my father's house." Annie gestured toward the main house.

"How old is he?" There was a strange look on Serena's face that Annie couldn't decipher.

"He just turned four." Annie kept her gaze on Serena. "Do you have any kids?"

"No." Serena's face closed up and she looked down into her lap.

Annie stayed quiet, wondering whether this was a sore topic for Serena. Maybe she wanted kids and a husband. She was suddenly curious about the other woman.

As if sensing that Annie was softening toward her, Serena looked up. "I gather you're close to your family, if you're all living together on the same property. I meant it when I said I envy you. You just seem so together and with it. Like you know what you're doing in life." Serena pointed to herself before letting her hand drop. "Me? I'm a big mess."

Annie was taken aback that this was how a stranger saw her. Perfect life? She wished. "You have no idea how wrong you are. I definitely don't have the perfect life."

"Yeah right." Serena laughed, and Annie wondered if she'd imagined the bitterness in it. "From the outside, your life looks pretty ideal. At least compared to me." She gestured to the wine bottle. "You know what, I think I changed my mind. Can I have a glass?"

Annie walked into the kitchen and opened the cabinet where they kept the glasses. She pulled down a second glass and poured the cabernet sauvignon for Serena. Thank goodness. Now she wouldn't feel like a lush. She handed it to Serena and regarded her curiously, before walking back to the breakfast bar to her own glass. Despite herself, this woman had piqued her interest. What could cause her to envy Annie, a woman she didn't know? And maybe it did make Annie feel a tiny bit better, that someone thought her life was something to be envied. As if.

Serena took a dainty sip, her eyes visible over the top of her wineglass. They had grown distant, as if thinking of another time. "My fiancé left me, a few months before our wedding. It was devastating."

Annie gasped. "How awful. I'm so sorry." She placed her hands on the counter. She wanted to ask what had happened, but she didn't want to pry.

A look of pain flashed across Serena's face. "Yeah. It was horrible. It's been almost three years, and I still get sad thinking about it."

"I would too," Annie said, feeling genuine sympathy for Serena. Maybe they had more in common than she'd thought. Not that Brody had left her, but it sounded like she'd experienced heartbreak like Annie had.

"Thanks." Serena looked into her wineglass and took another sip, this one bigger. "What did you mean when you said your life is far from perfect? I'm not sure if I believe you." She looked up at Annie in a teasing way, but there was something hard about her expression. As if she really didn't believe Annie and thought she was lying.

Annie looked away from those piercing green eyes and gave a small laugh. "You don't want to know. It's a long story."

"Actually, I do want to know." Serena's eyes seemed to bore into Annie's. "And it looks like we might be stuck together for a bit if this storm doesn't let up." She smiled, and once again, Annie was struck by how a smile changed the other woman's whole face.

Annie's text alert broke the silence between them.

B: Hey, but seriously, maybe you should take a picture of her and send it to me in case something happens.

Annie shot Serena an apologetic face before she answered Brody.

A: How am I supposed to take a picture of her without her knowing?

B: Dunno. Maybe take a selfie together?

A: Right. But I guess it is a good idea in case I turn up dead . . .

B: That's not funny. Maybe you should tell her to leave. I'd feel better. I'm starting to get a funny feeling.

A: It's fine. She's not a murderer. And have you looked outside? I can't send her out in this. Especially with a dead car.

B: Well, better than a dead you. Keep your phone by you. Call me if you feel uncomfortable, Ok?

A: Yes, Sir.

B: Love you, Sexy.

A: Me too, My Fireman.

B: Stay safe.

"See, I don't believe you. Look at the way you're smiling, just texting with your husband."

Serena's voice had Annie looking up, and she realized Serena was right. There was a wide grin on her face, and she couldn't hide it. It'd been so long since Brody had called her "Sexy" and she'd reciprocated with "My Fireman," because Brody had worked for the FDNY. It was what they used to call each other when they first met. Back when they were so in love that they couldn't get enough of each other.

7

Laptop ANNIE file

I still remember how giddy I used to get when I first started dating him and knew I was going to see him that night. I'd never felt that electricity with anyone before. *At last,* I thought to myself. *I've found my person.* He was sweet and kind to me, we had intellectual conversations, but we could also be silly.

The first time we had sex was because I asked him to show me his toes. I have this fear of men with hairy toes. He wouldn't show them to me at first. He looked at me like I had grown two heads. I feared the worst. We laughed so much that day, me trying to wrestle his shoe off and then his sock and him putting up a fight but not really? It was an excuse for him to wrap his arms around me and feel our bodies touching, getting closer. After a while, we didn't even know what we were play-fighting about. We ended up doing it right there on his living room floor. After, he finally showed me his toes, and thank goodness they weren't hairy. I still remember sitting there, just smiling at each other in the goofy way that only first-time sex can bring. You know what I mean.

When did we lose all that? We had such big dreams. We were going to raise our family in our dream home on the lake. He had grown up going to Lake George every summer with his family and always loved the water. Any water: ocean, river, lake, it didn't matter. Which is why when we saw the house on the lake and it was in our price range, he couldn't believe it and wanted to offer right away. We'd just found out we were pregnant, and that was the house he wanted our child to grow up in. I saw how excited he was, how much his eyes lit up at the thought of living in the lake house, and it made me excited too. And it became my dream house.

Our kids were going to grow up in a real community, where kids run in and out of each other's homes, and mothers could relax at the beach knowing the bigger kids were watching out for the little ones. We would have barbecues on our back deck overlooking the lake and eat outside. Our kids would run around the fenced-in backyard and we were going to get a dog. It was the perfect house for our perfect family.

But then our dream fell apart. We had turned into strangers long before what happened to our son, not understanding each other, and not even speaking the same language. How did that happen? We should have come together when that tragedy struck our son. It should have bonded us, made us a united front. But instead, it pushed us even further apart. And that was when you became my solace. Only you could push that loneliness away, as I dreamed of the life I was supposed to live.

8

"You said you have a sister?" Serena asked.

Annie nodded as she sat on the other stool at the breakfast bar. "I have an older sister, Jeannie, and a younger sister, Sam. Sam lives in the main house with my father and her daughter, Cam. We're all close, even though Jeannie is back in New York." Except they didn't talk about deep things, like everything Annie had been going through these past few years. Feelings weren't discussed in detail in their family. They were glossed over, like they usually were in Taiwanese households.

"I wish I'd had brothers or sisters. I'm an only child." Serena shifted on her stool.

Annie gave her a wry look. "Well, sometimes when I was growing up, I wished I was an only child. Jeannie was the perfect Asian daughter. She got straight As, went to law school, married a Taiwanese man that our parents approved of, and has a boy and a girl. She makes me and Sam want to barf sometimes."

Serena's mouth quirked. "I bet."

"Seriously, though. On my father's side, all the Taiwanese aunties are so proud of Jeannie. They brag about her, using her as the shining example among our numerous cousins of a daughter who makes her parents proud." Annie wrinkled her nose. "Not like Sam and me."

"What's wrong with you and Sam?"

"Sam's the free spirit of our family. She drifted through school, doing well enough to get by but not really applying herself. She's had more career changes than most people have shoes."

"That doesn't sound like a bad thing." Serena's wineglass sat in front of her, as if she were so absorbed by Annie's stories of her family that she forgot to drink.

"Yeah, well, when she was thirty-one, Sam had a one-night stand with a guy named Mark. She didn't even know his last name. She never saw him again, but he left her with something, and let me tell you, that is not done in our family." Annie put her own wineglass down, wondering why she was telling a virtual stranger this. But there was something about Serena that made it easy to talk to her.

"What? Her daughter?" Serena arched an eyebrow.

"Yup. My mom was horrified. She was more progressive than my dad, but even she thought you needed to do things in the right order: marriage, then babies. We all thought my dad would flip out, since he's so traditionally Taiwanese, but Sam has always been his girl."

Annie thought again how it wasn't fair the things Sam got away with, with their father. She could do no wrong, including coming home with a child out of wedlock, which Annie knew was a huge source of embarrassment to her father. But he'd stood by his youngest, shutting down his sisters, especially Big Auntie, whenever they brought up Sam's shame.

"And you?" Serena asked.

Annie waved the question off. "Let's just say I was a disappointment to my Taiwanese family too, in other ways."

"Is your mom Taiwanese too?" Serena put her elbows on the counter and leaned her chin into her hands.

"No. She's half-Chinese and half-Hawaiian." Annie gave a laugh. "It's been interesting growing up with all the different traditions."

"I bet it was fun. I'm just boring old English, and I think some Irish, as far as I know." Serena gazed at her. "Being Taiwanese is different from Chinese, right?"

Annie looked at Serena in surprise. "Yes. But most people don't realize that. Like, my Taiwanese family are really pro-Taiwan. There's a lot of political stuff I try not to get involved with, but basically, there's the pan-Green camp, who want Taiwan to be an independent country, and the pan-Blue camp, who think Taiwan should reunify with China. And my dad is always saying how Taiwanese products are much better than Chinese."

"Didn't that cause tension with your mom?"

"No." Annie shook her head. "My mom was born and raised in Oahu. She met my dad when they were in college in New York, and after they got married, they moved to Taiwan for a few years, where Jeannie and I were born. Sam was born in New York when we moved back to the States."

"Wow." Serena's eyes were wide. "You've lived such an interesting life."

Annie shrugged. "I guess." She'd never thought of it that way before.

"Hey, did you guys go to the Chinese New Year celebration at Kukui Grove in Lihue?" Serena's eyes lit up. "I was there. I loved the drumming and the lion dance."

"Yes. Finn and Cam loved it too." Annie's mouth curved. "Although my dad grumbled that it's not just 'Chinese New Year.' He thinks it should be referred to as 'Lunar New Year.'"

Annie stopped, suddenly remembering that she'd lost her expensive pair of sunglasses that day. She'd been sure she'd put them in the outside pocket of her purse when they went into the shopping center for the celebration, but when they got home, the glasses weren't there. She'd searched her car, and nothing. She'd always been so careful with them. Had she dropped them, or had someone taken them right out of her purse? Why was she always losing things?

"What? What's the matter?" Serena looked at her in concern.

"Nothing." Annie waved off the question. "Just remembering that I lost my favorite pair of sunglasses that day."

"Oh." Serena trained her eyes on Annie, a sympathetic look on her face.

"Never mind." Annie shook her head, mourning the loss of her sunglasses again.

Serena looked at her for another moment, then spoke. "It must be so nice to have your sister close again."

"It is and it isn't." Annie's mouth twitched. "Sam's really blunt, and we clash sometimes. We get on each other's nerves a lot. Jeannie has also been the one to balance us, and without her here . . ." She shrugged.

"When I was growing up, I would have given anything to have a sister or brother to fight with." Serena pressed her lips together.

"I guess the grass is always greener on the other side." Annie lifted her shoulders. "Sam can be such a pain in my butt sometimes."

But then again, Sam had done many kind things for Annie too. Like being willing to take Finn whenever Annie needed time to herself. Sam was also the one who had suggested to Annie that she volunteer at the Kauai Humane Society.

They'd been sprawled on their stomachs on the private dock that only the residents on their dead-end street could use. It had been a warm afternoon only a couple of weeks after Annie and her family had arrived in Kauai, and Annie was trying to relax, to enjoy the sunshine and the piña coladas that Sam had whipped up for them.

Sam had turned to Annie with her eyes narrowed. "Why don't you do something for the community instead of moping around?"

Annie let out an unladylike snort. "What, you mean like, volunteer at a shelter?"

Sam nodded. "Yes. The Kauai Humane Society is always looking for volunteers. And you love dogs."

Annie was about to protest, but then she stopped. She did love dogs. And these days, she preferred the company of animals to people. They didn't ask any questions or want to know how she felt all the time.

"You know what? I think I might do that." She was surprised when the words popped out of her mouth.

"Great. It'll be good for you." Sam reached out and bopped Annie on the head. "You're an emotional wreck, your son is afraid of you, and your husband looks miserable half the time. Life's too short. You need to get your head out of your ass."

"Why is she a pain?" Serena's question had Annie focusing on her again.

"Because she thinks I've got my head stuck up my ass and that I should let the past go and enjoy being in Kauai. She thinks Brody's going to leave me if I don't try to make things better." Annie clapped a hand over her mouth. Had she really just said that to someone she'd just met? And she couldn't even blame the wine. She hadn't even had half a glass yet.

"What?" Serena sat back on her stool, her mouth open. "No way. You and your husband look so solid."

"Yeah, well, like I said before, things have been a bit rough lately." Annie fell silent, not wanting to talk about everything that had happened.

"Hey," Serena said, seeming to sense that Annie wanted to change the subject, "why isn't your son in preschool? Isn't he that age?"

Annie's face flushed. "Yeah, he should be. We were going to put him in the one that Cam went to, but our neighbor basically implied that would be a mistake." Annie grimaced as she remembered how Kalani had informed them a few weeks ago that they wouldn't be able to get Finn into a good school in the middle of the year. She'd said you had to be on the wait list practically as soon as you were pregnant.

"Why is that?" Serena tilted her head.

"Sam works an assortment of odd jobs. She's a dog walker, bartends at Duke's on Kalapaki Beach, and she's also the caretaker of a few properties for people who live on the mainland and rent out their condos. You can imagine her income isn't very high, plus she's a single mom. What our neighbor Kalani was trying to say to us was that the school Cam went to is in a low-income area, since Sam qualifies for low-income services."

Even though Kalani had said that in the nicest way possible, it had still irked Annie. When Kalani offered to put in a word for them since a classmate of Leila's had moved away because of her father's job transfer to the mainland, Annie wanted to turn her down out of spite. But she knew she couldn't. On one hand, she wanted to defend Sam's choices. But on the other, she did want what was best for Finn. She and Brody had known when they decided to move to Kauai that the school system wasn't as good as what they had in New York. Shouldn't she want to put Finn in the best school possible?

Kalani had further enforced this belief when she told them that the quality of care and early education given to the children in Leila's school was better than could be found at schools where there wasn't a wait list. And they provided food for lunch, which some of the other preschools didn't.

Annie had swallowed and forced a smile on her face, telling Kalani it would be lovely of her to put in a word for Finn. Brody had poked her in the side at her use of the word "lovely," while Kalani had beamed at them and said she'd do her best to try and get Finn into Leila's class. They had an appointment to visit the school later that week.

Annie's cell rang right then, and when she saw who was calling, she quirked an eyebrow at Serena. "It's Sam. Think she heard us talking about her?"

Serena sniggered as Annie picked up the call.

"Hey, Annie. The storm's getting bad. Why don't you come over here?" Sam's tone was rushed, and Annie could hear the concern behind her sister's words. But she could barely hear Sam over the loud music and screaming coming from the background.

"I'm fine." Annie glanced back at Serena. "I have someone over here."

"Oh, a friend? That's great." Sam was practically shouting to be heard over the music. The reception wasn't great, and she was cutting in and out. ". . . Kalani?"

"What?" Annie shouted back.

There was a burst of static and fuzz.

"I'll call you back on the landline," Annie said, and then hung up.

She dialed her father's line, and when it was picked up, all she heard was the loud music and the kids screaming again, but much clearer this time. Holding the phone away from her ears, she heard her father say, "*Wei?*"

Annie shook her head. He still answered the phone like he was in Taiwan, even though he'd been in this country for so long. "How's Finn? I guess they're having a good time."

"Yes, so loud."

"Is Sam there?"

No reply from her father, and then her sister was back on the phone.

"Much better," Sam said. "Cell service is already getting bad. I think we're going to lose power. Who do you have over there with you? Kalani?"

Annie rolled her eyes. Why did everyone want her and Kalani to be friends so bad? Yes, once, she probably would have been friends with their cheerful neighbor. But these days, she couldn't handle all that chipper energy. She had more of a connection with Serena in just the short time they'd met.

"No, just someone I . . . know." There was no reason to tell Sam how Serena had come to knock on her door and Annie had thought she was there to kill her at first.

50

"Okay, well, it's really bad out. You guys should plan on staying put for the time being. I'm glad you have company." One of the kids yelled something in the background. "Hang on," Sam yelled back before returning her attention to Annie. "You should pack a bag in case we need to evacuate. Baba doesn't think we need to, since the house is built up, but you never know."

Annie's eyebrows rose. "You think it's going to be that bad?"

"Could be, especially since we're right on the river. Just be prepared, okay? I'll touch base in a bit." Sam's words rushed out. "And don't worry about Finn. He can stay for dinner."

"Oh, okay. Thanks."

"I gotta go. My dance partners are getting impatient." And with that, Sam hung up.

9

Annie put her phone down and stood, stretching her arms overhead. Despite the growing dread from the storm, she realized she felt great. She was enjoying Serena's company. She'd been missing her two best friends, Julia and Izzy, who were back in New York. Talking to Serena was a lot like talking to her old friends, and it made her wish they were here with her.

She'd met them twenty years ago, when she was freshly graduated from SUNY Purchase with a BA in dance, on the first day of a professional training program at a ballet company. She'd wanted to dance professionally, and her parents had been horrified. They'd thought she should get a "real" job, but she'd held her ground.

They had gravitated toward each other, the only people of color in the otherwise all-white program. Julia, tall at five eight for an Asian, with a strong, solid build more suited for modern dance than ballet, and skinny, scrawny Izzy from Barbados, who hadn't filled out yet back then and was always partnered with Annie, the only woman smaller than him.

The three of them had stayed fast friends as their dance careers advanced. Izzy was now a dancer in *The Lion King* on Broadway, and Julia was with an Asian American modern dance company. They were both single and still dancing professionally in New York City, while Annie's career had stalled when she'd lost her company and studio.

"Everything okay?"

Serena's question snapped Annie's attention back to her new friend.

"Sorry. I was just thinking about my friends from back home." Marley came up next to her, and she scratched him behind his ears. "I miss them. It's nice having someone who's not my family to talk to again. And not have to chase after a little boy for an afternoon." Annie made a face. "Does that make me sound like a bad mother?"

"No, of course not." Serena leaned her elbows on the breakfast bar, her face open. "I saw you two together. You're great with him."

Annie paused in her scratching of Marley. "When did you see me with him?" A prickle of uncertainty started at the back of her neck. What was Serena talking about?

"I just realized I've seen you before." The younger woman's expression was all innocence, but that prickle on Annie's neck turned into a spark as uneasiness traveled down her back.

"You said we've never met." Annie gazed at Serena in challenge.

"We've never met formally. But I just realized we saw each other yesterday at the beach at Lydgate. Your son kicked sand on me, and I kind of freaked out." Serena ducked her head, so that her curls swung in front of her face.

"Oh." Annie paused for a moment, and then her mouth fell open. *That* was why Serena looked so familiar. She was the woman on the beach with the giant floppy hat who had yelled at Finn and then stormed off.

Serena's glance skated away when she saw Annie making the connection. "I know I wasn't very nice. I'm sorry I yelled at him. I was having a bad day and took it out on him." She gave a rueful look. "Maybe I shouldn't have admitted I was that woman. Doesn't make me look very good, does it?"

"Yeah." Annie agreed that it wasn't nice of Serena, but she wasn't going to push the point. She herself hadn't exactly been a ray of sunshine for a while, and she'd definitely yelled at Finn for much less. "I knew I'd seen you before when I answered the door. It's been bothering me." Annie blew out a breath and dropped her shoulders. "Whew. Glad it wasn't something creepy, like you'd been following me or something." She gave a laugh. "It was just that we've run into each other before."

Serena opened her mouth and then snapped it shut, two bright spots appearing on her cheeks. Annie peered at her closely. She'd only met the woman, but she was already learning her body language. Right now, Serena was very uncomfortable. Should Annie not have said that about being creepy? Had she offended her?

Serena forced a laugh, and an awkward moment of silence hung between them before she broke it. "You said your marriage is strained right now? It's funny how we never really know what goes on in someone else's life. From my point of view, you have the best marriage to a reliable man."

Annie made a noise with her mouth. "The last four years have been pretty bad. I know it's mostly my doing, but I don't know what to do to change things." She paused, unsure why she was telling Serena this. But there was something in Serena's expression that made Annie feel that she understood. She took a breath and continued.

"Every morning I wake up and say, 'This is the day I'm going to be nice again. I won't yell at Brody. I will be patient and not be so grumpy and grouchy.' And every day, before we're even done with breakfast, I'm already snipping at him." She shook her head. "One of my best friends, Izzy, tells me I'm depressed and I need therapy, but I think it's just circumstances, you know? I don't need a therapist. How is a therapist going to make things better?"

Serena's face brightened. "I know exactly what you're talking about. People said the same thing to me when . . . well, when something bad happened. Said I needed a therapist. I told them I was fine. I've done therapy before, and it didn't really do anything. I'm fine. I mean, look at me. I'm dealing. Right?"

Annie nodded and Serena beamed back at her. A look of understanding passed between them, and Annie felt a bond with this woman that she hadn't felt since she met Julia and Izzy. There'd been this same instant connection with her two best friends, a feeling that they got her, no matter how different they were from each other.

"My friends are protective of me." Annie wrinkled her nose. "Izzy loves his therapist and keeps trying to get me to go. The last time we FaceTimed, he was on my case again."

Her friends had been concerned and wanted to know how things were going in Kauai.

Annie had said, "You'd think drinking mai tais in paradise would make me feel better."

"Have you found a therapist yet?" Izzy had asked.

Annie had blown out a breath. "I'm fine. I don't need to see anyone."

"But, Annie, you haven't been happy for years . . . and then when you disappeared after you lost your company . . ." Izzy had trailed off.

"I'm fine," Annie had said again, and she'd given Izzy a big cheesy fake smile. "See? And I didn't disappear." She'd looked away from the phone, not wanting them to see her discomfort.

"She didn't. She just needed"—Julia had struggled for the words—"a rest. And she doesn't need a therapist. If something good would just happen . . ."

Annie had been grateful that Julia understood. Julia Zhang's family was from Shanghai and clung to many of the same traditions that Annie's family did.

"What is it with you two?" Izzy had sounded exasperated. "There's nothing shameful about talking to a professional. I love mine."

"Tell that to my family." Julia's voice had been bitter, and Annie had agreed with her. "Asian people do not have mental health issues."

"You just need to find the right person." Izzy hadn't been ready to give up.

"No, I don't." Annie had pursed her lips. She could never bring shame to her family. She'd never talked to her father about how she had struggled when her life fell apart. They just didn't talk about problems like that. And even her sisters knew only the surface level of everything going on inside her.

They'd stared at each other until Izzy's lips quirked up. "I give up. I'm not arguing with two Asians who think using Vaseline on their eyes at night will keep wrinkles away."

Annie had caught Julia's eyes and a laugh escaped. "It works. We swear by it."

Izzy shook his head. "All you're doing is clogging your pores. You poor dears. You poor misinformed dears."

And Annie and Julia had burst into laughter, as Annie silently thanked Izzy for giving in, and always knowing when to let things go.

She told Serena now about what Izzy had said, and they laughed together.

"Your friends sound so fun," Serena said.

"Oh, they are. Izzy is hysterical. He hates to see me down on myself. When we first got to Kauai, they'd text and FaceTime all the time to check up on me." Annie stopped and frowned. "Come to think of it, they're still checking up on me daily." She looked at her phone. "They'll probably text or call sometime today."

"That's nice to have friends who care so much, though, no?" Annie detected that wistful note in Serena's voice again.

"Yes, you're right. They'd do anything for me." Annie met Serena's eyes across the breakfast bar, and that feeling of connection zinged between them again.

The lights flickered, and they both looked up and then back at each other, eyes wide.

Serena made a face. "This storm is scary."

While they'd been talking, the rain had slowed and was no longer as loud. But now it was picking up again, the patter on the roof intensifying. Annie walked to the window by the front door and gasped at what she saw.

"What?" Serena rushed to her side.

"Look how beautiful the sky is." Annie pointed. With the sun starting to go down, the sky had turned a deep navy blue, a color that she had never seen before. Every once in a while, lightning flashed, lighting up the sky and illuminating the clouds against the velvety sky. It was beautiful in an eerie way. The rain pelted down, and the wind whipped the palm trees and shrubbery around so hard that she hoped it didn't rip one right out by its roots.

"I've never seen a sky that color before." There was awe in Serena's voice.

"Me either." They both stared out for a few more seconds before Annie turned away. "I hope we don't lose power," she said. "Sam thinks we might. Oh, and that reminds me. She said to pack a bag in case we need to evacuate."

Serena gestured to her windbreaker hanging by the door. "That's all I have with me. I left my tote in my car."

"Okay, well, if we need to leave, we can grab yours on the way out. I'll throw a bag together in a bit." A moment of silence passed between them, but it wasn't awkward like it had been when Serena first came into the ohana. Even Marley was lying quietly by the couch, no longer growling. "I'm glad you're here," Annie said.

"Me too." Serena's eyes gleamed, and something inside Annie lit up. Maybe she could make new friends in Kauai after all.

10

Marley suddenly shot off the floor and ran for the front door, barking.

"Marley!" Annie jumped, one hand flying to her heart as she walked over to the dog. "You scared the crap out of me. What's going on?"

She looked out the window again and at first didn't see anything unusual, besides the heavy rain and wind. But then she thought she heard a creaking sound over the loud splashing of water, and before she could figure out what it was, a tree on her father's property fell to the ground, right across the backyard.

"Oh my god!" Annie's eyes widened in fear. The tree had missed both the main house and the ohana, but she eyed the others in the yard. What if another one fell? Would it hit them?

Serena rushed to her side and inhaled sharply when she saw the tree on the ground. They turned to each other, and as if synchronized, they both reached out at the same time and grasped each other's hands.

"What do we do?" Serena asked in a scared voice, squeezing Annie's hands.

"I don't know. I guess stay away from the windows?" They scooted away, still connected at the hands. Although that was stupid. If a tree was going to fall on the ohana, not being near a window wasn't going to make a difference.

Annie let go of Serena's hands and surveyed the backyard. "I think we're okay. The trees in the yard aren't very big." She bit her lip, doing a mental measurement of the angle of the trees in relation to the two buildings. "I don't think they'd fall on either house if they topple over." She should have paid more attention in geometry.

Her phone dinged and she looked down. It was a text from Sam.

S: You okay?

A: Yeah. That was scary though.

S: Stay inside. Baba doesn't think any of the trees would hit the house or ohana.

A: That's what I thought. We're not going anywhere.

Annie kneeled down and wrapped an arm around Marley. "Good boy. You must have sensed it, huh?"

"He is a good boy. I've always wanted a dog." Serena took a step toward Marley, and the hair on his back stood up. "I don't think he likes me very much."

"He just doesn't know you yet." Annie stood, looking at Marley. Why was he so alarmed by Serena?

"You're so good with dogs. He's not your first, right?" Serena crossed to the end table and picked up a picture of Lili.

"No. That's my first dog." Annie pointed to the frame in Serena's hand. "Her name was Lilikoi, Lili for short."

"Passionfruit?" Serena asked.

Annie nodded and walked to her side. "Our family has always loved coming to Kauai, and Lilikoi just fit her."

"It does. She's so cute." Serena handed the picture to Annie.

Annie stared at Lili, who wore a pink collar in the picture, and suddenly remembered something that had happened recently. She'd just finished volunteering at the humane society, and when she got to her car, an odd shiver had run down her spine. She'd paused, one hand on the handle of the door, and looked around. It had felt like there were eyes focused on her. She'd scanned the parking lot but hadn't seen anything out of the ordinary. She'd quickly opened the car door and frozen when she saw what was on the driver's seat: a pink collar with white paw prints on it, much like the one Lili used to wear. Her heart pounding and blood roaring in her ears, she'd slowly reached down and picked up the collar. Before she could read the name on the black bone-shaped tag, she knew what it would say.

And she was right. LILI, it said in all caps, with Annie's cell number under it. What was it doing in her car in Kauai? She looked at the tote bag on her shoulder, remembering that she'd found it at the back of her closet when they were packing to move from New York. Had this tag been in the bag, forgotten all this time, and fallen out when she got out of the car? She could have sworn there was nothing in the bag when she packed it that morning. But how else in the world could an old collar from Lili have gotten into her car in Kauai?

"Annie?"

She started, her eyes returning to focus on Serena's concerned face. Goose bumps broke out all over her skin, just like they had that day she'd found the collar.

"I . . ." She stared at Serena, but she wasn't really seeing her. Because this was just another worrying reminder that she was doing and finding things she couldn't remember. And that feeling of someone watching her . . . She'd had that same exact feeling when they had first moved to the lake house in New York. She'd thought back then that she was being paranoid, new to the neighborhood and not yet used to living in the country, since she was such a city girl. Now she wondered: Was it paranoia, or was she losing her mind?

"Do you need some water?" Serena's voice broke into her thoughts again. "You look really pale."

"No, I'm fine." Annie tried for a smile, knowing she was failing miserably. "Just remembering something upsetting."

"I'm sorry I'm bringing up bad feelings." Concern was etched all over Serena's face.

Annie gave her head a shake, trying to clear it of the echoing doubt in her mind. "You're not. I love talking about Lili. She really was cute, and the best dog. So loyal and loving . . ." Her voice trailed off, and she was surprised to find her throat clogging up, even after all these years. Lili had been more than a dog. She had been Annie's first child.

"Lili is exactly the kind of dog I would have gotten if I had one," Serena said. "She's a mini dachshund, right?"

"Yes. She was stubborn too, like all dachshunds." Annie cleared her throat. "You know, she chose my husband for me. She didn't like any of the men I was dating, but when she met Brody, it was love at first sight. She put a paw on his leg and that was it." Annie forced out a laugh, remembering the look of surprise on Brody's face when Lili claimed him as her boyfriend. "The wiener had spoken."

"See, how perfect is that?" Serena sat down on the couch. "Your dog picked your husband for you. That is so sweet."

Annie let out a breath. It *was* sweet. It'd been more than eight years since she'd met Brody at a friend's party. Lili had been right: he was perfect for them, and Brody had loved Lili too, for the almost five years he'd known her. When they'd moved to the lake house four years ago, they'd been so full of hope for the family they'd raise there. Finn had been born two months after the move, and everything had seemed to be going as planned. Annie hadn't anticipated how gutted she'd feel when Lili passed away suddenly only a couple of months after Finn's birth.

"You look sad." Serena's voice broke through Annie's thoughts. "Do you want to talk about it? I'm a good listener."

"Um . . ." Annie shook her head and sighed. She was about to brush off the question, but then she realized she wanted to tell her. The thoughts in her mind were starting to drive her crazy with worry. Maybe talking about it with someone who was sympathetic and seemed to understand her would help. They didn't know each other, but something about Serena made Annie want to open up. Sometimes, it was easier to talk to a stranger. And something about being stuck together while a storm raged outside, the uncertainty of what was going to happen, made her feel closer to Serena.

"I didn't mean to pry." A furrow appeared between Serena's eyebrows.

Annie crossed to the breakfast bar, picked up their two glasses, and brought them over to the couch. Handing Serena hers, she sat and took a sip. "You're not prying. But it's a long story, and we're going to need fortification. Are you sure you want to hear it?"

Serena nodded. "We're not going anywhere for a while, are we?"

Annie gave her a rueful look and sank back into the cushion. Marley walked to her side and settled on the floor. "I guess not."

Annie reached down and threw Marley's favorite stuffed alligator to him. He caught it between his two front paws and settled down, gnawing on a foot and squeaking the squeaker every once in a while. She watched him for a moment before taking a breath.

"So Lili died from a severe case of pancreatitis two months after Finn was born. We did everything we could to save her. We even tried holistic medicine and acupuncture. But she kept getting sicker and sicker. I was supposed to be on tour with the dance company I founded, but I stayed home. Then she rallied, and I flew out. I hadn't even been there a full day yet when our vet, Dr. Shane, called me and told me to come home right away. Dr. Shane loved Lili too."

Annie stopped, taking a sip of wine. "Lili had had a seizure and was going downhill rapidly. Dr. Shane knew how special Lili was to me and knew I'd never forgive myself if I wasn't with her. She called me home because she thought it might be time to end her suffering." Annie looked down at Marley and took a breath, blinking back the tears. "But Lili took matters into her own hands. I got off the plane and Brody drove me right to the animal hospital. They put her in my arms and everyone left the room for a moment. It was just the two of us. Lili looked up at me, and then her whole body relaxed and she went limp. She had waited for me to come back. She passed away in my arms."

"Oh, Annie." There were tears in Serena's eyes, and Annie blinked fast, fighting her own.

"I knew it was going to be a bad year after that. And it was. My mother died here in Kauai five months after that, and then the next month, I lost my dance studio and company and had to file for bankruptcy because I had personally guaranteed the company loans." Annie put her wineglass down before she dropped it; her body was trembling slightly from the memories. "Now aren't you sorry you asked?"

"No." Sincerity flooded Serena's face. "I'm glad you told me, that you trust me. That's awful. I feel so bad for you."

"Yeah." Annie looked down. "My mom . . ." She stopped, not wanting to get into what had happened, and switched topics. "I was dancing professionally in New York City, and had started a modern dance company. I also had a studio on the Upper East Side for almost ten years." Annie paused, picturing her studio, which had been on the third floor of a walk-up. The excitement the day she'd found the space, building the sprung dance floor, having mirrors and barres installed, and decorating the changing room. She'd loved her studio, spending hours in there taking and teaching classes, choreographing new pieces, and rehearsing her company. She'd spent more time in leotards and tights or leggings than regular street clothing, her hair either up in a bun or twisted and clipped up in a wide barrette. Dancing had been her life, her passion.

"What happened to your company?" Serena reached out and put a hand on Annie's arm briefly, offering support.

"My landlord wanted to sell the building, but instead of telling me, he raised the rent by more than forty percent, knowing I'd never be able to afford it." Annie's mouth twisted as if she'd eaten something sour, thinking back to that time. "He also decided I owed him back property taxes, which he had said verbally that I didn't need to pay when we first signed the contract. He'd said it in front of his lawyer, who remembered, but because we never formally wrote it down, my lawyer said he was within his right to collect on the back taxes. They totaled more than $100,000."

Serena gasped. "No. I guess you didn't have the money?"

"No." Annie frowned. "And we weren't doing well financially. Just barely getting by every month. My lawyer advised me to file for bankruptcy and get out." She stared off into space, lost in thought about that horrible year. "That was the last straw. To lose Lili, then my mother, and then my career and everything I'd worked so hard for, not to mention my financial credibility, it was too much. I . . ."

Serena reached out again, this time leaving her hand on Annie's arm and squeezing. She didn't say anything, just waited for Annie to continue.

"I kind of . . . I don't know. Lost it. No one could help me. I wanted to die. I couldn't take care of Finn. I just wanted to disappear."

"Oh, Annie. I understand perfectly. I've felt the exact same way before." And with those words, Serena took Annie's hand in hers and their eyes met. Understanding passed between them, and all Annie felt in that moment was relief that someone finally, *finally*, understood her.

11

Annie's cell rang, breaking the spell between them. Taking her hand back from Serena, she picked up her phone and saw it was Brody.

"It's my husband. I should take this."

"Of course." Serena nodded and pulled out her own phone. "I'll check my social media while you talk."

"Thanks," Annie said before picking up the call. "Hi, Brody."

"Everything okay?"

Annie laughed, happy to hear his voice, and the sound was a welcome relief from the somber mood just a minute before. "Yes. Still here. But the storm is awful. A tree fell in the backyard. I'm afraid the power or cell service is going to go out."

"Oh no. Are you all okay?" Worry tinged Brody's words.

"Yes. My father doesn't think any of the trees should hit either house if they fall. But I guess we're safer staying put for the time being. How's Lihue?"

"Horrible. I don't think I'm going to make it back anytime soon." Brody paused, as someone shouted something in the background. "I'm going to wait and see if the storm lets up."

"That's probably for the best. The news is telling people to stay off the roads." Annie glanced over at the TV.

"I'll get something to eat with the guys. You going to eat all the food your father brought over this morning?" Brody chuckled.

Annie realized how much she missed laughing with Brody and teasing each other. "I'm fine. Serena and I actually have a lot in common." She turned to Serena, who looked up at the sound of her name. "We're getting to know each other."

"I'm glad." Brody's voice softened. "It's good you're making friends."

"I know." Annie stopped, wanting to say so many things to him. How she was sorry for everything. How awful she knew she'd been to live with and how she really did want to try and make their lives better again. But with Serena there, she knew this wasn't the right time. "Let's talk more when you get home, okay?"

"Yes. Love you, Sexy."

"Me too, My Fireman." Annie's heart gave a bump, happy they were reaching out to each other. She hung up, a soft smile on her face, and looked up to see Serena watching her.

An intensity in her eyes gave Annie pause. She tilted her head in question at Serena, wondering what was going through the other woman's mind. But then Serena gave a small shake of her head and her eyes cleared. Annie wondered if she'd imagined it. If the storm and the uneasiness it caused were making her see things that weren't there.

Serena spoke, her tone light and teasing. "I don't know if I believe you that your marriage is in trouble. Didn't sound like it from here."

"That was not normal." Annie pursed her lips. "I think the storm is making us be kinder to each other. Or," she corrected, "it's making me nicer to Brody."

"Mm-hm." Serena looked like she didn't believe Annie.

"Trust me." Annie drummed her fingers on her phone. "We've been having a rough time. But I hope things will get better."

"I'm sure it will." Serena's voice was soft, a yearning in her tone.

Annie studied Serena, and then on the spur of the moment, she decided to be bold. They'd found common ground just a little while ago, and she really could use a friend here. "Seeing as how we're stuck together for the foreseeable future, how'd you like to have dinner with me?" Annie paused, then plunged ahead with an invitation. "Finn's staying at my father's for dinner, and Brody is stuck at the airport. There's plenty if you want to eat with me. My dad made me a pot of *lu rou fan*. Do you know what that is?"

Serena shook her head.

"I guess I should ask first, do you eat pork?" Annie was actually excited to share this very Taiwanese dish with her new friend. Back when she was in grade school, she had hated the ethnic foods her parents would pack her for lunch, knowing the American kids would make fun of the braised pork belly rice her dad made. But now that she was a grown-up, she realized how special their Taiwanese cuisine was, and it always delighted her to introduce someone to foods so different from what Americans thought of as Chinese food.

"I eat everything. I love food." Serena's face lit up when she said that.

"Me too. Another way we're so alike." This storm and Serena's broken-down car were turning out to be good things. Who knew they would have so much in common? "Anyways, *lu rou fan* is usually finely chopped pork belly that's slow-cooked in an aromatic soy sauce with five spices. But my dad doesn't chop up the pork belly. He leaves it whole, which has a whole other name, I think *kang rou fan*, or something like that. But we just call it *lu rou fan*. He spoons the pork belly over hot rice with the sauce. He adds hard-boiled eggs in the sauce too, along with sliced carrots. So it's like a stew, but the sauce is amazing."

"That sounds great." Serena smacked her lips. "I love trying new foods."

"I was going to make a Taiwanese cucumber salad to go with it. My dad grows Japanese cucumbers in his garden." Annie's mouth watered, just thinking of what they were going to eat.

"You're making me hungry." Serena groaned, holding her stomach. "My mouth is watering."

Annie looked at her. They really were in tune with each other, having the same thoughts at the same time. "I was just thinking the same thing."

"We can read each other's minds." Serena grinned. "What's in the cucumber salad?"

"Just rice wine vinegar, a little sesame oil, garlic, and a bit of sugar." Annie stood. "I miss the vegetable garden I had back home, but I'm glad my dad has one here. I didn't know what I was doing when I decided to try to plant a garden, but I managed to grow tomatoes, cucumbers, green beans, kale, zucchinis, and a whole bunch of herbs. It was great to just go out there and pick something for dinner."

"I have a black thumb." Serena wiggled them. "I can't keep anything alive."

"I thought I did too, until we moved to the lake house. We also had a flower garden in the front that the previous owner had planted." Annie walked into the kitchen. "I'm going to make the cucumber salad now, so it can marinate for a bit."

"Do you need help?" Serena asked.

"No, you just relax on the couch with your wine. Put a movie on if you want. There's not much to do." Annie opened the refrigerator.

"I feel bad just sitting on my butt." Serena came toward Annie. "Let me help."

"Okay."

They exchanged another warm look, and then Annie began to gather the cucumbers her father had brought over that morning. She pulled out a cutting board and a knife, humming under her breath. She was so glad Serena had knocked on her door. Having her here was better than drinking alone in the storm. The howling wind and loud raindrops had become background noise, more like a soothing soundtrack than anything threatening, as they were warm and dry inside the ohana.

"You want to peel the cucumbers?" She handed Serena the peeler.

"Sure. Leaving a bit of peel on okay with you?" Serena picked up the first cucumber.

Annie nodded and they got to work. They were in sync as they prepared the salad together, never bumping into each other in the tiny kitchen the way Annie and Brody did. They chatted as they worked, about the different beaches in Kauai, and which ones were their favorites. Annie loved Poipu Beach because of the kiddie area for Finn, and Serena said she liked Hanalei Bay because it made her feel like she was on a deserted island, far from civilization and all the worries in the world.

"What kind of worries?" Annie asked, as she mixed together the marinade. She leaned in and inhaled, loving the umami smells that bombarded her nose.

"Everything," Serena said, cutting the cucumbers into thick chunks and then smashing them a bit so they'd absorb the marinade better, just like Annie showed her. "Work, money, friends, what I'm doing with my life, if I'm going to be single forever. Just to name a few." She gave a self-deprecating laugh.

"Life is hard." Annie nodded to acknowledge Serena's feelings. "Do you want more wine now or wait for dinner?" She held up the bottle. Neither had finished their first glass yet, but Annie was in a celebratory mood. When was the last time she'd felt so comfortable around someone, when she wasn't on edge and feeling bad about herself? It was nice, nice to feel like the old Annie, entertaining a friend for the night.

Serena dumped the cucumbers she'd sliced into the pineapple-shaped bowl that Annie had pulled out and held out her wineglass for Annie to top off.

Annie filled her own, and then they clinked glasses. "Cheers," she said. "To new friendships and to living on Kauai."

Serena's eyes twinkled at her over the top of her glass.

While Annie rinsed the rice for the *lu rou fan* in cold water, Serena sat back down at the breakfast bar with her wine. "Are you looking for a house? Or just going to stay here?" she asked.

Annie threw an amused look over her shoulder. "We're definitely not staying here. It's too small for the three of us. We've been looking at houses." She fell silent, because really, Brody had been looking at houses while, until recently, Annie had been dragging her feet. She didn't know why. Maybe because she missed the lake house and wasn't ready to find a new house. Or maybe she was just being difficult.

"See anything you like?" Serena asked.

Annie nodded. "We just saw a one-level home in the Wailua Homesteads, up the mountain about ten minutes from here. It was really nice, definitely a contender." She added two cups of water to the cleaned rice and set it in the rice cooker before placing the lid on. She leaned back against the counter as she told Serena about the house they'd seen.

It had a newly renovated kitchen with light brown cabinets and tan speckled granite countertops. All the appliances were stainless steel, and there was a large island in the middle of the kitchen. Annie had always wanted one. Their kitchen in the lake house was spacious but didn't have an island. Something about people gathered around an island when she entertained had always appealed to her. Not that she entertained much lately.

She'd also liked the layout of the house. The three bedrooms and two baths were on one end of the kitchen, and then down a few steps on the other side was the living room. It had a fenced-in, flat backyard lined with flowering plants and fruit trees, perfect for Finn and Marley.

"Think you're going to offer?" Serena played with the stem of her wineglass.

"Brody wants to, but I'm not sure . . ." She did like the house, but somehow, putting in an offer on a house made this move permanent. By staying in the ohana, it was almost like they were just on an extended visit, and would go home to their New York life soon. But they'd sold the lake house as soon as it was on the market. And did she want to go back, after what had happened in August? Would she be able to walk by the woods next to their lake beach and not picture Finn being carried out, covered in blood and crying hysterically?

"You don't like the house?" Serena's question snapped the gruesome image out of Annie's head.

"I do. And there's some amazing fruit trees on the property. There's avocado, lime, mango, banana, and an orange tree." Looking at the rice cooker, Annie realized she'd never turned it on, so she reached over and flipped the switch down before leaning back against the countertop.

"That sounds amazing." Serena clasped her hands together. "Can you imagine? You could get up in the morning and pick bananas and mangoes for breakfast, and make fresh orange juice. Or make guacamole with the avocado and limes."

"Hm." Annie tapped a finger to her lips. "That does sound good. The house is nestled right at the backside of Sleeping Giant with the northwest trail about sixty yards away. And it's a dead-end street just like this one, which is great for Finn and Marley."

"I haven't hiked on Sleeping Giant yet. I heard it's great." Serena took a sip of her wine. "Why's it called Sleeping Giant?"

"Because it looks like a giant sleeping on his back." Annie laughed. "Finn thinks its real name is NoNo Mountain."

"It's not?" Serena angled her head.

"Its real name is Nounou Mountain. But I guess it's close enough to Finn's interpretation." Annie's lips curved. "We'll probably take Marley hiking there one day. If it ever stops raining, that is." They both glanced out the kitchen window, where the rain continued to pour down in torrential sheets. "And the views up there are incredible."

"I'm not very athletic." Serena gestured to her body, which was curvier than Annie's but nicely proportioned. Annie envied Serena her

71

curves, since her own body was more like a boy's, flat chested with no hips. "But I definitely should hike part of it, from everything people say."

"You can come with us." Annie threw a look over her shoulder as she covered the cucumber salad and placed it in the refrigerator. She was surprised when the words left her mouth, but realized she meant them. It would be fun to have Serena go hiking with them.

She looked back to see Serena smiling at her as she toasted Annie with her wineglass. "I'd love that."

Annie smiled back. "It's a date, then."

12

When dinner was ready, they sat at the small table and dug into the food. The *lu rou fan* was delicious: salty, yet slightly sweet, the sauce sticky and rich, making it perfect with the white rice. The tang and crispness of the marinated cucumbers were a great complement to the fatty pork belly dish, and Serena actually moaned out loud in pleasure as she ate, making Annie laugh. It was the perfect comfort meal for a stormy night. The torrential rain continued to rage outside, but in here, it was warm and cozy. The food was delicious, not to mention the new friendship that was forming. Contentment spread through Annie's body as she took another bite.

"This is so good," Serena said. "Do you cook much?"

"I didn't used to, but in the past few years, I've started to try new recipes." She didn't add that she'd started cooking when she'd lost her company because she was suddenly without a job and had nothing else to do. Annie took a bite of the cucumber, enjoying the way it crunched between her teeth. "Do you cook?"

"A little. Not a lot. It's no fun cooking for one person. When Danny—that's the name of my ex-fiancé—and I were together, though, I used to cook for us a lot." Serena got quiet, and Annie glanced over at her new friend. She looked so sad, and Annie wondered again what had happened to make Danny break up with her right before their wedding.

"Have you seen the monk seal and the honu at Poipu Beach yet?" Annie asked to distract her.

"Honu?" Serena looked confused.

"The Hawaiian green sea turtle." Annie was surprised that Serena didn't know what a honu was, if she lived on Kauai. "They sometimes come up on the sand to bask in the sun, and you have to keep at least fifteen feet from them. Finn loves seeing them."

"I've been to Poipu but haven't seen any animals." Serena shrugged. "But maybe I wasn't looking for them."

"You can't really miss them," Annie said with a laugh. "There's always a large crowd gathered around them, taking pictures. The turtles usually come up on the kiddie area, where the water is shallow and calm." She passed the bowl of cucumber salad to Serena. "The monk seal come up on the regular side of the beach."

"I like the kiddie side." Serena took another generous scoop of the cucumber. "I can't swim, so it's perfect for me."

"You live in Hawaii and you can't swim?" Annie widened her eyes at Serena in mock horror and was rewarded with a giggle.

"Yeah. I guess I should learn. Especially if I end up staying here." The laughter died and Serena's expression sobered. As if she'd just had a thought that made her unhappy.

"You never said what you're doing here." Annie looked at her new friend, and when she saw the way Serena's mouth pinched, she added, "Sorry, I didn't mean to pry. You don't have to tell me if you don't want to."

"You're not prying." Serena put her fork down. "I'm just not sure what I'm doing. I'm kind of at the point in life where I feel like I need a change, and Kauai seems like a great place to live. I'm not really a tourist, but I'm not from here either. I'm thinking of staying permanently. To figure out my life. I mean, this is paradise, right? If I can't figure out my life here, where else can I do it?"

"You're right. That's kind of why we're here in Kauai too. To start over after what—" Annie stopped herself. She didn't want to bring down the mood by mentioning what had happened to Finn. And she didn't like seeing the shadow pass over Serena's face, so she changed the subject. "Speaking of paradise, where do you think the best mai tai is on this island?"

"Oh, definitely at Tahiti Nui in Hanalei. I love Hanalei. I think I want to find a place up there." Serena's face lit up. "I went there one day to go to the beach, but it was raining, so I ended up at happy hour at Tahiti Nui. Their tsunami fries are so good, with that furikake and teriyaki sauce on them." Serena's eyes cleared, and Annie noticed they were an unusual shade of dark green now, when earlier, they'd been a lighter green.

"I think Duke's has the best ones." Annie was glad to have distracted Serena from whatever thoughts were distressing her. They continued to debate the mai tais around the island while they finished dinner.

"You're so lucky to have family around you." Serena stared down at her empty bowl.

"Where's your family?" Annie was curious about her friend.

Serena dropped her hands into her lap and didn't answer at first. Annie thought she hadn't heard or was ignoring the question, but then Serena spoke. "They're dead. At least my dad is. He died in a car accident when I was in college."

"Oh no." Annie reached across the table to squeeze Serena on the arm briefly, returning the comfort the other woman had offered earlier, when Annie had told her about the year her life fell apart.

"And I don't speak to my mom." Serena stared off into space. "She disappeared when I was ten, and I haven't seen her since."

"What?" Annie's forehead scrunched up. "What do you mean, she disappeared?"

Serena continued to stare off for a moment, then turned to look at Annie. "I meant she left. She left me and my dad one day. It's as if she just disappeared." Serena flicked both hands in the air. "Poof." She giggled, but the sound was not a happy one.

"I'm so sorry," Annie said.

"It's okay." Serena looked up, her words at odds with the way her mouth turned down and her eyes glittered, as if with unshed tears. "It's been a while. I'm used to being on my own."

"But I bet it doesn't make it easier. What about sisters or brothers?"

"I was an only child. I have an aunt and uncle somewhere on my mom's side, but we don't keep in touch. I really am all alone in this world." Serena gave what Annie thought was a brave smile, making Annie's heart go out to her.

"That must be so tough. As much as my family drives me up a wall sometimes, I don't know what my life would be like without them in it."

Serena shot Annie a look. "Exactly. That's why when I found Danny, I was so hopeful he'd be my family. He promised to love me always and be my best friend, my new family." Her expression changed as she looked off at a point above Annie's head. "But then he left me. When things got tough."

"That's terrible." Annie tried to temper her shock. "What happened? Do you want to talk about it?" Serena had listened with compassion earlier. It seemed only fair to offer an ear for what obviously had been a very difficult time of Serena's life.

Serena met Annie's eyes and shook her head slightly. "It's . . . I can't. Not right now. Things had been difficult for a while, ever since . . . but we were excited about the wedding. At least, I thought we were excited. *I* was excited. But it turned out, he wasn't." Serena's eyes glazed over, as if she'd been transported back to her past. "And then something happened, and he told me he couldn't do it. He couldn't marry me. It wouldn't be fair to either of us, he said. He wanted me to . . ." She broke off, and the look of pain flashed over her face again. "He said he couldn't live with me anymore."

"I'm so sorry." Annie frowned. She didn't know the whole story, but that sounded devastating to her. Just as devastating as losing her mother and Lili and her business.

"It was a weird time." Serena sighed. "He said I was 'acting funny.' That one minute, I'd be the Serena he knew, and then the next, I'd be this stranger." She looked up and met Annie's eyes, her forehead bunched up. "I have no idea what he was talking about. He made me sound like I had a split personality or something. I don't." She reached a hand out to Annie. "I mean, do I seem normal to you?"

Annie nodded. "Yes. I've only just met you, but you seem very steady to me."

"Right?" Serena shrugged again. "But it wasn't just that. He'd turned into a stranger too. He wasn't the Danny I knew when we met. I asked if there was someone else." She fell silent.

"Was there?" Annie was almost afraid to ask. That was what usually happened, right? Someone cheated and a couple broke up?

"He never answered. Just looked at me with this mournful expression, and then he said he was sorry and left." Serena licked her lips and then took a sip of her wine. She gave a grim smile. "That's why I'm single now. I don't trust men after Danny. He promised me the world, and then he left me all alone. Even knowing that I had no one. No family to turn to."

Annie got up from the table and walked over to Serena's side, leaning down to give her shoulders a squeeze before picking up their dirty dishes. She wanted to offer Serena some comfort, but she didn't know how the other woman would react if Annie hugged her like she would have hugged Julia or Izzy if something had happened to them.

Serena stayed seated while Annie cleared the table, and Annie knew she was getting her emotions under control. She loaded their dishes and utensils into the tiny dishwasher, then turned to look at her friend, who now looked composed, her hands folded in her lap.

"Hey, I picked up slices of lilikoi pie from Hamura's earlier. We can have it for dessert. Have you ever tried it?" Annie took down two glasses and got a pitcher of water from the fridge, holding it up with a question at Serena. Serena nodded, and Annie filled the glasses with ice and then water. She brought them to the table.

"Thanks. I didn't realize how thirsty the red wine and *lu rou fan* made me." Serena took a healthy swallow and then said, "I've never had lilikoi pie before. Is it good?"

Annie rolled her eyes. "So good. It's really refreshing and so light. I think Hamura Saimin has the best lilikoi pie on the island. The three of us always get it after saimin when we eat there."

"What's saimin?" Serena looked at her with curiosity, and Annie was glad she'd distracted her.

"You've never been to Hamura's?" Annie's mouth dropped in disbelief. "It's usually everyone's first stop after landing at the airport. It's like Hawaii's version of a ramen noodle soup. The restaurant is nothing fancy. It's counter service and no frills but such great food. I'll take you."

"Really?" Serena rested her chin in the palm of one hand. "Are you just saying that to be polite, or do you mean it?"

Annie was struck by the vulnerability in Serena's voice. She'd had so many disappointments in her life—no wonder she was wary of a simple invitation. "I mean it. I promise." She pointed at Serena before going to the fridge. She took two clear plastic clamshell containers out and popped one open, placing it in front of Serena along with a plastic fork. "Here, try it. I don't know why, but it always tastes better to me with a plastic fork."

Serena speared a piece and made a humming noise when she swallowed it. "It's so light and airy, and the passionfruit filling isn't too strong. It literally melts in my mouth."

"Right?" Annie sat down and took a bite of her piece. "Yum. This," she said, pointing to her slice, "is one of the best parts of Kauai."

Serena didn't say anything because her mouth was full, but she nodded in agreement. There was silence for the next few moments, as they both focused on the pie. When Annie was almost done with her slice, she asked, "Where are you from?"

"New York. I lived on Long Island," Serena said.

"We're from New York too. Another thing we have in common." She raised her fork in a mock cheers, and Serena copied her.

Annie gestured out the window when a gust of wind howled like it wanted to tear inside the ohana. "It doesn't sound like it's letting up. I haven't seen a storm this bad in Kauai before." She placed her fork down and stretched. "I'm going to clean this up, and then I should probably pack a bag, like Sam said."

Serena stuffed the last bite in her mouth and sighed in contentment. "That was one of the best meals I've had in a long time. I'll help you clear up." She got up and collected their empty containers and took them into the kitchen. "Thank you for the meal. Really. It was great."

"Anytime." Annie gathered her water glass and wine and placed them on the counter in the kitchen. "Oh, I should feed Marley." The dog walked up to her as soon as he heard his name.

Serena nodded and leaned against the counter watching them, another contented sigh leaving her lips. As Annie scooped the roasted chicken and vegetables she'd made for Marley into his bowl, she felt alive, really alive, for the first time in a long time. The old Annie was bubbling just under the surface, waiting to be let out again, after being beaten down for the past few years. And it was all thanks to Serena, the first person to really get her since her life fell apart.

13

Annie paused in the doorway of the bedroom. "You want to keep me company while I pack a bag?"

"If you don't mind me being in your bedroom?" Serena questioned back.

"Don't be silly." Annie gestured with her hand.

Marley followed them in and sprawled out at the foot of the bed. Annie looked at him. "I'm going to have to let him out to pee soon. I hope he doesn't wash away."

"Does he mind the rain?" Serena settled herself on the single arm-chair in the corner as Annie pulled a small rolling suitcase out of the closet.

"He doesn't love it, but he'll go out." Annie pulled open a few drawers and took out changes of clothing for herself and Brody, just in case, as well as for Finn. "Lili hated the rain, though, which is typical dachshund behavior. She absolutely refused to go out when it was raining. Thank goodness she was pee-pad trained."

"I bet she'd look cute in a pink raincoat." Serena giggled.

Annie looked up sharply. "How did you know she had a pink raincoat?"

Serena widened her eyes. "She did?"

They stared at each other, and then Annie laughed. "We really are in sync, aren't we? It's as if we can really read each other's minds."

"I know." Serena nodded before her eyes landed on some pictures on the dresser. She pointed to them. "Can I look at them?"

"Sure." Annie walked out of the bedroom and grabbed toiletries from the bathroom before coming back in. She stowed them in the suitcase and then walked up next to Serena to get her brush and phone charger from the top of the dresser.

"You have such a beautiful family." Serena was looking at a picture of Annie's whole family that had been taken right before the trip to Kauai when her mother died. They'd all met at Annie's parents' condo in New York—Annie, Brody, and Finn; Sam and Cam; and Jeannie and her husband and two kids—to celebrate their mother's birthday before everyone except Annie's family left for Kauai.

Annie took the picture from Serena and gazed at it. They all looked so happy, except for her. She had sunglasses on and wasn't smiling; she was looking off to the side instead of at the camera like everyone else. She dimly remembered posing for the picture. Brody had dragged her there, when all she wanted to do was sit by the lake at home and stare at the water. She was barely functioning, still distraught over Lili's death, overwhelmed with taking care of baby Finn, and also dealing with problems with her landlord.

They'd all gathered around a hot pot that night, the kids at a separate table, as the others had laughed and argued, cooking meats, vegetables, and various fish cakes and fish and squid balls in the boiling water in the middle of the table. It was one of Annie's favorite family traditions, but she'd barely eaten a thing that night, not even the bean thread noodles she loved so much. Brody had mixed her sauce—made with a raw egg and soy sauce, Chinese barbecue sauce, scallions, and hot sauce—and placed it in front of her. Hot pot signified family to her, but she'd been so wrapped up in her own misery that night that she'd barely paid any attention to her mother, not knowing that was the last time she'd see her.

Her mother had held Finn in her arms most of the night, so proud of her newest grandson. How Annie wished she could go back in time and snap out of it, hug her mother while she held Finn, and breathe in the familiar smell of the face cream her mom had used. If she'd known that was the last time she'd be with her mother, she would have slapped herself and woken up from that fog, cherishing every moment they had left.

"I like these sunglasses." Serena's voice broke through Annie's thoughts. "Did you get them here in Kauai?"

Annie looked up from the picture to find Serena holding a pair of sunglasses in her hands. She stared at them, not sure if her eyes were playing tricks on her. She reached out and took them from Serena.

The breath caught in Annie's chest, and she suddenly found it hard to breathe. "Where did you get these?"

"They were right here on the dresser, next to this basket of barrettes." Serena cocked her head to the side. "What's the matter? You look like you just saw a ghost."

Annie only stared at the sunglasses, turning them over in her hand, not quite believing what she was seeing. They looked just like the pair she'd lost at Kukui Grove when they'd gone to see the Chinese New Year celebration. But how could that be? She would have seen them if they were on the dresser all along, since she used this dresser every day. And she was almost positive they hadn't been here. Where had they come from?

"Annie?"

Annie turned to Serena. "I . . ." She couldn't form a coherent thought. What was happening to her? Had she found them and placed them here on the dresser herself? But then why couldn't she remember that she'd done so? The panic started in her chest, and her body tingled. Dimly, she was aware that Marley was at her side, pressing his body into her legs as her vision darkened. But no. She refused to give in to a panic attack, not when something good was finally happening. She would not embarrass herself in front of her new friend and lose control. She dropped the sunglasses and photo on the dresser and clenched her fists at her side. She would not give in to the darkness that was clawing its way through her body. She took a deep breath and blew it out through her mouth, then took another one in through her nose. In and out, slowly, as Serena stared at her, eyes wide and not moving a muscle.

When Annie felt slightly in control again, she loosened her fists and heaved out a breath. "I'm sorry." Tears wanted to spill out, but she wouldn't let them. "I get these . . ." She struggled for words. How to explain a panic attack to someone who'd probably never had one?

"Panic attacks?" Serena asked in a gentle tone.

Now it was Annie's turn to stare at Serena. "You know? I mean, you've had them?"

Serena nodded. "Unfortunately."

Annie drew her lips into her mouth, not sure what to say.

"I get it, Annie." Serena's voice was soft. "It's okay. I've been there. Whatever it was that set it off, I'm here, okay?"

Annie nodded, not trusting her voice. But she was grateful to have Serena there, someone who understood. Who'd experienced these terrifying attacks and knew how she was feeling without her having to put it into words.

14

Once Annie could function like a normal human being again, they made their way back out to the living room. Annie collapsed on the couch while Serena poured more water for both of them and brought it to the coffee table. Annie gulped it down like she'd been in a drought, and when she'd had enough, she placed the glass on the table.

"Better?" Serena asked, from where she stood beside the couch.

"Yes." Annie closed her eyes briefly and then opened them. "Thanks. For being here and not freaking out."

"I get it, Annie. I really do."

Their eyes met, and then Annie looked away. "Do you mind getting my wineglass? I need more wine." In her head, she knew that was probably the last thing she needed, but it would soothe her nerves.

Serena got their glasses and then sat on the couch next to Annie, who had Marley at her feet.

"How did your father get this house? It's such an ideal location, right on the water." Serena glanced out the big picture window behind the sink at the rain, which was still falling steadily. "Well, I guess it's ideal when there's not a crazy storm out."

Annie let out a breath, glad Serena was bringing the conversation away from her panic attacks. "I couldn't believe it when my father got the house." It had a private backyard with a canal that connected to the

Wailua River, just steps away. They could kayak or paddleboard to the river right from their own yard, or use the private dock a few houses down and through a bamboo tunnel for the residents of this street.

"It does seem like a prime piece of real estate in Kapaa." Serena was still looking out the window toward the main house.

"He bought this on the same trip that my mother died, if you can believe it." Annie took a shaky breath, glad her heart rate had returned to normal.

"What?" Serena turned toward her.

"Yeah, crazy, right?" Annie thought back to that time. All three sisters had thought he'd lost his mind. "He didn't tell anyone that he came to see this house in the days following my mother's death. He bought it and then didn't tell us until he was back in New York." Annie shook her head. "After the funeral, at the dinner for family who'd come, he announced that he was selling their condo and moving to Kauai. That's when he told us all he'd bought our mother's dream house here."

"No way." Serena sat forward, leaning toward Annie.

"Yup. Apparently, they'd been looking at houses because they were going to move here. But they didn't tell us. And she'd loved this house when they went to see it right before the hiking trip. He bought it in her memory."

"That's actually really romantic." Serena had a dreamy look on her face. "And sad."

Annie nodded. "Sam decided to move with him, which actually made me and Jeannie feel better, since we were worried about him. She and Cameron have been living with him in the main house for the last four years, and they've been really thriving here."

"They must have been happy when you and your family decided to move here."

"I think so. It is nice to be around family again." Annie paused, thinking again how Serena was making her appreciate her family. It had taken an outside perspective to get her to see that she was lucky to have them.

"Tell me about your mom." Serena picked up a couch cushion and hugged it to her chest.

Annie's lips curved, thinking about her mother. "She was great. Loving and kind, but she was serious about instilling responsibility and great work ethics in all three of us. She believed in keeping your word. That if you promise to do something, you follow through. Otherwise, don't promise."

Serena's brows rose. "My mother said the same thing too. She always said, if you commit to something, you have to stick it out." Her mouth turned down, as if the thought were an unpleasant one.

Annie shook her head. "Mothers."

"Right." Serena blinked a few times in rapid succession.

Annie peered at her, wondering if she was okay before continuing. "She was so much more outgoing than my father. She would have had a party for the whole neighborhood within a week of moving in." She looked off into the distance.

"She sounds great." There was a look of longing on Serena's face.

"She was. She loved to talk to people. Always wanted to know their story, what they're doing in life, their aspirations. She cared about people and loved gathering them together. Organizing parties, planning the food." Annie paused, thinking about the parties Finn had missed. Her mom had loved planning birthday parties for Jeannie's children, as well as Cam.

"What was her name?" Serena asked.

"Well, I think I told you she was half-Chinese and half-Hawaiian. She had a Chinese name but went by her American name, Chrissy."

"And what's your father's name?"

Annie grinned. "His American name is Jack."

There was a pause as Serena thought. "Wait. Jack and Chrissy? Like on *Three's Company?*"

Annie broke out in a big smile. "Yup. Exactly like that. It was their favorite show."

"And you have one sister named Samantha and another named Jeannie?" Serena raised her eyebrows, understanding dawning in her eyes. "Like *I Dream of Jeannie* and Samantha from *Bewitched*?"

Annie couldn't help the snort of laughter that escaped. "Exactly like that. I thought you'd be too young to get the reference. But yes, our whole family is named for American sitcoms. Except me—I'm named for the redheaded orphan. And my parents gave themselves American names when they got married. I guess they got tired of telling people how to pronounce their Chinese names."

Serena laughed right along with her. "So is your real name Anne?"

"Nope. Just Annie. My mom was obsessed with the movie. The one with Carol Burnett and Albert Finney. I think I learned how to sing 'Tomorrow' before I learned English."

Serena choked on her laughter, and Annie thumped her on the back, even as she herself gasped for air. Once Serena had caught her breath, she looked over at Annie, and it set them off again. Annie actually rolled off the couch, landing on Marley, who looked at her with displeasure. Which just set her off on another gale of laughter until, finally, she quieted. Looking up, she saw Serena catching her breath before reaching out a hand to haul Annie back on the couch.

"I haven't laughed like that in so long," Annie said, wiping the tears out of the corners of her eyes.

"Me too," Serena said. "I totally needed that."

"I'm so glad you're here," Annie said, when she could finally talk again without choking. "Let's take a selfie to remember this day." She gestured to Serena, who came to her side, and Annie snapped a picture.

Serena looked over her shoulder as Annie zoomed in on the photo. They both looked so happy in it.

"Have you been to Kauai before? Is that why you came here this time?" Annie asked, putting her phone down next to her.

"No. I've never been. But I wanted to be somewhere warm, to get away from the snow and freezing-cold weather. I didn't want to be in New York; plus, I lost my job, so there was no reason to stay. I figured I could start over somewhere new."

"So it was random?" Annie tucked her legs up under her, getting more comfortable. "You just pointed to a place on the map?"

Serena gave a small laugh. "Something like that." A light flickered in her eyes, making them glow like an animal's in the dark. "It was more . . . a feeling that I should be here. It's warm, and everyone always says how beautiful it is."

"I'm glad you picked it. Otherwise we wouldn't have met." Marley made a small snoring sound and Annie looked down, surprised he'd fallen asleep despite all the commotion.

"I'm glad I'm here too." Serena reached down and petted Marley. He opened an eye and looked at her but then closed it again. She straightened up. "I do miss New York City, though. All that hustle and bustle, the energy. It's gorgeous here, but sometimes at night, I get a little creeped out, all by myself."

"I miss the food in the city," Annie said. "Food here is good, but the diversity back in New York was great. You can get anything you're craving."

"Yeah." Serena nodded. "When I used to work there, on my days off, I would take the subway and just get off at any stop, then walk around until a restaurant caught my eye. I miss that, eating my way through New York City."

"Well, we'll just have to eat our way through Kauai together." Annie shot her a grin.

"I'm down for that." Serena leaned back. "Are you glad you moved here?"

Annie rocked her head from side to side. "Yes and no. I wish we could have brought our lake house here. It was so perfect for us and really hard to let go of."

"Why'd you sell it if you loved it so much?" Serena leaned forward, her face curious and her lips slightly parted.

"We couldn't stay there. Not after what happened." Annie paused, not wanting to think about what had made them move to Kauai, much less tell Serena. "But anyways, it was perfect. The lake life was good for Finn."

"What happened?" Serena asked.

"Nothing." Annie shook her head and waved a hand in the air. "We just had to. We needed to get away."

"But if you loved it so much . . ." Serena's voice cracked and she cleared her throat, giving Annie a puzzled look.

"It's . . ." Annie knew she was being evasive, but she couldn't get into it now. "I'll tell you another time. But believe me, we wouldn't have if we weren't kind of forced to. We were only there for four years. We thought we'd be there for much longer." Annie paused, lost in thought of her days in that house, of the tranquility of sitting by the lake staring at the water. "It was right on the water, one of only about seven houses whose yard backed up to the lake. We were so lucky to get it."

"Just like your father was so lucky to get this house." Serena stared at Annie. "Your family must have a lot of good luck."

"Some, and we also have a lot of bad luck too." Annie shrugged. "But the lake house was perfect."

"Perfect," Serena echoed, and her eyes got that faraway look again, making Annie wonder what she was thinking about.

15

Laptop ANNIE file

We loved that house on the lake. From the moment the Realtor took us to see it, we were instantly in love. We turned to look at each other, unable to believe that this house, this beautiful glorious house, was on the market. Until that moment, we never thought we could afford to buy a waterfront property. But there it was, the perfect house, tucked away about an hour and fifteen minutes north of Manhattan, in a town that the real estate agent called the "hidden gem of Westchester County."

The house wasn't huge, only about 1,700 square feet. But it was so well laid out and allowed so much natural sun that it was almost like living out-doors. I love bright houses. You can't be depressed in a house that lets in so much sunshine. I know you know what I mean.

My first apartment in the city was this tiny one bedroom that I shared with a friend, the two of us packed in there like rats. Our apartment faced an alleyway adjacent to another building, so it was always dark in there. We never knew if it was sunny or raining. The only way to tell was if one of us stuck our entire body out the window and craned our neck to look up and find the tiny patch of sky between the buildings. I really thought one of us would fall out of that window at some point. After living there for a year, I knew I never wanted to live in a dark apartment or house again. I crave bright open spaces. And this house was gloriously bright and happy.

It had three back decks overlooking the lake, about a hundred feet away. Three! It was the most amazing outdoor living space. To sit there and stare at the lake, watching the egrets and great herons, the ducks and geese on the water, listening to the burbling sound of the creek that ran down the side of our house into the lake. It was so soothing and everything felt better there. We could have a canoe or a rowboat and go boating right from our backyard. We could pack a cooler with beers and wine and just drift out there in the middle of the lake, the peaceful, peaceful lake. We would get a paddleboard, maybe two, so we could go out together.

The main bedroom upstairs was spectacular. It was huge, with its own bathroom and walk-in closet and a small balcony. The views from that balcony! I could stand out there all day. In the appraisal, the guy who wrote it called the views "superior." I couldn't have said it better myself.

This was it, the house where we would raise our family. The commute to the city for work would be a bit farther than we had planned but so what? It was worth it. To be able to come home to this every day. Who cared how long the train ride would be?

We were ecstatic and even the Realtor's warning that there would be a lot of bids on the house didn't dampen our mood. This house was meant for us. You know that, right? I could feel it in my bones. We put in a full-price offer and we got it! But I wasn't surprised. I knew we would. And the timing was perfect. We'd move in, and then our child would be born a few months later. Everything was perfect. And then you came along.

16

"Should I turn on some music?"

Serena nodded, and Annie muted the TV but kept the news on in case there were any updates on the weather. She picked up her phone and went to her music, picking a mellow mix. A deep male voice wafted through the small ohana from the Bluetooth speaker on the kitchen counter.

"I love Lewis Capaldi," Serena said from her end of the couch. Marley stood and stretched on the floor. He looked over at Serena and took a step back, going on the other side of Annie before settling on the ground again. Annie had bought him two dog beds, but he seemed to prefer to lie on the ground next to her.

"Me too. Brody doesn't like his voice. Said it's too soulful. Whatever that means. I think his voice is beautiful." Annie leaned into the couch cushions as the rich, throaty voice washed over the ohana. Music always made her feel better. She patted the couch next to her, and Marley jumped up. He pressed his body against hers, as if keeping a distance between himself and Serena. Annie wondered why he was still wary of the woman. She'd have to work on socializing him better if he was afraid of strangers. When she looked up, she found Serena watching them, a sad look on her face.

"What're you thinking?" Annie asked.

Serena bit her lip. "It's just . . . I was thinking about something Danny and I had once wanted." She grimaced and then shook her head. "Never mind. There was so much we were going to do. It's not important anymore. It's all in the past. No sense dwelling on it."

"You can tell me if you want." Annie studied Serena's face. "You listened to me before. It might help to get it off your chest." She turned the volume on the music down, then stroked Marley's back, grateful for the warm body next to her. She hadn't thought her heart would ever be ready for another dog again after Lili, but here was Marley, making his way into her heart. He was so different from Lili, but maybe that was what had made it possible for her to open her heart to him. He was his own dog.

"It's okay." Serena took a breath and blew it out. "I don't want to relive the past. I'm here in Kauai now, and I'm having a great time with you." But the expression on her face was still sad.

"I'm having a great time too." Annie's heart went out to Serena. As much as Annie had been struggling, it sounded like Serena had even more of a burden to carry. There was nothing like hearing about someone else's tragedy to bring your own life into perspective. Opening the door to Serena hadn't been a mistake after all. She was bonding with a new friend in a way she hadn't with anyone in a while. And Serena was making her feel better about herself. Maybe Annie wasn't such a failure, as a person, wife, or mother.

"I'm glad my car chose your street to conk out in," Serena said, breaking into Annie's thoughts.

"I was just thinking the same thing. What were you doing on our street, anyways?" Annie had been meaning to ask Serena that. Theirs was a private dead-end street, and not many cars usually turned down it.

"I made a wrong turn and was turning around." Serena shifted on the couch. "The rain confused me, and then the car just died."

"Oh." Annie nodded to accept Serena's answer, and then the corners of her lips lifted. "Did you know, when I first opened the door to you, all I could imagine was that scene from *Criminal Minds* where the homeowner opens the door and then . . ." Annie shuddered. "Anyways, I'm glad it was you and not someone who wanted to hurt me."

Serena threw her head back and laughed, causing Marley to turn his head in her direction. "Me? A danger to you? No way. I can't even kill a bug. I always screamed for Danny." Her face sobered and her laugh sputtered to a stop. "But I guess those days are long gone. I've had to deal with bugs myself for a while now."

"That's tough." Annie made a face in sympathy.

"It's fine," Serena said. "What happened to your mom? You said she died in Kauai?"

"Yes. They were here on vacation. It was supposed to be all of us, Jeannie and her husband and two kids, Sam and Cam, and me and Brody and Finn. But I was having . . ." Annie trailed off, the events of that summer flashing through her mind. "It was a hard year. I told you about it. I didn't end up going. I couldn't muster the energy." She took a deep breath. "I always wondered if I could have saved my mom somehow if I had gone."

"Oh, Annie." Sympathy oozed from Serena, and Annie looked up.

"I know there was nothing I could have done. But I can't help but play the what-if game. You know?" Even all these years later, Annie still felt responsible for backing out of the trip at the last minute.

"Yes, I do." Serena nodded.

Words started pouring out of Annie's mouth. "My mom had always dreamed of hiking the eleven miles of the Na Pali Coast to camp at Kalalau Beach. You need a permit, and they're hard to come by. But we all surprised her and planned this trip for her birthday. She was so excited." Annie paused, remembering the look on her mom's face when they told her. "She started training, dragging my dad and Sam on hikes in New York. She wanted me to train too, but . . ." Annie trailed off, pausing for a moment before continuing. "It was going to be the four of us doing the hike. Jeannie and the men were going to stay behind to watch the kids."

"What happened?" Serena asked after a few minutes when Annie didn't speak.

Annie turned to her. "Since I didn't go, it was only the three of them. I don't know if you know anything about this hike, but it's pretty dangerous. You're basically hiking along the cliffs, and some areas are really narrow—one misstep and you can fall to your death. Plus, you have to cross a lot of streams, and people have died from trying to cross them when they were flooded."

"Was that how your mother died?" Anxiety flooded Serena's face.

"No. They made it to the beach in one day. My mom was so excited. My father, not so much. He's a homebody. He's fit, but he doesn't like camping. He'd rather sleep in a bed. But it was her dream, so he went. They camped out for the night and then started back early the next day. They'd gone most of the way, maybe had two miles or so left." Annie's heart twisted as she remembered the frantic phone call from Jeannie that day. Like Annie, Jeannie had blamed herself for not going on the hike, even though there was nothing either of them could have done. Jeannie hadn't been back to Kauai since that trip. She'd been the closest to their mom and took her death the hardest.

"It rains a lot here, if you haven't noticed yet." Annie and Serena both turned to look out at the rain, which showed no signs of letting up.

"They thought maybe she slipped on a muddy patch, but later they realized it wasn't that." Annie blinked hard, willing the tears to stay away. "I wasn't there. I only know what Sam and my father told me, and they didn't really see it happen. One minute she was next to them, and the next, she was on the ground and unconscious."

"Oh, Annie." Serena scooted closer and put an arm around her. "I'm sorry."

Annie's anguished eyes sought out Serena's sympathetic ones. "There's no cell reception up there, no emergency service. Sam said she basically sprinted, trying to reach the end of the trail to get help. My father stayed with her, and he was able to signal to a helicopter, so they got help before Sam reached the end of the trail." Annie shook her head. "It was a brain aneurysm that had ruptured. That trail is not equipped for emergencies. By the time they could get her out, she'd suffered a stroke too. A few hours after they got her out by helicopter and got her to the hospital, she was gone."

Serena gasped. She grabbed Annie's hand and squeezed, the warmth soothing Annie's cold fingers. After a moment, Annie withdrew her hand to wipe the tears off her face. Marley looked at her without moving. Lili used to lick Annie's tears away whenever she cried, but Marley only stared at her, his head still as he studied her with a serious expression. A fresh burst of longing for Lili and for her mother shot through Annie's heart, and she placed a hand to her chest.

"I am so, so sorry for your loss, Annie." Serena sniffed, wiping away her own tears.

"I don't know why I just told you all that. I didn't mean to make us both cry." Annie gave a little laugh, suddenly embarrassed to have shared this with Serena. She must think it was too much info for a virtual stranger.

But Serena pulled Annie in, and suddenly, they were hugging and Annie let her guard down. She was just as comfortable with Serena as she was with Julia and Izzy, and right now, it felt good to have a friend hold her. They stayed like that for a moment, and then Annie pulled away. She needed a tissue, or she was going to snot all over Serena's shirt.

She stood and pulled a tissue out of the box near where Finn slept. She blew her nose and then walked into the kitchen to wash her hands. Then she turned to face Serena, giving her a rueful look.

"We're really just going for those deep conversations tonight, aren't we?" Although it felt good to talk about it. Maybe that's what Izzy had meant when he kept saying she should see a therapist. But for Annie, talking to someone like Serena was a much better alternative.

Serena picked up her wineglass and toasted her. "I'm glad we are. That you feel comfortable enough with me to tell me about your life, the good and the bad."

They fell silent, each lost in her own thoughts, listening to the music, which had continued to run, cycling to a song by Imagine Dragons. Annie glanced at the muted TV screen, where the meteorologist was gesturing in front of a weather map showing the line of severe thunderstorms currently moving across all of Hawaii. She was worried about Brody, stuck at the Lihue airport, and worried for them—if the river should flood, they'd have to evacuate. But right now, this very moment, it was nice to be all warm and cozy inside, having just shared an intimate talk with someone. Not just small talk or obligatory talk with a mother of Finn's friend. But the way she could talk to Izzy and Julia.

"This is nice." Annie voiced her thoughts out loud.

"I know." Serena met her gaze. "I didn't expect this. Not at all. I didn't think I'd like you quite so much."

Annie paused, wondering what Serena meant. She'd thought Annie was a bitch when she first opened the door? She smirked to herself, about to comment, but then Serena held up her glass again.

"To new friendships and new adventures."

Annie raised her own glass and echoed, "To new friendships."

17

The relentless deluge of rain continued to rage outside, as the strong wind gusts whistled through the air. Annie peered out the window by the front door, but all she saw was darkness and the pouring rain. She turned on the outdoor light, grateful the power was still on. Was it her imagination, or did the backyard look like it was flooding? She turned back to the news, but there wasn't any mention of flooding along the Wailua River yet, or a need to evacuate. All the same, she checked in with Sam in the main house.

A: Think we need to leave?

S: Baba doesn't think so. He thinks we'd be fine even if it flooded, since our property is up higher than the river. And the house is built up one story too. You guys okay?

A: Yes, we're dry and we have wine. ☺

S: ☺

A: Finn behaving?

S: He's good. It's good to see him laugh.

A: Thanks for watching him.

S: NP

Annie looked up from her phone. "I'm going to have to try to get Marley outside. He usually has to go after he eats." She turned the music off from her phone and then put it down and clapped her hands together. "Marley, come."

He trotted to her side, and she clipped a leash on his martingale collar. For longer walks, she used a harness, but for short distances, the collar worked. He usually went out in the backyard without a leash, but with this rain and wind, she didn't want to chance having him blow away.

Annie slipped on flip-flops and threw on her black windbreaker, which come to think of it, looked just like Serena's hanging on the hook by the door. With a glance back at Serena, who gave her a thumbs-up as if rooting for her against the storm, she took a breath and reached for the front door.

"Ready, Marley? Let's go!" She threw open the door and gasped as the cold rain hit her square in the face, soaking her. Marley looked at her, then stepped just enough outside to get his butt out the door and lifted a leg to pee, right on the lanai.

"Smart boy," Serena called, laughing.

"This rain is insane." Annie's hood flew off as the wind whipped through her hair. "Come on, Marley, hurry."

Marley finished his business and rushed back inside. He shook himself as Annie slammed the door shut. "You're spraying water everywhere." Annie held up her hands and turned away.

She took off her drenched windbreaker and hung it up next to Serena's. "Look," she said, pointing to their matching jackets. "Twins."

"Even our jackets have something in common."

Annie took the towel she'd used earlier off the hook and dried herself and Marley. "I can't believe how much rain there is. And it's kind of chilly with all that wind. You want a blanket?"

"Sure," Serena said from the couch. Annie walked to the closet next to the bathroom and pulled out two burgundy-and-white fleece blankets that they'd brought from New York. She hadn't thought they'd ever have to use them in Kauai, but now she was glad to have them.

She tossed one to Serena, then pulled out a chew bone for Marley. He grabbed it in his mouth, and after she'd settled on the couch under her blanket, he jumped up next to her.

"It's so cozy in here." Serena gestured around the room.

"It is." Annie nodded in agreement. And to think, just hours ago, she'd looked forward to an afternoon of drinking by herself. This was so much better.

Serena pointed in the direction of the main house. "I've always wanted to be part of a big family." Her voice was a mixture of longing and something hard that Annie couldn't identify.

"You said you were an only child?" Annie wanted to know more about Serena. It felt as if they'd started their friendship backward. They'd told each other their deepest thoughts without knowing the basics first.

"Yes. My parents divorced when I was young. They were so nasty to each other." Serena twisted her fingers together on top of her blanket. "My mom was a sociopath and a pathological liar."

Annie almost laughed out loud, thinking Serena was joking, but the sharp look on the younger woman's face stopped her. Her face had turned to stone, and a frown furrowed her forehead. "I mean it. She was crazy. She had no empathy and no idea what simple human compassion was. She wanted to hurt my father, to come out ahead of him no matter what, even if it meant hurting me in the process. She didn't want me. Never had. But she knew he did, and so she fought him."

"I can't even imagine." Annie rubbed Marley on top of his head as he gnawed on the bone, her heart going out to young Serena.

Serena's face turned almost ugly as she spoke, her mouth twisted and her eyes narrowing into two slits. "I hated her so much. Hated how she used the fact that courts usually grant custody to the mother against my father, lying about him under oath and twisting events around to make him look bad. Even though she was the one who was an alcoholic. She used to leave me by myself to go off on a binge when my father was working. But he didn't want to use that against her. It wasn't until she got really nasty that he finally told his lawyers about it."

"She sounds . . ." Annie trailed off, catching herself before she said something bad.

"Mean, crazy, awful?" Serena supplied, her face scrunched up in pain or hatred, Annie couldn't be sure. "She was. She dragged the divorce on for years, fighting my father at every turn. Eventually, the forensic psychiatrist recommended that she not even get visitation rights without a social worker present. That's how scared I was of her." Serena's mouth hardened. "I was only six when my father filed for divorce, and I was already scared to death of her then."

Sympathy for Serena bloomed in Annie's chest. "What an awful situation to grow up in. But your father eventually got full custody?"

Serena nodded. "Yes. Four years later. That's how long the divorce took. I was ten by then. We were both so relieved we cried the day we found out. He didn't care how much money he had to pay her. He only wanted me. And I never saw her again."

Annie's mouth opened in shock. "I don't understand how a mother can just leave her child like that." The lights flickered as if in reaction, and they both looked up. When the lights stayed on, Annie breathed out a sigh of relief. "Let me dig out flashlights and candles just in case. But keep going."

Serena shook her head as Annie stood. "She disappeared. For all I know, she's dead. Or she has a new family and is torturing them like she did us. I don't know." She narrowed her eyes and stiffened her spine. "I don't know and I don't care. She's dead to me."

Annie placed a hand on Serena's shoulder briefly before going to the closet by the bathroom. She had no words to comfort Serena, who was staring off in space, lost in her thoughts.

"I think she blamed me for everything bad that ever happened to her. She didn't want a child. She didn't want me. She told me over and over again: if her birth control hadn't failed, she'd never have had me."

Serena's eyes glittered. "The way she used to look at me when I was little—I still remember the hatred in her eyes and the way she'd stare at me as if she wished I'd disappear." Serena's voice dropped, and her tone froze Annie's blood. "You'd think a mother would love her child, even a little. Well, she didn't."

She turned to Annie, her eyes finally focusing. Annie held still in front of the closet, wanting to hear more, yet at the same time, her heart hurt for ten-year-old Serena, who'd had to grow up knowing her own mother hated her.

"My father told me they thought she had postpartum depression when I was born, but looking back, I know it was more than that. While some mothers fall in love with their children at first sight, she fell in loathe with me." Serena let out a dry laugh and pushed her blanket aside. "I never knew mothers were supposed to be loving until I was in kindergarten and would watch the other mommies come into class to volunteer for parties and events. I didn't understand what was happening when I saw the way those other mommies hugged and kissed their kids, and helped them with tasks and making sure they got their cupcakes and drinks."

"Oh, Serena." Annie's voice was soft.

Serena swallowed hard and stood, walking to Annie's side. "In my experience, mommies hit you if you annoyed them. Mommies locked you in small closets if they thought you were being too loud. Mommies left you home alone if they needed a drink and there was not a drop of alcohol in the house. Mommies stayed in bed for days, leaving you to find food for yourself. Those mommies I saw at school were so strange to me. I thought they were acting in a movie or something."

"Your mother hit you?" Annie whispered, holding in her hand two flashlights that she'd found in the closet.

"Yes." Serena was matter-of-fact, as if they were discussing the weather. "But I had my father, and he more than made up for her."

"But how could he let her do those things to you?" Annie couldn't stop her mouth from dropping open, imagining all that Serena had gone through.

"He didn't know. My mother scared me into not saying a word to him. She told me she would take me away from him if I ever told him any of the things she did."

"Oh my god."

"I lived." Serena shrugged. "The good times with my father more than made up for anything my mother did to me." She paused, her face softening at the thought of her father. "Him I miss so much. I would give anything if he was still here on Earth with me."

"He sounds wonderful. You two must have been so close." Annie thought of her own relationship with her parents. She knew they loved her, but she wasn't especially close to either parent, not the way her mom had been with Jeannie and her father was with Sam.

"We were." Serena's voice grew thick. "But he died when I was only a sophomore in college. And suddenly I was an orphan." She looked up and let out a short laugh. "I mean, technically I wasn't since everyone presumed my mother was still alive, but I might as well have been. I wouldn't be surprised if my mother had pissed someone off and they'd killed her." Her face twisted. "For all intents and purposes, I was alone in the world."

Annie wanted to reach out again to offer her sympathy, but something in the tilt of Serena's head stopped her. Serena was staring off in space, and Annie could tell her mind was in the past. *How do you console someone who's been through something like that?* Annie suddenly understood why people had a hard time talking to her the year everything happened. It was so hard to find the right words to express sympathy without sounding trite.

Instead, she handed a flashlight to Serena. "Let's see if these work." She pressed the button on hers, but nothing happened. Serena did the same. Nothing. "Shoot. We need batteries." She focused on Serena's face. "I'm so, so sorry for what you went through."

Serena flashed her a look of thanks. "My father left me well off. I had money, but no family. I was over eighteen so technically considered an adult, but I was still such a child."

Annie shut the closet door and made her way to the kitchen to look for batteries. "I can't imagine what that must have been like, to be alone in this world at that age."

Serena still stood by the closet, her gaze far off. "I had a breakdown that year." She stopped and her mouth quirked. "Maybe I shouldn't tell you that. Might scare you away, and I don't want to do that. I feel as if we're friends already, you know?"

"I do know. And that's not going to scare me away," Annie said, stopping in the middle of the kitchen.

"Thanks."

Annie nodded and watched Serena walk back to the couch. She sat and pulled the blanket over her lap. "I fell apart when my father died. I didn't leave the house . . . I wallowed for months." Her eyes got that faraway look again.

"Months?" Annie couldn't look away from those forlorn eyes.

"No one cared. I had no family. My friends were all at college." Serena drew her feet up on the couch and wrapped her arms around her legs. Her voice broke.

"Oh . . ." Annie walked to the junk drawer to give Serena a moment. She opened it, rummaging around, but there wasn't a single battery to be found.

"I wanted to die like my father."

Annie looked up at those words, her breath catching. She closed the drawer and made her way back to the couch, sitting down next to Serena.

Serena waved a hand in the air. "I just . . . wanted to disappear, you know? I didn't want to live my life anymore." She gave a little laugh. "That's why I understand how you felt the year your life fell apart."

"Yeah." Annie nodded, picking up her wineglass from the coffee table.

Serena's face suddenly lit up. "We both seem to have diarrhea of the mouth tonight, don't we?"

Annie had just taken a sip of the wine and snorted. Some of it shot up her nose. She clapped a hand over her mouth before it could spew out of her mouth. When she could talk again, she said, "Don't say things like that when I just swallowed a mouthful of wine."

Serena grinned at her, and Marley watched them, the bone dangling out of his mouth. Annie reached out to rub him on the head, and he returned his attention to gnawing on the bone.

"That's why I was so excited when Danny proposed. I mean, I loved him and was so happy to marry him, but he had a big family. A brother, a sister, and like a million cousins. They had huge family get-togethers for the holidays, and they welcomed me when we were together. But ever since we broke up, they won't speak to me anymore. I don't know what Danny said to them, but they blame me for what happened . . ."

Annie frowned when Serena didn't continue. "What happened?"

A dark cloud came over Serena's face, and suddenly, the mirth that had just filled her face was replaced with something darker. "It's complicated. Let's just say they blame me for the breakup, even though he was the one who ended things with me." She spoke through clenched teeth.

Annie eyed her, trying to gauge her mood. Was Serena still angry with Danny for breaking up with her? Or was she sad that she had lost the big family that had once welcomed her? "Life's been a bitch to you, hasn't it?"

"Yes, yes it has." Serena's eyes shifted, and suddenly, she was the warm, friendly person Annie was beginning to like a lot. "This is why I feel so comfortable with you. You just get me. I don't usually tell people about my past. It sounds so awful." She chuckled, and a chill went down Annie's spine. The sound was so hollow, so devoid of emotion, that she felt bad for her new friend. As much as Annie's life had gone downhill four years ago, others were having just as tough a time, if not tougher.

"You're welcome to share my family." Annie wanted to do what she could to make Serena feel better. "Jeannie is supposed to come visit soon with her family, and then it'll get even louder."

"That sounds so nice, you have no idea."

Annie tipped her head. "Jeannie hasn't been back here since our mother died. I think she's afraid to. But Sam and I talked her into coming for spring break. Her kids miss this place. And we miss them."

"I'm sure she'll be happy to be with family again." The wistful tone was back in Serena's words. "I can't tell you how often I used to look at families who were out together, even doing something simple like taking a walk or having a picnic at the beach, and wish I was part of it. It was just my dad and me for most of my childhood, and then once he was gone, it was just me. And for a while I thought I had Danny and his family, but now, it's just me again."

She looked so sad that Annie wanted to reach out and hug her. The thing was, Annie could picture Serena's longing perfectly. To think your life was going to go one way, to plan for it, wish for it, and finally have it in reach, only to have it all fall apart. "I know this doesn't help, but I'm really sorry for what you went through as a child. I don't know what happened between you and Danny, but I know what it's like to have your dreams crushed and to lose someone."

"It does help. Especially because I've always thought you were so perfect. I never thought you would understand all this." Serena was looking away, not meeting Annie's eyes.

"I do understand." Annie was going to say more, but then she stopped. What had Serena just said? That she'd always thought Annie was so perfect? That made no sense—they'd just met today.

Before Annie could think more about what Serena meant, Serena suddenly reached out to clink her glass against Annie's. Except she did it a little too hard and wine sloshed out of Annie's glass and onto the blanket covering her legs. Annie made a soft sound of surprise and used the napkin in her hand to try and clean up the spill.

"Oops. I'm so sorry." Serena giggled. Annie stopped dabbing at the blanket and looked up. Serena sounded drunk. But how could that be? They hadn't even finished their second glass of wine. Maybe she was a lightweight?

"It's okay." Annie didn't want her to feel bad and tried to make light of the spill. "The wine will blend in with the burgundy part of the blanket." She got up to get paper towels and a cleanser for the spill.

"I'm so clumsy sometimes." Serena sank back, relaxing into the couch cushions as if she hadn't just told a story of an awful childhood and the loss of her fiancé. Annie nodded at her, thinking that Serena was putting on a brave face to cover her hurt.

"I'm clumsy too." Annie turned back to the stains and dabbed at them. "I'm always walking into tables and chairs and giving myself bruises."

Serena's face brightened as if Annie had just said Santa Claus was real and coming to town. "Oh, me too! I call them Unidentified Party Injuries."

"UPIs!" Their laughter filled the ohana, and Marley paused in his chewing to stare at them again. After cleaning up the spill and opening another bottle so she could top off their glasses—Hadn't Annie promised herself she'd have only one glass? But she wasn't drinking alone, so it didn't count, right?—she settled back on the couch, the conversation now on the different restaurants in Kauai and which ones they had tried. But even as Annie relaxed on the couch with her delightful new friend, her mind kept returning to what Serena had said earlier.

What had she meant when she said she hadn't thought Annie would understand? That she was so perfect? Had Annie heard her wrong? Or was she just implying that she didn't think they would have connected so quickly and strongly?

18

Annie's phone dinged while she was in the bathroom, peeing out some of the wine she'd consumed. She washed her hands and then picked up the phone.

B: Just checking in. Everything okay?

A: Yes! I'm feeling pretty good right now. <smirking emoji>

B: Oh yeah? Good in what way? 😉 Should I battle the storm and get home now?

A: Haha, you're so funny. How're you doing at the airport?

B: There are worse places to be stuck at. There's food and drinks and company. Can't ask for more than that. But hope the storm lets up enough soon for me to drive home.

A: Me too. But the news is saying it's getting worse.

B: I know. I'm going to try to get home now.

A: Okay, but if roads are bad, maybe you should stay at the airport.

B: I'll see. But what's making you feel good? You haven't felt that in a long time.

A: Really? 😠 You really think I am one giant grumpy potato don't you?

B: Hey, if the spud fits . . .

A: 😣 That was lame. You're so not funny.

B: Yes, I am. But tell me why you're happy. Seriously, that's good to hear.

A: I think I made a new friend.

B: Who, Kalani?

Annie rolled her eyes. Seriously? Had Brody not heard a word she'd said about how she hadn't connected with Kalani? Why was her whole family so intent on throwing their neighbor at her?

A: No. Serena!

B: Oh, right. What's she like?

Annie looked toward the door. She'd had to pee so bad earlier but had held it, trying to figure out what Serena had meant when she said she'd always thought Annie was so perfect. But then she couldn't hold it anymore and had made a beeline for the bathroom, making Serena crack up.

What was Serena like? There was so much about her that Annie liked, and they shared so many similar experiences and had supported each other as they talked about both of their pasts that it was hard to believe they'd only just met. But at the same time, how well did she know the other woman? Yes, they'd bonded, and yes, Annie was sure they were going to be good friends, but what did she really know about Serena? For all she knew, she was a very good actress who had an ulterior motive. But what motive and for what gain?

B: Hello? You there?

Annie shook away the doubts, determined not to let her imagination get the best of her. Serena was not here to hurt her or get something from her.

A: Yeah, sorry. I really like her. She gets me. We're having great conversations.

B: She's still there?

A: Have you looked outside? Of course she's still here. We had dinner and now we're having a drink on the couch and just talking.

B: You guys ate the lu rou fan that your father made for us didn't you? 😠

Annie stifled her laughter. Brody loved her father's cooking and had been looking forward to the *lu rou fan* ever since her father had brought over the pot that morning. Brody couldn't get enough of her father's cooking. His favorite was the *niu rou mien*, Taiwanese beef noodle soup, a hearty dish with a broth seasoned with star anise, peppercorns, and other Asian spices, with chunks of tender beef and crisp green vegetables. Her father made his own noodles, and Brody always had seconds whenever her father made it.

A: Sorryyyyyy!

B: 😠 But wait. I thought you said Serena gave you a weird feeling.

A: It was only because she looked familiar. But we figured out why. Finn and I saw her when we went to Lydgate Beach yesterday.

B: Oh.

A: I really like her.

B: I'm glad you've made a friend. Really, Annie.

A: But? I hear a "but" there. Even though we're texting and I can't hear you, I hear it.

B: You realize that makes no sense, right?

A: Yes, it does. And you're not answering my question.

B: Just . . . I don't know. Something seems off. Your intuition has always been spot-on. And you had a funny feeling about her earlier.

A: I told you, it was only because she looked familiar. There's nothing off about this. I made a new friend. Period.

B: Don't get mad, A. We were just having a nice chat.

A: Until you decided to be judgmental.

B: I'm not . . . Look. I'm happy for you, okay? Just . . . be careful.

Annie didn't answer and made a face of disgust. Ugh. Why did Brody have to rain on her parade? He was the one who wanted her to make new friends here, and now he was questioning her judgment?

With a sigh, Annie looked down when her phone dinged again.

B: Are you going to let her stay there if this lasts into the night?

A: I don't know. I guess. I can't kick her out, can I? And what about you? What are you going to do about sleep if you're stuck there?

B: Don't worry about me. I'm more worried about you.

A: Would you be worried if I were with Izzy or Julia?

B: No, I'd be glad you had company.

A: Same thing. Serena is a friend. I have a feeling we're going to be good friends.

B: Okay. But I wish your new friend is Kalani.

A: Oh, god, not this again. Kalani's nice but I didn't connect with her like I do Serena.

B: But your family knows Kalani. We don't know anything about this Serena. I don't like this. Maybe she wants something from you.

A: I'm leaving now. Goodbye.

B: Wait . . .

Annie closed out of the text exchange and opened the bathroom door.

"I thought you'd fallen into the toilet." Serena had the remote in her hand, clicking through the channels.

"Sorry. Brody was texting me. I don't know how he's going to get home." Annie walked to the couch and plopped down on it.

"He was a fireman with the FDNY, right?" Serena continued to surf the channels.

Annie nodded. "How'd you know?" She racked her brain, trying to remember if she'd told Serena that. She must have, though. How else would Serena have known?

Serena shrugged. "I think you told me?"

Annie stared for a moment and then said, "Right. So yes, he was a fireman. He loved his job so much. It was hard for him to leave it and retire to move here."

"Isn't he young to be retired?" Serena questioned.

"Sort of. But with the FDNY, he could have retired after twenty years on the job. He had twenty-one years, so it wasn't unheard of, but he had wanted to wait until he had twenty-five years." Annie sighed. She knew Brody had given up a lot to move here. He'd loved his job so much, and the camaraderie he'd built with his fellow firefighters. Yet he'd given that all up, plus leaving his entire giant Irish family in New York to come here so they could start over. He'd sacrificed a lot for this move.

"If he loved his job so much, why didn't he wait until he reached twenty-five years?" Serena turned her attention to Annie, placing the remote on the coffee table.

"We had to . . ." Annie stopped herself. She'd already told Serena so much about her life, and she suddenly wondered if it was wise to tell her more. Especially because the reason they'd moved here was all tied up in Annie's guilt at not protecting Finn when he'd needed her. Brody's skepticism was getting into her head.

Serena regarded Annie and waited, but when Annie didn't continue, she popped off the couch. "I have to pee too. All this water and wine we're drinking. Be right back."

Annie sat on the couch, lost in thoughts about Brody as she stared blindly at the news, which Serena had ended back on. She knew her husband didn't blame her for what had happened last summer, but she hadn't realized he didn't trust her with Finn until they'd moved to Kauai.

It was a week after they'd arrived on the island, and they were in the ohana unpacking a box because Brody had finally gotten tired of searching through them all whenever he needed something.

"Annie, you're in paradise, yet all you've done this week is sit on the lanai. Why don't you come with us to the beach? Visit all your favorite places?" Brody pulled household supplies like scissors, pens, notebooks, and books out of a box as he spoke.

"I'm settling in." Annie leaned her hands against the counter and didn't feel the need to elaborate that she'd been feeling so heavy and listless, even though she knew she should get off her butt and do something. Unpack, get to know the neighbors, enjoy the beautiful sunshine and ocean breeze. Take Finn for shaved ice and malasadas, the puffy orbs of fried dough, almost like doughnuts, that he loved so much.

"I thought with your father and sister here to help, it would be better—" Brody broke off and stuffed his hands in his pockets, hunching his shoulders forward as if against the cold.

Annie let go of the counter and slowly raised her head to stare at her husband. "You don't trust me with him." Her voice was so low it came out as a whisper.

Brody opened his mouth, but nothing came out, and Annie saw the truth in her husband's eyes. Silence settled over the kitchen like a blanket of snow as they stared at each other, the tension so thick it almost choked her.

And as always, it was Brody who broke the tension. He'd heaved a big sigh and then reached out to draw Annie close to him, enveloping her in his strong arms. She'd melted into his chest, desperate to find her way back to him. Why couldn't she shake off this malaise that had settled over her the last few years? She wanted to find that type A go-getter she used to be.

Brody spoke, his deep voice rumbling in Annie's ear. "Remember our first date?" His voice was husky, caressing the air between them.

"Yes." Her voice was barely above a whisper, and she smiled into his chest. She wished they were still those two people from back then, just discovering one another.

On their first date, at a dimly lit wine bar on the Upper East Side of Manhattan, Brody had grabbed her hand in the middle of a story she was telling him. They'd been getting on so well, and there was definitely chemistry between them. When he took her hand, the spark that shot up between their joined hands had startled them both. And she'd further surprised them by placing a hand on his crotch. She had no idea what possessed her to be so bold and inappropriate. But she'd been burned on too many dates, thinking each might be a keeper and then finding out they weren't interested. She wanted to know if Brody was interested in her.

Where had that excitement gone, when she couldn't wait to see him again? Where was the anticipation of a date with him, when she used to dance to music as she put on makeup, knowing she'd see him soon? How had they gotten to this point, where she let small irritations take over, when once, they hadn't been able to get enough of each other?

As if he knew she was thinking about him, Annie's phone rang.

"I was just thinking about our first date," she said in lieu of a greeting when she picked up.

Brody laughed. "That's good. Just called to make sure you know I'm glad you made a friend. I just want you to be safe."

"I know." Her voice softened. She paused and then added, "I'm sorry."

"It's okay." He paused. "I just talked to Finn. You're not going to believe what he said to Jeannie when they FaceTimed with her and her kids earlier." The hilarity in Brody's voice lifted Annie's spirits. She vowed again to get her act together, to throw herself into life in Kauai and finally pull herself out of this pit she'd somehow landed in.

"What did he do?" Knowing their son, it was probably something outrageous.

"Sam and Jeannie were talking about Jeannie and her family coming to visit for spring break, but Jeannie was kind of dragging her feet. Finn told them they should come because Ah-Gong missed Jeannie's kids so much. Jeannie teased Finn and asked if they could borrow Ah-Gong for a while, if he missed them so much." Brody paused to catch his breath. "And do you know what that little rascal said?"

"I can't even imagine." Annie could already feel the anticipation of mirth coming on.

"He told Jeannie that he and Cam need their Ah-Gong. But he said he'd go online and order a new Ah-Gong for Jeannie's kids, so they could have one too. And he said he'd find an old one, so it would be cheaper." Brody let out a bark of laughter and Annie joined him.

"He did not," she said when she could talk.

"Yup. That's your child." Brody chuckled. "Where does he get these ideas from?"

"No clue." Annie heard the toilet flush and turned toward the bathroom door. "I'm going to call him and hear it from the source."

"Okay, glad things are good over there. I'll keep you posted."

"Same here." She paused. "Thanks, Brody." And she hung up, snickering at how clever their son was.

19

When Serena got out of the bathroom, Annie told her what Finn had said about buying a new grandfather for Jeannie's kids.

"He didn't." Serena's lips twitched, and when she caught Annie's eyes, the two collapsed on the couch in laughter.

"Kids," Annie said, shaking her head. "The things that come out of their mouths. Do you mind if I call him real quick? I just . . ." She was about to say that she usually had such a hard time connecting with him and this seemed like the perfect opportunity to try to bond with him.

Serena waved her hand in the air. "Call him. Don't mind me. You've already been so kind, letting me crash here and feeding me. You do what you have to with your family."

"Thanks." Annie flashed her a smile as she dialed her father's landline.

Finn answered the phone with a breathless "Hello?"

"Finn." Annie's heart contracted. "I heard you wanted to buy a new Ah-Gong for your cousins."

"Yes." A loud crash sounded, followed by a serious of rustles and muffled conversation. Annie pulled the phone away from her ear and set it on speakerphone.

"Hello?" Finn finally said again.

"Did you drop the phone?" Annie asked, shaking her head.

"Uh-huh." More rustling.

"Have you ordered a new grandpa yet?" Annie teased.

"No. Sam won't let me use her computer."

"You're so silly, you know that?" Annie held back her laughter, but she could imagine him grinning from ear to ear, proud of himself.

"Not silly," Finn said. He chortled, deep in his belly, in the way that always made her and Brody stare at each other in delight, before cracking up themselves. These were exactly the kind of moments she needed more of with her son.

"And what's this I hear about a discount for an older grandpa?" Annie pretended to be stern. "Who even taught you that?"

"Nobody." Finn yelled that out so loudly that Annie winced, even though she didn't have the phone against her ear. She saw Serena glance over at them. "I learn-ned that all by myself!"

"That really is silly." Annie tried to sound firm but couldn't help the laughter that crept into her words.

"No, it's not. New things are more 'pensive, so older things get a discount." Finn sounded proud of himself.

"Can't argue with his logic," Serena whispered.

Annie hooted. It felt so good to let go, and she'd done more of that today than she had in the last few years. When she could speak again, she asked Finn, "So what does Ah-Gong think about this?"

"Dunno. Cam needs me. Bye!" And with that, Finn was gone, leaving Annie with a dead phone.

"Did he hang up on you?" Serena asked.

"Apparently." Annie looked at her phone, which had definitely been disconnected.

"What a clever boy." Serena sounded proud, as if she knew Finn. "You're a really good mother, you know that?"

Annie swallowed in surprise. "Really? You think so?" She'd doubted herself all Finn's life, so to hear someone say the opposite had a glimmer of hope lighting up inside her.

"Yes." Serena nodded. "Look how good you were with him on the phone. He obviously loves you and has a good rapport with you. You've taken such good care of . . . of your, um, son." Serena stumbled over the end of her sentence, and Annie wondered again if she was getting drunk. But they'd only just opened the second bottle between them, and the drinks had been spread out over several hours. She herself didn't feel drunk, just pleasantly happy, as if nothing could bother her today.

"Thanks for saying that, because most of the time, I don't feel like a good mother. I don't know what I'm doing, and I'm usually so awkward and not motherly toward Finn." Annie stood and paced the ohana, reliving her conversation just now with Finn. It was the most natural they'd been around each other in a while, and that spark of optimism bloomed even more in her chest. Maybe she could do this.

"I don't believe you." Serena's firm voice had Annie turning to her.

"Don't believe me how?"

"That you don't know what you're doing with him."

"Oh, thanks." Annie nodded. "Well, here's an example: I didn't even plan his birthday party a couple of weeks ago, or pick out his gifts."

"How come? I think that's something I'd love to do if I had a child." Serena got that faraway look in her eyes again.

"We don't know anyone here, so Sam said she'd be in charge. And I don't really know what Finn likes . . ." Annie scrunched up her nose, thinking back to the birthday party they'd had at the big covered main pavilion at Lydgate Beach Park, next to Kamalani Playground.

Sam had thought that was a good place to have Finn's party, since the mazelike wooden play structure was one of Finn's favorites. It was huge, and decorated with keiki art, whimsical and colorful carvings of sea animals and other artwork for kids. Finn had had a blast with Cam, Leila and her two sisters and one brother, along with a few other children that Sam had invited. It had made Annie happy to see Finn climb all over the wooden play structure and run screaming on the gigantic grassy area with the other kids, playing their own version of tag.

"What?" Serena frowned, bringing Annie's attention back to her. "What do you mean you don't know what Finn likes?"

Annie flushed and her face went hot. "I just . . . I don't know. Brody is the one who always knows what Finn is into. He picked out Finn's birthday presents." She was suddenly embarrassed. She thought back to the party, when she'd watched Finn open the present from her and Brody.

Finn had been sitting under a picnic table with the largest present, his cheeks red. He bounced up and down, wound up from the excitement of his party. Brody had told him to wait until things calmed down before opening his presents, but while no one was watching, he'd ripped it open. She'd smiled to herself, not blaming him for being unable to wait. He'd opened the box and pulled out a remote-controlled transformer car.

A while later, Sam had started collecting empty plates and glasses after everyone had left and it was just family. "Did you have a good day, Finnie-boy?" She had leaned down to rub him on the top of his head.

"Yes, the best." Finn shook the box in his hands, a smaller one than the one he'd opened in secret.

"If you want to open the present from Mommy and me, go ahead," Brody said, taking a long sip from the bottle of Kona Longboard beer in his hand.

"I want to open this one." Finn shook the box again.

"I thought you wanted to open the big box?" Brody looked around. "Where is it?" He spotted the box under the picnic table and got up to get it. "Did you open this already?"

Finn turned innocent eyes to Brody, his face clear. "No, Daddy. I think Leila did."

Annie's mouth had dropped open at how easily Finn had lied to Brody. She was about to say something, but then Brody asked, "This was just what you wanted, right?"

Finn nodded, and a flash of remorse went through Annie. What kind of mother didn't know what her four-year-old wanted for his birthday? Good thing Brody had known.

"Don't feel bad, Annie." Serena's voice brought her back to the ohana. "I wouldn't have guessed that he'd want a transformer car either. Maybe it's just that Brody is more in tune with what little boys like, because he was once one himself?"

"Or maybe it's because I don't pay as much attention to my child as I should?" Annie had meant that to come out jokingly, but instead, it fell flat, leaving Serena staring at her in silence for a beat.

"I'm sure that's not it?" Serena's sentence ended in a question, much like it had when she'd first showed up at the ohana, making her sound uncertain. She cleared her throat. "I mean, I know it's not that."

"Thanks—you're good for my psyche." Idly, Annie played with the ends of her hair, twirling it around her finger. Midtwirl, her hand stilled.

An odd little shiver ran down her spine. What had Serena just said? Her mind spun. Why did she know so much about Annie and her family? Annie was almost sure she hadn't told her what Brody had bought for Finn. Or had she?

20

It's my son's birthday today. When I was pregnant, I was sure I'd be one of those ridiculous moms who planned elaborate birthday parties for their babies. I'd invite all the kids we knew and their parents, and have lots of food, cake, and games. Wine and beer for the adults. I'd buy our son presents I knew he'd love, and he'd grow up knowing birthdays are special. Yet here it is, my son's fourth birthday, and I can't do anything. I don't know anything about him. I don't know what kind of toys he likes, or what movies. I don't know if he prefers cars, or balls, or arts and crafts. I don't know anything. But you do. You get to be with him, smiling proudly as he blows out his candles.

I haven't felt like myself ever since that . . . incident with my son. I can't even say it. I try not to think about it because otherwise, it would make it true. I know he blames me, and truth is, I think it is my fault. Sometimes I don't remember doing things. It's like I wake up and can't remember my dreams but it's real life, not a dream. One time, I apparently sold stock in the middle of the night and I didn't even know I did it until two weeks later, when I got the statement. Another, I made a date with a friend (back when I went out with friends) for lunch and never showed because I didn't remember doing that.

So maybe what happened with my son was my fault. Maybe I did something and I can't remember. But how could I have done that? Even if I'd blacked out, wouldn't I remember if I did something that would have hurt my little boy? Wouldn't I always protect him, even if I was in a blackout and don't remember anything? Isn't that what a good mother would do?

I am a good mother. I am. I just never knew being a parent was so hard. When he was little, he'd cry and cry and I'd cry right along with him because I didn't know what to do. I thought there was something wrong with him. Then I thought there was something wrong with me. That something was broken in me and that's why I couldn't bond with my little boy.

But then I found out the truth. I realized why we never bonded. And I knew what I had to do. I knew

I had to tell you the truth, that you'd help me. But people kept telling me I was depressed. They told me I needed help.

I feel better now, being in Kauai. The sun has cleared my head and the mai tais have lifted my mood. My son had a great time at his birthday party, which I didn't plan. But I was there, watching him play with the kids, eating his favorite foods, and blowing out the candles on his cake. I watched him open his presents, presents that I didn't buy. But soon, soon, I'll get to know him again and know what he likes because I'm going to follow through on my plan. He's the most precious being in the world to me and I'll do whatever I have to, to get him to love me.

21

"It's my best friends, the ones I told you about." Annie held up her phone so that Serena could see the incoming FaceTime call. "They like to check in on me." She gave her a wry smile. "They want to make sure I'm not about to kill myself or something."

A tic jumped in the corner of Serena's right eye, and Annie realized too late that she shouldn't have made a joke about suicide. Especially after what Serena had confided in her. But before she could apologize, the other woman smoothed a hand over her forehead and said, "Right. Happens to me too. Danny had me hospitalized once because he thought I was going to harm myself."

"What?" Annie spun around in surprise to fully face Serena. God, she was the worst. She'd just stuck her giant foot in her mouth, making a joke about something that wasn't funny. She wanted to ask Serena more about what she'd just said, but she had already picked up the call and Izzy's loud voice distracted her.

"Annie! Are you okay?" he shouted, holding his phone so close to his face that all Annie could see were his perfectly arched eyebrows. "We saw on the news that there's a huge storm going on there. Flooding and everything. Wanted to make sure you're okay."

Annie recoiled from the loud voice and traded a look with Serena. Before she could speak, Izzy bellowed again. *"Can you hear me?"* He brought the phone up to his face.

Annie winced at Izzy's high-pitched yell. This close up she could see every pore of his clear brown skin.

"For heaven's sake, Isaac Michael Griffith, how many times do I have to tell you, you don't need to yell on FaceTime?" Julia's face scrunched into a scowl and Annie suppressed her grin. "Get that phone away from your face."

"Don't call me Isaac. It's Izzy." Izzy moved the phone away and stuck out his tongue.

"So mature, *Isaac*." Julia's voice dripped with disdain.

Annie did laugh then, grateful that her two best friends were behaving exactly as she'd left them, and also completely ignoring her. "Hello? Remember me? The one you called?"

"Go ahead and take the call," Serena mouthed at Annie as she made to stand up. "I can wait at the breakfast bar."

Annie waved a hand at her. "No, no. Stay. I want to introduce you to them."

"Who're you talking to?" Izzy's curious face peered at her.

"Hang on a sec." Annie beckoned to Serena. "Come over here so they can see you."

Serena scooted over on the couch, her face clouded in uncertainty. "Are you sure?"

"Yes!" Annie gestured to her again. "Come on." She turned back to the phone and angled it so that Julia and Izzy could see Serena. "This is my new friend Serena."

"Hi." Serena waved at them, a tentative smile on her face. Even with her hesitancy, Annie could see how luminous her face was when she smiled, as if lit from within.

"Hi, Serena." Julia waved, but then she must have dropped her phone, because all they could see was some blurred and jerky movement before her image came back on the screen.

"Serena and I are stranded inside because of the storm. Wait, isn't it really late there?" Annie checked the clock. "Like after one?"

"Yup." Julia grinned, and Annie could see for the first time how red her face was.

"You guys went out?" Annie stuck out her bottom lip, half pouting that her friends were together in New York City partying it up while she was stuck inside in a storm.

"Julia met me after the show. She wanted to introduce her new love to me." Izzy wiggled his eyebrows, and both Annie and Serena laughed.

"And?" Annie raised her eyebrows back at Izzy.

"I like her. I think you would too." Izzy gestured to Julia, whose face was turning a darker shade of red. "I think she's in love."

"Julia, you look like you got a sunburn. How much did you drink tonight?" Annie teased, thinking of how the Asian glow always affected her and Julia when they drank.

"A lot." Julia had a goofy look on her face. "But I was nervous. It's the first time Sheilah has met any of my friends."

Julia had just met Sheilah through a friend right before Annie moved to Kauai. She'd rounded up Annie and Izzy for bubble tea to discuss it. "I really like her, but my parents aren't going to approve." Annie remembered how Julia's eyes had clouded when she said that. Julia was bisexual, and her traditionally Chinese family didn't know.

"Maybe this is the universe's way of telling you to finally come clean with your parents. It's going to be hard, but maybe in time, your parents will come around?" Annie may not have known how to fix her own life, but she had no problem giving advice to someone else.

"Yeah." Julia had heaved a deep sigh.

Now Julia happily told them about the night and how well Sheilah had gotten along with Izzy. Annie studied her friends' faces as Julia spoke. They looked so relaxed, so happy in their own skin. They knew what they wanted—to dance in New York City—and were still pursuing their dreams. While her dreams had crashed and burned and she was left wondering what to do next. What did she do when there was no place to channel all the passion she'd once put into dance?

The more she listened to Julia and Izzy talk about Sheilah and what was going on in New York, the more Annie missed her old life. She had a focus back then. She knew what she wanted and was doing what she loved. Teaching, rehearsing with her modern dance company, performing in and around New York City, and going to schools for lecture demonstrations. She'd even enjoyed the administrative side of the studio—hiring teachers, dealing with advertising copy, maintaining the website, ordering supplies, and the myriad things to do when you ran your own business.

She'd thrived on the fast-paced life of a performer, the thrill of getting up in front of a crowd, no matter how big or small, and the joy she took in movement, whether in a class or on a stage. She had never thought it would all end so abruptly, and all because the landlord had raised her rent. One minute she was planning the winter schedule for her dance studio and dreaming up new choreography for the company, and the next, her lawyer was advising her to file for bankruptcy.

Even though Julia liked to point out that her company had been in trouble financially, Annie liked to think she would have figured out a way. She always did. But she didn't get that chance. Her landlord took that choice away from her. And now she was in Kauai, at loose ends, not sure what she wanted to do.

"Are you listening to me?"

Annie blinked, brought back to the present by Izzy's voice. He'd taken over catching her up on his life. And no, she hadn't been listening.

She'd been dwelling on her past, on what her life could have been if she hadn't lost everything. She hadn't even wanted to dance anymore after that. She had always taken so much pleasure in dance classes. But she hadn't stepped foot in a studio in three and a half years.

"I wish I was there with you. I miss you guys," Annie said instead of answering Izzy's question. She missed her friends so much. Why had she and Brody moved to Kauai?

Both Izzy and Julia paused, and Annie saw them exchanging a look.

"Enough about me. How's Hawaii?" Izzy asked.

Annie shrugged. "You'd think drinking mai tais in paradise would make me feel better. But most of the time I just feel so blah and gross."

"You're fierce and you know it." Izzy snapped his fingers in the air. *"Fierce."*

Annie blew out a breath. "Yeah, I'm as fierce as a hippo." She rolled her eyes at Serena, whose eyes twinkled back at her.

Izzy gave her the side-eye. "Hippos are fierce. Don't put yourself down. If you can still do a split, you've still got it. Get up. Now."

"What?" Annie made a face. Was he serious?

"Do a split. Now." Izzy stared at her so intently that it made Annie sit up straight.

"I'm not doing a split right now . . ."

"Get up!" Izzy barked, and Annie jumped up.

"Fine." She scrunched her nose at him but gave her phone to Serena and slid into a split. Serena held up the phone so Julia and Izzy could see, and Annie said, "Are you happy now? I can still do a split. Without warming up."

"Now the other leg," Izzy ordered.

Annie scowled but switched legs, throwing her hands in the air for good measure. "There. Are you satisfied?" She looked up to the sky and yelled, "I'm fierce!"

"Yes, you are!" Serena yelled back, caught in the moment.

Annie rolled to her side and took her phone back from Serena. "Are you happy now?" she hissed into the phone. "I just made a spectacle of myself in front of my new friend."

Izzy guffawed. "Girl, in show business, a spectacle is never a bad thing."

Annie glared at him but then dissolved into giggles, unable to resist him. He always knew how to make her laugh.

"So, where's your friend? We need to get to know her." Izzy brought the phone close to his face again. "Give her the phone."

Annie passed it to Serena with a little apologetic shrug, but Serena didn't look upset. She took the phone eagerly and gave a little wave. "It's so great to meet Annie's friends. She's incredible, isn't she?"

Julia's head cocked to the side. "We think so. But why do you?"

"Julia!" Izzy sounded affronted. "You're being rude."

Julia shook her head. "Sorry. I'm a bit drunk. When I get drunk, I have no filter. But Annie is our friend. We don't want to see her hurt."

"Oh, of course." Serena's eyes opened wide, and she looked the picture of earnestness. "I just meant that I've never met someone who I instantly connected with like we did. She's so great."

"How do you know each other?" Julia asked.

"Um . . ." Serena floundered, and Annie reached to take the phone back from her.

"Her car broke down on our street and she rang my doorbell. I almost didn't let her in. I was being silly and thought she was a serial killer or something."

"So, wait. You've only just met tonight?" Izzy's Barbados accent tended to come out when he was excited or nervous, and right now, it was out in full force.

"Yes, but I feel like I've known her forever." Annie felt the need to defend her friend. "Like she's one of us."

"Oh." That was all Julia said, but Annie could read a lot into that one word. *Oh, what do you really know about this woman you've invited into your home? Oh, who is she? Oh, and why are you so chummy with her? You're the one who's always warning us about potential killers and you let a stranger into your house and now compare her to your best friends?*

"Hey." Annie said this quietly, but she hoped they heard her warning. She didn't want them to insult her new friend.

"Right." Izzy nodded. "Well, I'm so glad you're making new friends there, Annie. Keep an eye on our girl, would you, Serena?"

"Sure thing." Serena beamed at Izzy, seemingly at ease now that the interrogation into how long they'd known each other was over. "I'm just glad she wants to be my friend."

"Tell me more about Sheilah." Annie tried to steer the conversation away from Serena.

"She's awesome." Izzy's face took over his square as he brought the phone close. "So perfect for our Julia. Not uptight at all. In fact, I think she makes Julia loosen up and live a little, instead of always following the rules."

"Hey." Julia glared. "I'm not uptight. I just like to do the right thing."

"I know what you mean." Serena joined in the conversation as if she'd always known them. "I like to follow the rules too. It makes life easier, doesn't it?"

Julia tilted her head to one side and seemed to be considering what Serena had just said. "Yes," she said slowly, drawing out the word. "That's exactly it. It's easier to follow the rules. Less messy."

"Right." Serena nodded her head enthusiastically. "When I stray from the rules, I always get confused and usually land in trouble. Like, is this right or wrong? Should I have done that? And then I start second-guessing myself. Like, maybe if I'd stuck to the plan, I wouldn't be in this mess right now. You know?"

Julia pointed her finger at the phone. "Exactly. See, guys, someone understands."

Annie caught Izzy's look, and they both rolled their eyes.

"I saw that." Julia pinched her lips together, glaring at her friends.

Annie laughed. "I'm happy for you, Julia. When are you going to tell your parents?"

Julia's face immediately dropped, her mouth turning down. "I don't know. You know how my parents are. They're always making anti-gay comments, like how unnatural it is. Like it's a disease or something."

Annie felt Julia's pain. Her parents were a bit more open, but they still had some hard-and-fast ideas of what relationships should be like. At the same time, maybe it was time Julia finally confronted her parents. "You're thirty-eight years old, Julia. Don't you think it's time to live your life the way you want and not be afraid of what your parents think?" Julia was four years younger than Annie and Izzy. She'd been only eighteen when they met all those years ago, and Annie and Izzy liked to tease her about how much younger she was.

"I know." Julia's chin dropped to her chest so all they saw was the top of her head, making her voice muffled. "I'm scared. But I don't want to hide Sheilah. I don't want to pretend she's my 'special friend.'"

"I wish I was there to help you." Annie felt helpless all the way in Hawaii and glanced at Serena, who was looking on, sympathy shining in her eyes, making Annie certain again that she was going to be a great friend.

Julia's head popped back up. "Hey, that's a good idea. Can you come back here and go with me to tell my parents? They love you. They'd listen to you more than me. Maybe you can convince them."

Izzy piped up. "Julia! She just got to Kauai. She can't fly all the way back here just to hold your hands while you talk to Mommy and Daddy."

Annie shook her head. "I wish I could. But I'm just getting settled here. And besides, you need to be a big girl and do it yourself."

Julia nodded glumly. Then her face brightened. "But you could take a quick break and come home and help me. I mean, you don't even have a job yet, do you?"

Annie opened her mouth to answer when a booming crack of thunder shook the house. She turned to look at Serena, whose eyes had widened in alarm.

"What was that?" Izzy asked, bringing the phone close to his face again.

"Thunder." Annie walked to the window just as lightning jolted across the sky, lighting up the darkness for a moment. What she saw made her blood freeze. The driveway, illuminated by the outdoor lights, and front yard were completely under at least a few inches of water.

22

"Annie, is everything okay?" Julia peered at her, concerned.

"I need to call my sister. It's starting to flood." Annie exchanged a look with Serena, who was clutching her wineglass with both hands.

"Oh no." Izzy gasped. "You need to get out."

"My father thinks we're safer staying here since we're up high from the river." Annie bit her bottom lip. "I have to call them."

"Okay, but call us right back, okay?" Julia's worried eyes focused on Annie's face.

"I will," Annie promised, then disconnected.

She immediately dialed her father and was relieved when Sam picked up. "Did you see the river is flooding?"

"Yes." Sam's voice was calm. "Baba thinks we're okay. He thinks it will be fine."

"What do you think? Do you think we're safer trying to drive somewhere?" Annie was worried. What was the right thing to do? Stay or leave? But where would they go?

"Unless there's a surge from the mountains, he thinks we'll be safer here."

"But the news said earlier that parts of Kauai might need to evacuate." Annie tried to keep her voice from rising in panic, turning to the TV to see whether there was any breaking news.

"Yes, the low-lying areas. I don't know." Sam sucked in a breath. "We've had flooding before, and it never reached the house because of the way it's built. But then again, we've never had a storm this bad since we moved here."

Annie swung her attention to the news. On the breaking news ticker at the bottom of the screen, they were warning people to stay put because of damage from the storm. Kuhio Highway was partially closed between Lihue and Kapaa, due to downed trees across the road. Annie gasped when she saw that. There was no way Brody was getting home anytime soon, since that was the only way into Kapaa from Lihue.

"The news says to stay put," Annie said into the phone to Sam.

"I think that's for the best too. So does Baba. You okay over there?"

Annie swallowed before answering. "Yes, okay."

"Come over," Sam urged. "If this is freaking you out."

Annie looked at Serena and admitted to a reluctance to leaving the cozy ohana. If her father thought it was okay to stay here, then she'd rather stay inside and dry and not get soaked running over to the main house.

"We're okay. Give Finn a hug and kiss from me, okay?"

"Okay. I'll let you know if anything changes." Sam said goodbye and then hung up.

"Do you think we're safe here?" Serena asked.

Annie pasted a cheerful look on her face. "I think we're better off here than out in the storm. Let me just call Brody to see where he is."

She dialed his number, but he didn't pick up. She texted him, asking if he was still at the airport, but no answer. She waited, but still nothing. Frustration and worry bubbled up inside her, wondering if he'd lost cell signal at the airport. A new text popped up, making her heart jump, but it was only Izzy, asking if they were okay.

"I should call them back. I know Izzy, and he won't go to bed until he sees that we're fine," Annie said.

Serena nodded and Annie called her friends back on FaceTime.

Both of them immediately connected to the call.

"How bad is it?" Julia asked.

"Bad. But we're fine. Let's not talk about the storm."

"Fine. Did you get a job?" *Trust Julia to get right to the point.*

"She's volunteering at the Kauai Humane Society," Serena said. She took the phone and angled it so they could see Marley, who rumbled low in his throat. "You know she adopted Marley, right? He was so sad, but now he won't leave her side."

Annie laid a hand on Marley's head. "I'm so glad I adopted—" She broke off. Something hovered at the edge of her mind.

"That's great, Annie. I know losing Lili almost killed you." Izzy's voice was soft.

"Yeah." Annie frowned.

"Lili was such a great dog," Serena said. "She was so cute in her pink harness and leash. Marley would look better in a different color." She looked down at Marley and missed the look Julia and Izzy exchanged, but Annie caught it.

"What?" Annie mouthed.

"How do you know about Lili, Serena?" Julia's voice was sharp.

"What?" Serena flushed, as if overheated.

"I told her," Annie said.

"All about Lili, down to the color of her harness and leash?" Julia's eyes lasered out from the phone.

"Yes." Although, wait, *had* she told Serena that? Annie turned to Serena. "I did, right?"

"Oh, um. I think so." Serena brought a hand up to her face. "Plus, I think there's a picture in here somewhere . . ." She gestured around the ohana.

"Well, whatever. Lili did have a pink harness, and she was cute." Annie jumped in to take the heat off her new friend.

Serena worried her lip, and Annie gave her a slight nod to reassure her everything was okay. Serena spoke again. "Yes, and she loved taking walks around the lake, right? I remember wishing I had a dog like her. She was so devoted to you."

Annie's head swam. What? For a second there, she thought she'd heard wrong. Was she drunker than she thought? But before she could gather her thoughts, Julia's voice hissed out from the phone.

"Annie . . . abort . . . you . . . abort . . ." The phone crackled as reception went in and out. Julia's face froze on the screen for a moment as she said the code word they used to whisper to each other whenever one of them needed to get away from a situation. Annie would have laughed, but the look on Julia's frozen face made the laughter die before it could erupt.

"You need to pee now?" Annie was confused. They were on the phone. Why did Julia want to go to the bathroom with her?

"Yes . . . badly." Izzy nodded his agreement. One minute, she could see and hear her friends clearly, and the next, they froze for a few seconds.

Julia said, "Sorry, Serena . . . right back. It's a thing . . . We . . . together. You don't mind if Annie takes us to the bathroom, do you?" The last part of her words came in loud and clear.

"I don't have to pee." Annie didn't want to be rude and leave Serena in the middle of the conversation when they were all getting along so well.

"Well, I do. And you're coming with me." Julia stared at Annie until Annie shrugged and stood up.

"I'll be right back." With a glance over her shoulder at Serena, who must be so confused about why her friends were going to watch Julia pee, Annie walked into the bathroom and closed the door. "What was that?" she hissed at her friends in a whisper. "That was kind of rude."

"Annie." Izzy's voice was quiet, the reception now stable. "How long have you known Serena?"

Annie's voice was edged in impatience. "I told you: I just met her this afternoon. I mean, we saw each other yesterday at the beach, but this is the first time we've talked."

"Why does she know so much about you?" Julia's brows were knit together in concern.

"We've been talking for the last few hours. I told her a lot about my past. It was amazing. It's as if we share a mind." Annie shook her head. "What's going on?"

Izzy frowned. "I don't know. I just got this weird feeling. And I know Julia did too. She seems perfectly nice, but she seems *too* nice. Acting like she's known you for years."

"Izzy . . ." Annie started, but then she stopped. What was it that Serena had said that made her pause earlier? She frowned, and then it came to her: Serena had told Annie's friends that Annie was volunteering at the humane society. But now that Annie thought about it, she hadn't told Serena that. Had she? She'd told her about adopting Marley, but she didn't remember saying anything about volunteering. But she must have; otherwise, how would Serena know that? And wait, had she told Serena what Brody had gotten Finn for his birthday? She'd thought she'd just been thinking about it, not saying it out loud. But how else would Serena have known that Finn had gotten a transformer car for his birthday? Was Annie once again doing things she couldn't remember?

"What?" Julia was staring at her. "What're you thinking?"

"Nothing." Annie didn't want to voice her suspicions out loud. It wasn't even a suspicion. There had to be a good reason for all of it. She refused to believe that there was something sinister about Serena. There couldn't be, not with the way they'd bonded. She trusted Serena, almost as much as she trusted Julia and Izzy. Which was saying a lot, since just a few hours ago, they'd been strangers.

"Annie?" Julia was looking at her with concern. And Izzy had his head cocked to the side, as if he were contemplating something. "Who is she? What's she doing in your house?" Julia's tone sent goose bumps up and down Annie's arms.

"Don't worry. Everything's fine. Really. Um, I got to go. Check on this storm. I'll call you tomorrow, okay?" And with that, Annie ended the call before Julia or Izzy could protest. Annie needed answers. Her friends were right, even if she wouldn't admit it out loud to them.

How did Serena know so many details about her life when Annie was almost positive that she hadn't shared them with her? Or had she, and she was starting to lose it? She needed to know, for her own peace of mind. And there was only one way to find out. She had to ask Serena.

23

Annie marched out of the bathroom, her face resolute, ready to get to the bottom of this. There had to be a very good explanation. She trusted Serena, she really did. Maybe she'd told Serena these details when she was talking about the past and had forgotten. But that thought was scary too, because it would only reinforce that she was doing things she didn't remember. Feeling a buzz of adrenaline rush through her body, she walked toward Serena, determined to get some answers.

But she halted when she found the woman huddled in a corner of the couch, her knees drawn to her chest. She'd bunched up her napkin and was crying into it, so softly that at first, Annie wasn't sure what she was doing.

She went to her side. "Serena, what's wrong? I'm sorry my friends were rude. We weren't trying to hurt your feelings." Annie touched her on the shoulder.

Serena raised her tearstained face. "It's not you guys." Tears dripped down her face and into her arms, which were crossed over her knees. She pointed to her phone. "I was just scrolling through my phone and saw pictures of my son. It made me sad."

Annie sat next to Serena. "Your son? You have kids?" She hadn't mentioned she had a son when they were talking about Finn.

Serena buried her face back into her arms so that her answer came out muffled. "I had a son. He died when he was almost a year old."

Annie gazed at her new friend in dismay. What should she say? That had to be a parent's worst nightmare. What words of comfort could she possibly give to someone who'd lost her baby? And this poor woman had already been through so much in her life. Annie's head was fuzzy from the wine and this revelation, and she scrambled to find the right words.

"I'm so sorry." That was all Annie could think of, hoping she could convey the depth of her sympathy with those three words.

"Thanks." Serena picked up her head to look at Annie, her mascara pooling under her eyes. "He would have been four now. It was awful."

"I'm sure it was." Annie's forehead wrinkled with concern. Impulsively, she reached out and hugged Serena, who clung to her for a moment. "Same age as Finn." Her heart broke a little, thinking about losing Finn. "What happened? Do you want to talk about it?"

Serena pulled away and wiped her eyes with the napkin. "His name was Johnny. Danny and I were so proud of him. We weren't married . . . I told you that. I got pregnant by accident, but we both wanted him. We were going to have such a great life together." She sighed, the depth of her grief filling the room. "I found him in his crib a month before his first birthday. He wasn't breathing. He was gone."

"I'm so, so sorry." Annie couldn't think of anything else to say and winced at how trite the words sounded. "What a horrible thing to have happened to you."

Serena turned tearstained eyes to Annie. "Danny blamed me. His whole family did. They think I did something to him, but I didn't. It was sudden infant death syndrome. But Danny and his family said ninety percent of SIDS happens before six months of age, and Johnny was eleven months old." She reached out and placed a hand on Annie's arm. "I swear, I didn't do anything. He had gone down for a nap, and when I went to check on him, I found him like that."

"What a nightmare." Annie shuddered involuntarily, thinking of what she would do if she ever found Finn unresponsive. As much as she had trouble bonding with him, she knew she would have been destroyed if that had happened to her son. She reached over and hugged Serena again. "I know words are inadequate, but I'm really so sorry for you."

"Thank you." Serena sniffed. "I'm sorry. I was just looking through my phone while I waited for you, and it hit me all over again when I saw the pictures." Annie was about to ask to see them, but then Serena turned her phone facedown on the couch and took a big breath. "But I don't want to be sad and bring you down."

"It's okay." Annie stopped when Serena's eyes flashed and her mouth turned down. "But we can talk about something else if it will make you too sad."

Serena gave a brave smile. "Let's talk about something else. Tell me all about your marriage. How do you two make it work?"

"My marriage?" Annie blinked slowly at Serena's words. "What do you want to know about it?"

"My relationship was such a disaster. I want to know how you guys do it." Serena's face softened and she leaned forward, as if anticipating Annie would impart words of wisdom.

"Um . . . I told you. We're not exactly doing well." Annie got up and retrieved the box of tissues from Finn's bedside. "We're trying, but it hasn't been the way it was in the beginning."

"But you're still together." Serena took the box from Annie and wiped her eyes. Then she picked up the throw pillow next to her and hugged it to her chest. She seemed to draw comfort from having something in her arms. "I guess I see you two as really well matched. He's attentive to you but respectful and you look like you have your own life figured out, but you can count on him. Like, he wouldn't abandon you if something bad happens."

Annie did a double take. That was how Serena saw them? When she hadn't even met Brody? "How do you know all this?"

Serena sighed. "Doesn't matter. I just know. I wish I had a relationship like yours. I thought Danny was the one. There hasn't been anyone since him, and that was three years ago."

"Three years is a long time. You haven't met anyone else in all that time?" Despite herself, Annie's curiosity was piqued.

"No. And it is a long time. But it still seems like yesterday to me. I just can't trust guys anymore. We met online, did I tell you that?"

Annie shook her head. "No way. Izzy and Julia have been trying that, but neither are having any luck. Julia met Sheilah through a friend. I'll have to tell them internet dating does work." She stopped and grimaced. "Oh, sorry. I guess it didn't really work."

"It's okay." Serena brushed off her apology with a hand. "It did work at first. We were happy for a while." She turned to Annie. "He's Chinese. His full name is Danny Chao."

"Oh." Annie's face remained neutral, even though inside she raised an eyebrow in surprise. Nothing Serena had said before had given Annie a hint that Danny was Asian.

"Yes." Serena widened her eyes. "Another thing we have in common. We both had, or have in your case, interracial relationships." She sighed. "I loved everything about him, from his black hair to his beautiful body—slender but not too thin, just muscled enough but not a hulk." Her face relaxed as she thought back. "I loved his Chinese heritage and the foods he introduced me to. I'd only ever had American Chinese food, as he called it, so when he took me to meet his family and I tasted their home-cooked meals, I was just blown away." She looked off in space dreamily. "It was exactly what I wanted. This loud, noisy family, all gathered around the dining table, the kids at a separate table since not everyone fit around it. There was so much food, really good food. Dumplings, and soups, sticky rice with shiitake mushrooms and bamboo, thinly sliced beef stir-fried with wide noodles. I even loved the *fuqi feipian*, the thinly sliced beef heart, tongue, and tripe, tossed in a numbingly spicy sauce. I mean, if you'd told me what it was before I ate it, I probably wouldn't have. But it was surprisingly good."

Annie stayed silent, sensing that Serena needed to get this out, to talk about her relationship with Danny and what she mourned about the loss.

"I loved his family. Did I tell you that already?" Serena turned questioning eyes at Annie, who nodded. "It was so full of cousins and relatives, and I couldn't wait for all the holiday get-togethers when I would finally be a part of a large family. He was so kind to me back in the early days. He lived in lower Westchester and worked in NYC, so it was easy to see each other. I was in Long Island, but we'd meet after work for dinner, and he'd either come to Long Island for the whole weekend or I'd go to him. He always called when he said he would, made sure I got home safely after our dates, picked me up to drive me into the city for a night out even though it would have been easier if I took the train and met him in the city."

"He sounds like a very considerate person," Annie said.

"That's what I thought." Serena's expression darkened. "Things were great for the first year. We were both happy when we got pregnant by accident. We had our lives mapped out. We found our dream house." Her breath hitched. "Then we lost our dream house, and that's when everything fell apart."

Marley lifted his head and listened for a moment before letting out a soft woof. Annie cocked her head, but all she heard was the storm still raging outside. She put a hand on Marley to comfort him, and he put his head back down.

"Sorry," Annie said. "I hope he didn't hear something we didn't."

Serena was silent for a moment too, listening, and when nothing happened, she continued her story. "He said I changed. That I wasn't the same person he had met. I don't know what he was talking about. I was still me. How had I changed? I was a mother now, yes, but everything else was the same. I think he was the one who changed. What happened to the man who promised me everything? We hadn't even said our vows—'In sickness and in health, through the good time and the bad,' or however the hell the vow goes. And he left as soon as tragedy struck."

Serena turned anguished eyes to Annie, and all Annie could do was shake her head and reach out to grip the woman's hands. All the tragedies they'd each endured in the past few years; was that what was bringing them together?

"It's almost eerie, isn't it, how similar our lives are in so many ways? As if we're living parallel lives," Annie said. Was that why Serena seemed so familiar with her?

"We're like two halves of the same person."

Annie nodded, but a fissure of unease washed over her. "I'm not sure if that's accurate, but I see what you mean."

Serena took her hands back and bent her knees up on the couch, wrapping her arms around her legs. "We were going to get married a few months after Johnny's first birthday. For the first time since my father died, I felt like I belonged to someone."

"He just left you after Johnny died?" Annie couldn't fathom it. She knew if this had happened to them, Brody would have stuck with her and they would have been united in their grief. At least, she thought they would have.

"Yes. He loved Johnny. So much." Serena shook her head. "I think he needed someone to blame, and I was the most obvious person." She gestured to Annie. "If this had happened to you guys, would your husband have blamed you and left you?"

Annie shook her head, thinking again how Serena was always able to read her mind. "I don't think so."

"See, this is why I've always thought you had such a great life."

"Is it . . . lonely? Being by yourself?" Annie couldn't even imagine. As much as she and Brody hadn't been getting along, she was grateful to have him in her life and for Finn. To know she had a family she could count on. She didn't miss the days when she was single and living in the city by herself, wishing for companionship until Lili came into her life.

"It is." Serena nodded. "You have no idea. I literally have no family at all. If I just disappeared tomorrow, no one would be looking for me." She frowned, her mouth pulling down. "Do you know what that feels like? To know no one would miss me?"

"What about your friends?" Annie couldn't imagine having no one care if she disappeared.

Serena gazed off into the distance. "They're all married now and have their own lives. They don't have time for me. And the friends I had when I was with Danny all took his side. They don't talk to me." She brought her gaze back to Annie. "That's why I realized it was time to take charge. To live my right life now."

Annie stared at Serena, thinking it was a strange phrase. *Live my right life.* What did that mean? Was Annie living her right life? Was Finn? Maybe he was living the wrong life and would have been better off with a different mother.

She stood, immediately appalled at the thought. She was Finn's mother, and they *were* living their right lives. They were.

24

Serena narrowed her eyes when Annie jumped off the couch. "What? What are you thinking? I can tell something is spinning around in your mind."

Her tone had Annie lifting a brow. "How do you know that?"

Serena's smile was crooked, and the spark in her eyes that Annie had thought she'd seen earlier flashed again for a brief moment. "I know we just met, but I feel as if I know you. Like I can anticipate what you're feeling and thinking."

"Hm." Annie bit her bottom lip. Even though Serena's statement should have creeped her out, it actually warmed her heart. To have someone know her like that, without her having to spell it out, was nice. Could she really tell a stranger something she'd been ashamed to say to even her sisters and best friends? But Serena had said it herself—it did seem as if they'd known each other for years, not just a few hours.

"You can tell me." Serena's voice was soft, almost gentle. "I won't judge."

Without answering, Annie went down to her knees on the floor and sank back into child's pose, her hips reaching back over her calves, her spine flat. She stretched her arms forward, tenting her fingers on the floor to maximize the stretch.

"What're you doing?" Annie could hear the confusion in Serena's voice.

"When I was dancing and stressed out, child's pose always helped me." Annie's voice was muffled, her forehead touching the ground. She knew Serena wouldn't judge—that was why she was about to tell her—but it felt safer to say the words from down here.

"Okay." Serena got on the floor next to her, imitating Annie's pose. "I guess I'll try it too."

Annie took a breath and let it out. "I didn't feel that maternal instinct everyone talks about when Finn was born. Of course I love him, but I didn't get that, I don't know, mothering feeling and that all-consuming love I kept hearing about." She reached both hands to the right as she let her hips sink to the left, deepening the stretch down her left side.

Serena copied her. "Not everyone feels the same. Don't compare yourself to others."

Annie moved her hands to the other side. "But it was weird because right after the birth, when they first put him on my chest, I did feel a moment of connection. Like he was fiercely mine." She lifted her head to look at Serena, who was still copying her moves. "But I never had that feeling again." Shame washed over her, and she dropped her head down to the floor again.

"There's a reason for that." Serena's voice was low.

Annie stilled at the strange statement. *Reason? What reason?*

"Don't beat yourself up." Serena sat back on her haunches. "It doesn't mean you love him any less. Some women just don't get all gushy and mushy. But let me ask you something: If Finn were in danger, would you think twice before trying to save him? At your own risk?"

Annie was about to say that his life had been in danger, and she'd been sleeping on the beach, but she snapped her mouth shut. It was one thing to admit she hadn't had that maternal love at first sight, but she wasn't about to give Serena an example of how she was a bad mother. She thought about the question. Would she? If the house were burning down and she knew Finn was inside, would she run in and save him? And relief coursed through her when she realized the answer was yes.

She sat up and faced Serena. "I would. I would save him from a burning building. I would save him if someone was trying to hurt him." *If I had known he was in danger in the woods, I would have run to him. I thought he was safe with Lindsay.*

She wished there were something she could do to help Finn. When he was awake, he was fine, as if nothing had happened. But at night, it was a different story. He'd had another nightmare the other day. She'd been reading on the couch after he'd gone to bed and Brody was in the bedroom watching TV.

Images from that night flashed through her mind. Finn had mumbled something in his sleep from the mattress on the floor, and Annie had tensed. She waited, hoping he'd quiet down and stay asleep, but the mumbling got louder until she could make out words. She stood, ready to soothe him, but it was too late. He shot up in bed, yelling, "No! Lindsay! No! Lindsay! Lindsay!"

In the next instant, she was by his bed and knelt to gather him into her arms, rocking him as he sobbed against her. She made soothing noises, listening to the anguish in his voice as he cried and mumbled Lindsay's name over and over again.

Then she'd looked up at Brody standing in the bedroom doorway. Their eyes met. Annie knew he felt as helpless as she did. They hadn't been with Finn when he'd needed them most. They had no idea what had happened to Lindsay, the teenage girl who'd been watching him while Annie napped at the lake beach.

Annie's mind brought up an image of Lindsay's face as she imagined it'd looked that day, her eyes staring sightlessly up at the sky. Had whoever killed Lindsay threatened Finn, told him not to tell anyone what happened or they would get him? Or had they been after Finn too, and he'd escaped before they could get him? Coldness stabbed through her heart at the thought. Even after months of therapy sessions, all the therapist had been able to get out of him was that there had been a woman in the woods with them. Finn hadn't said much to the therapist in New York. She'd said he was detached, just sitting there, no expression on his face. He hadn't drawn anything that would have given them a clue when the therapist asked him to draw what had happened. It was only at night, while he slept, that his terror came out.

When Finn had finally quieted down, Annie wiped his face with her shirt and tucked him back into bed. She watched him for a moment, her poor tortured little boy. His forehead was creased, and even though he was asleep, he looked like he was carrying a heavy burden on his little shoulders. She'd been hoping being away from the place where the tragedy had happened would stop the nightmares.

Annie let out a sigh, confusion clouding her brain when Serena spoke. It took a moment for her to focus back on the other woman, as the echoes of Finn's screams receded in her mind.

"Well, there you go," Serena was saying. "You have the maternal instinct. It's just a different degree. Everyone is different." She got off the floor and went back to the couch, a satisfied look on her face.

Annie thought about what she said and suddenly felt lighter. Serena was right. Who had ever said there had to be a certain amount of instinct for one to be considered maternal? Why hadn't anyone else in her life ever understood her the way Serena did? Feeling bolder, she decided to share more with her new friend. "I really thought there was something wrong with me. That, because of all the bad luck that happened to me the year Finn was born, I was broken somehow."

Serena wrinkled her nose. "I don't think there's anything wrong with us. They just don't get it."

"But you do." Annie swallowed the sudden lump that appeared in her throat. "You get it. I'm so glad I invited you in."

"Me too." Serena picked up her glass again and swirled the wine in it. "It feels like we've been friends forever." She looked at Annie, suddenly shy.

"I know." Annie tilted her head. "It's weird, right? Why do you think we feel like this? Is it all a coincidence, or do you think there's something sinister going on?" She had meant it as a joke, but Serena suddenly put her glass down and sprang up.

She rubbed a hand over her eye and grimaced when it came away with makeup. "Ugh, I must look like a raccoon. Why didn't you tell me? I need to wash my face."

"It's just a little smudged. You don't look like a raccoon."

But Serena had already bolted into the bathroom. Annie stared after her. She realized she'd never asked Serena why she'd made references that suggested she knew Annie better than she should when they were on the call with Julia and Izzy. She'd been distracted by finding Serena crying over Johnny.

Annie looked down at Marley, who gazed back at her. "What do you think, Marley? Can we trust her?" He growled and she pulled back. "Really? That's what you think?" She wanted to believe Serena, to believe that she was sincere.

Marley let out a yawn, then put his head down, as if disinterested. "Thanks for your conflicting input." Annie shook her head, but her mind was working. She knew Serena wasn't there to harm her, but she couldn't shake the feeling that there was more to the story than Serena was telling her. She looked at the other woman's phone, which was still facedown on the couch. Keeping an eye on the bathroom door, Annie walked to it and turned it over. She touched the screen and it came to life, showing a picturesque view of a body of water on a sunny day. Annie peered at it. Why did it look so familiar? Was it somewhere here on Kauai?

She went to open the phone and then cursed under her breath—of course the phone was password protected. Did she have enough time to try to figure out Serena's password? How could she possibly even guess at it? But she couldn't stop the urge to try and see what was on the phone. Maybe the pictures would give her a clue. Or her contacts. Something, anything. With another glance at the bathroom door, Annie began punching in numbers, starting with obvious ones like 123456 and 654321.

25

When Annie heard the water shut off in the bathroom, she placed Serena's phone facedown and picked up the remote, turning the volume up on the TV. She did her best to look like she'd been just sitting there watching the news when Serena came out of the bathroom.

"How's the storm?" Serena asked. "Is it slowing down yet?"

"Yeah, no." They both stared at the meteorologist, who was talking about wave heights approaching forty feet just north of Kauai and warning of "giant disorganized waves" that could cause unprecedented coastal flooding. Annie scrunched her nose—her mind felt as disorganized as the waves. Serena was a puzzle, and Annie was determined to get to the bottom of things.

"Serena . . ." she started.

But before she could say more, Serena picked up her empty wineglass. "Mind if I get a refill? This storm is freaking me out." She waved the glass in the air. "I need reinforcement."

"Oh." Annie glanced at the window, not wanting to admit that the meteorologist's words were freaking her out too. "Of course, help yourself. I just opened a second bottle earlier."

As Serena filled her wineglass in the kitchen, Annie went to the window and peered into the darkness.

Illuminated by the outside light, she could see the flooding in back wasn't as bad as in the front because it was higher up. The rain was slowing down some, and maybe it would blow away into the ocean and not pummel Kauai. She hoped so.

Turning back to Serena, Annie said, "I really need to ask you why you seem to know me better than you should." She grimaced, realizing that sounded wrong. "I mean, we just met and you know things . . ." She watched Serena fill her glass, searching for a way to ask how she knew so much about Annie without offending her.

Serena returned to the couch. "Yeah, it's strange. I feel like you know me better than you should too. I mean, you understand me. You get what it feels like to have your life fall apart. To lose people you love and something you've always wanted." She set her glass down on a coaster and twisted her fingers together. "All I wanted was a family."

"That's not what I meant," Annie said. "I mean, how do you know so many details about my life that I'm pretty sure I didn't tell you?" There, she'd said it.

"What do you mean?" Serena's eyes were wide with questions.

"Like, knowing Lili had a pink collar, and what we got Finn for his birthday, and I don't know, a whole bunch of stuff that you shouldn't know." Annie was finding it hard to concentrate, to remember what it was that had alarmed her friends and made her question Serena, with the way Serena was staring at her.

Serena cocked her head. "Annie, are you okay?" Her brows came together. "You told me all that. Don't you remember?"

Annie stared at her, a sick dread starting in the middle of her stomach. Had she told Serena and forgotten? Just like she'd forgotten packing that box of missing items, or finding and losing things all over Kauai? She searched her mind, desperate to have a concrete memory, yet the more she thought, the more confused she became.

Serena popped off the couch and walked to Annie's side by the front door. "It's okay, I'm here." She took Annie by the arm and led her gently back to the couch, where Annie collapsed, stunned. What was happening to her?

They sat in silence while Annie tried to make sense of it all. The news droned on, dire warnings about the storm continuing as the wind outside picked up again. She shook her head, wishing she could clear it.

"Did this start going on after what happened to Finn?" Serena finally spoke, her concerned gaze focused on Annie's face.

Annie turned to her. "Did I tell you about that too?" She reached a hand to rub the side of her temple, where a headache was creeping in.

"You just mentioned earlier that something happened to Finn and that's why you had to leave New York."

"Oh, thank goodness." Annie was positive that she hadn't told Serena what had happened. But Serena's next words made the anxiety come rushing back.

"You said only that he was found with Lindsay, some girl from the neighborhood."

The bottom dropped out of Annie's stomach. She was positive she'd never mentioned Lindsay's name. Had she?

"I . . ." Annie couldn't find the words. Her thoughts were swirling around too fast. "I don't get it. I don't remember . . ." Was she losing her mind? *How does Serena know all this?* She wanted to scream, to just let it all out.

"What happened to Finn, Annie?" Serena's eyes were full of compassion and kindness, and she sat down next to her. She placed a hand on Annie's arm, and at her gentle touch, all Annie's defenses dissolved.

She dropped her shoulders and, almost like she was in a trance, began to tell Serena about Finn and Lindsay. "Finn was found in the woods next to the lake beach with poor Lindsay Miller. I was supposed to be watching him." Tears pooled in her eyes and she stood, wanting to flee. She walked to the window again, staring out at the storm.

"I was so tired that day, tired every day, if I'm being honest. I don't know why taking care of Finn is so hard for me. It's like he's not mine, you know?" Annie glanced at Serena out of the corner of her eye. She was still seated on the couch.

"I know," Serena said softly.

"I sometimes feel like an impostor. Like I'm just playing at being his mom." Annie bit her bottom lip. "That day, when Lindsay came over and said she'd watch him, I was so grateful. I liked her. She was quiet and awkward, didn't really hang with the rest of the girls. She was a dancer, and I once showed her how to break in her pointe shoes. She loved listening to stories about my performing days and my company . . ." Annie trailed off, picturing Lindsay, the way she always had her sandy hair up in a bun or high ponytail, and the wistful way she stared at the other girls, giggling together in their tiny bikinis and trying to get the lifeguard's attention.

"Poor Lindsay." Annie dropped her head into her hands. "I should have given her more of my time. She wanted to be a professional dancer. Was always asking me questions. She invited us to a performance once. But I just . . ." She picked her head up and shrugged. "I didn't go. And now she's gone . . . at only sixteen."

"Sixteen." There was a hitch in Serena's voice.

"I know it was my fault. I should have been watching Finn, yet I was taking a nap when God knows what happened to Lindsay. And Finn was there. He talks about the woman that was in the woods . . ."

"He does?" Serena's quick words cut her off.

Annie turned and regarded her for a moment. "Yes. But he doesn't know who it was and won't talk about what happened. Only screams two words when he has nightmares, 'Lindsay' and 'no.'" Annie ran her fingers through her hair, pulling on the long strands. Anything to not feel the pain in her heart. "What if whoever hurt Lindsay had gotten Finn too? Nothing anyone can say to me is going to make me feel better."

"Oh, Annie . . ." Serena stood but didn't come to her side.

Annie blinked back her tears. There was no use crying. She knew it was her fault. By some miracle, Finn hadn't been hurt, but she shuddered now, picturing the scene in the woods. There'd been blood. Finn had some on him. The police had never figured out who the woman was, or what really happened to Lindsay. No one had seen anything. Only Finn.

Annie blew out a breath, knowing she'd never in her life forgive herself for not being there with him. This was why Brody didn't trust her with Finn. This was why the thought of disappearing, not having to face these feelings anymore, was starting to appeal to her. Because she couldn't get the blood off her hands for her part in Lindsay's death.

26

That THING that's become one giant capital-lettered thing is haunting me, pulling me back to that day, again and again and again. I know you understand. No one knows what really happened that day, not you and not even me, and I was there. I live in fear that one day, the police are going to show up on my doorstep because they've finally figured out what happened. And somehow trace it back to me, even if I can't tell them what happened.

But that doesn't exonerate me. It doesn't make me any less guilty. It's like that saying—if a tree falls in the forest and no one saw it, did it really fall? (Did I get that right? Probably not. I'm always mixing things up.) If you caused something terrible to happen but no one saw it, did you really do something terrible?

When my life fell apart, I "disappeared" for a bit. Everyone said I just needed a rest, that I could go somewhere and recharge, but I think you know what it really meant. I checked into a psych hospital. They were afraid I was going to hurt myself. They had no idea I'd already tried, but I stopped myself at the very last minute. I spat out all the pills I'd collected over time because I was too chicken to go through with it. I was disappointed in myself, that I couldn't even do this one thing right. For once, I wanted to be the one in charge, to decide my life, without fate intervening. Yet I guess fate did intervene, telling me it wasn't my time to go. It was what made me spit those pills out, after only taking a few.

So there I was, forced to face my life and everything I'd lost with the realization that I wasn't strong enough to determine my own fate. And I hated myself even more then, because I didn't have the courage to end it. I had failed again.

I thought I would hate being locked up. I thought it would make me claustrophobic, knowing I couldn't leave and do whatever I wanted. But surprisingly, being in the hospital turned out to be a restful time for me. It was like being on vacation (okay, maybe a forced vacation where we were locked up and couldn't come and go as we pleased but you get the idea), because I didn't have to deal with all the pressures of my life that made it hard for me to function. I didn't have to worry about anything. I just had to do as I was told, go here, go there, stay here, take my medication, sleep, eat, get better, get well. It was almost magical, that letting go of control. I was the perfect patient, doing everything they wanted, even going to group and private therapy sessions. I told them whatever I thought they wanted to hear. I knew the whole point of being there was to get well enough to function like the rest of society does. But what if I'm not made like everyone else? What if I'm just not strong enough to go on? How do you lose everything and then be able to pick up the pieces and carry on?

That's why when I finally came up with this goal, it gave me new life. It led me to you, the one who will make my life better again. But ever since I got to Kauai, I've been suspended in inaction. I've been enjoying the food and the beach and the whole Aloha spirit very much, but it's finally time to put my plan into action.

27

"That's why we had to leave." Annie turned her back on Serena to stare out at the storm. "I loved that lake house, but after what happened, I couldn't walk by the beach and the woods next to it without picturing Lindsay lying there in a pool of blood."

She wrapped her arms around herself. "I couldn't stop the guilt that ate at me whenever I think about that day, which is several times a day. I couldn't help thinking that it could have been Finn who had been found dead. Or both of them. How could we have gone on if something had happened to our little boy?"

Serena made a sound of sympathy behind her, but she didn't turn around. She stared out into the dark, listening to the pounding of the rain and the whoosh of the wind. "Brody was the one who said we needed to move. He saw how it was eating me up, and Finn was having nightmares every night, afraid to go to bed once it got dark out. He wouldn't walk past the beach, and he wouldn't let either of us out of his sight. He was supposed to go to preschool this year, but he refused."

A prickly feeling started at the base of Annie's neck, much like when she'd found Lili's collar in her car at the humane society. She whipped her head around to find Serena staring at her, sympathy shining in her eyes.

"Why wouldn't he go to preschool?" Serena asked.

Annie hesitated for a moment until that prickly feeling passed. "He screamed and had the worst temper tantrum the first day of school, and the psychologist said not to force him. We could do stuff with him at home."

"He's a smart little boy."

"He is." Annie nodded. "He misses his friends from New York, but Kalani was able to help us get Finn into her daughter Leila's preschool here. We're visiting the school later this week, and Finn is supposed to start there next week. He didn't want to at first, but his therapist was able to make him see that it's a good thing. I think he's finally ready."

"He's going to school?" Serena put a hand on her heart, her face a puddle of sentimentality.

"Yes. He said he wants to. I think being here, having my father and Sam and Cam, and meeting Leila and her siblings, has helped him start putting the past behind him. He still has nightmares." Annie stopped and thought about the one he'd had recently. "But they're less and further apart. And he no longer has the daily reminder of where Lindsay died confronting him every day."

"That's good. Do you think he misses the house?"

"I do." She nodded. "He talks about it, and about his room, where we'd painted two opposing walls blue, so it's as if you'd walked into an underground seascape. He mentions the backyard, saying Marley would have loved it." Annie hunched her shoulders. They really needed to find a house of their own soon. "We all loved that house so much."

"I know what you mean." Serena's voice was so soft that, at first, Annie could barely hear her over the storm.

She walked back to the couch and sat next to Serena.

"We found our dream house too," the younger woman said. "I told you. It was the house we were going to start our family in, to grow our family. Losing it was so hard for us." Serena looked away from Annie, her fingers working together. "I think everything would have been okay if Danny and I hadn't lost that house. I think that's when he started changing. I'd just lost my job, right as we were getting approved for a mortgage. And without our combined incomes, the banks turned us down. Twice." Her mouth twisted. "I had money from my father, but it was in a trust that I wouldn't get until I was thirty. Our mortgage fell through and we lost the house we were going to start our family in."

"Oh." Something about what Serena was saying sounded familiar. But what? And what a doomed life the woman had led so far. Annie thought her life had gone off the rails; Serena's was like a head-on collision with a Mack truck.

Serena squeezed her hands together. "That house meant everything to both of us. From the first moment we saw it, we fell in love. Hard. It was perfect, exactly what we needed to grow our family. But then we lost it." She worried her lip with her teeth, lost in thought.

"You've had such a rough time." Annie could commiserate, and she wanted to reach out to Serena, even as a feeling of unease poured through her veins. She was still worried about not remembering things, worried about the storm, and worried about her mental health. But Serena's life sounded so much worse than her own. "How long ago was this?"

Serena told her the year, and Annie's stomach clenched. "That's the year Brody and I were house hunting too." She tipped her head to the side, trying to tamp down that feeling that was now creeping through her body. A laugh escaped. "You know, it's just so weird how similar our lives are."

Serena gave Annie a long, cool look that made her think she shouldn't have laughed. "I believe there's such a thing as parallel lives," Serena said. "And you and I are living it. I believe it's possible to have two people living similar lives and they don't know it. And one of them would be a mess, and the other one would be living the better life. That other me is poised, a great mother and wife, and has a great career and knows who she is and what she wants to do in life."

Annie's jaw dropped open and she stared at Serena. She couldn't move. Something was about to happen. She could feel it. Her entire body was tingling.

The words spilled out of Serena, tumbling over each other. "That other me doesn't screw up like this current me. Everyone loves her and wants to be around her, and no one tells her she is depressed and needs to go to therapy. That other me has a son she loves dearly and would do anything for and who loves her just as much. She has a loving husband who would die for her and never leave her, even if she killed someone. He would stick by her and cover for her, so that she never goes to jail. He would go to jail in her place, that's how much she is cherished by him. I dream of that life. I see it, and I think that's who I'm supposed to be."

Silence settled over them, so that the only sounds came from the storm and the meteorologist saying, ". . . torrential rainfall . . . deep tropical moisture . . . very serious warning . . . never drive a vehicle through flooded roadways . . . we don't typically get this . . . stay inside . . . Kauai definitely getting pounded." Annie heard the words, but fascination at what Serena was saying held her motionless. What was Serena talking about? *The other me? Killing someone? What?*

Serena let out a rumble of laughter, breaking the tension. "Did you like that? I'm trying to write a book. A thriller. My creative writing teacher in high school said I had the best imagination. That was a passage from the book I'm writing."

Annie was speechless. Her brain hadn't caught up with what was going on, and when it finally did, she gave a weak chuckle.

"But I do think there's something to the parallel-lives theory, don't you?" Serena kept talking, as if Annie weren't frozen in front of her. "Maybe that's why we're so familiar with each other?"

Was that it? Was it possible to have parallel lives with someone without knowing it, so that everything in a seeming stranger's life was as familiar as her own?

"I've never had a friend who understands me like you do." Serena's face was open and cheerful again. "All our friends sided with Danny after Johnny died."

"Yeah." Annie walked over to her abandoned wineglass and took a sip. She had to get a grip. The evening was starting to take on an out-of-control feeling, as if she were in a movie and had no idea what her next lines were. She struggled for a moment, then grasped for the one topic that wasn't confusing. "I know I don't know him or his side of the story, but Danny was obviously not the right person for you."

"Thanks." Serena gave her a small smile. "And you and Brody found your lake house the same year Danny and I found our dream house, huh?"

"Yes. Brody kept complaining about how far away from the city it was." Annie thought back to that warm June day when their real estate agent had taken them to the very top of Westchester County to see the house on the lake, right when they'd found out they were pregnant with Finn. They'd both fallen in love at first sight and put in an offer that night, even though Annie hadn't put her New York City apartment on the market yet. But they'd been too late. There'd been multiple offers before theirs, and the buyers had gone with another one. After a summer of looking at more than fifty houses, she'd seen that their dream house still hadn't closed. Their agent had made a call and told them, "Make your best offer now if you want the house. The buyers just got turned down twice for their mortgage and are about to ask for a third extension. The owners are freaking out."

She and Brody had gone slightly above the asking price and the sellers had gratefully accepted, severing the relationship with the previous buyers.

"You were lucky to find it." Serena's dreamy voice brought Annie's attention back to her. "It sounds so nice."

"It was. Sometimes I wish everything hadn't happened and that we were still happy there." Annie sighed. "But there's no use trying to go back in time. Brody knew this was the right move for us. And I think he's right."

"He's such a great husband." Serena's voice was tinged with longing.

"Yes, but that doesn't make him the perfect husband." Although now, compared to Danny, Brody looked like a saint.

Serena's shoulders dropped. "I don't need perfect. I just need someone who will stick by me and not blame me and run away when things get tough."

Annie realized Serena had just described Brody. He loved her, even these past years, when she'd been at her worst. When had she forgotten that? He'd given up his life to move them all here, and yet here he was, making the best of things. He'd even gotten a job, even though he received a pension when he retired from the FDNY. While she was throwing temper tantrums and acting like an entitled princess. Annie was suddenly ashamed of herself.

"You're right." She nodded. "You're making me appreciate Brody more."

"You should hold on to him. Men like him are hard to find. Just like your lake house."

"You're right," she said again. "We sold it right away. We were just two houses down from the beach, so we could pile everything into a beach buggy and walk down. It was so nice for Finn."

"So nice," Serena echoed, staring into her wineglass, as if hypnotized by the ruby wine.

"It's rare to find that kind of affordable waterfront house in Westchester County." Annie let out a loud sigh. "It was perfect."

"I know. They are really hard to find." Serena gave her glass a swirl, still staring at the crimson liquid inside. "That was the perfect house."

Annie nodded, a smile on her face as she thought about the house, but then she faltered. "Wait, what?" She looked up at Serena, who finally tore her eyes away from her glass.

"I said it was the perfect house. Twenty-Five Lake Circle." Serena gave Annie a serene smile.

Annie stared at Serena, and it took everything inside her not to drop her wineglass. Her blood froze, and she could literally feel the color draining out of her face as a chill spread through her body. That was the exact address of their old house on the lake.

28

A flash of light lit the sky and lightning strobed through the ohana, making Annie think she was in a horror movie. A few seconds later, the loud crack of thunder made her jump as she stared at Serena, who hadn't moved at all. Annie knew her skin was probably so white now it would have pleased even the most die-hard Taiwanese mother who prized pale skin. The beating of the rain intensified outside.

Annie had to practically shout to be heard over the storm, which seemed to have reached an apex. "How do you know that address? Who are you?" She felt as though she were in the midst of a prank. Someone was going to jump out any minute and say, "Gotcha! Ha!" Because how else to explain all the eerie things that had been happening since Serena appeared on her doorstep? Marley, who had been taking a nap in his bed by the couch, suddenly lifted his head and growled.

"I'm Serena. Serena Kent." Her voice was loud, and she gave Annie a friendly smile, as if Annie should recognize her name. And as ridiculous as the thought was, all Annie could think was that she'd never asked Serena her last name, like Brody had told her to earlier.

Was she a celebrity? Someone Annie should recognize? Annie scrambled to think, to put a face to the name. Was she the woman in that rom-com that just came out, about the maid of honor who killed her best friend for marrying the man she loved? Wait, no, that wasn't a rom-com. Or maybe she was the woman in that Netflix show about the mother who could see dead babies? No. Try as she could, Annie couldn't place the name.

Serena cocked her head to the side. "You don't know who I am? And who Danny is?"

"No. Should I?" Annie tried to keep the panic out of her voice. "I don't get it. What's going on? Do we know each other? I mean, from before? How do you know my address in New York?" Her brain was scrambling, trying to make sense of the situation. She looked around frantically. Maybe she'd left a piece of mail with their old address lying around, which would explain everything. Otherwise, whatever Annie was imagining was enough to make her poop in her pants.

A look of satisfaction crossed over Serena's face. "Because that was the house we were going to buy. Our dream house. Me and Danny's." She gazed at Annie indulgently, as if willing her to catch up to the game.

"Wait." Annie's brows furrowed and her thoughts spun. That was why what Serena said earlier had rung a bell. "Brody and I got the house because the people who were supposed to buy it had something happen with their mortgage. It got turned down or something."

"Yes," Serena said calmly, as if they were having a conversation about the weather. "That was us. Our mortgage got turned down twice. Because I lost my job and, without our combined incomes, the banks wouldn't approve our mortgage."

"That was you? You and Danny?" Annie stared, her mouth dropping open. She took a step back, and Marley was suddenly by her side, as if sensing her apprehension. What weird twilight zone was she living in? What the hell was Serena doing in her house?

Serena nodded. "You didn't know our names, did you? I thought you would, but when I mentioned Danny's full name, your face didn't change. I guess they didn't tell you the names of the people you stole the house from, huh?"

Serena said it teasingly, but Annie heard the threat. How could that be? She *liked* this woman. They were bonding. She was going to be her new best friend here in Kauai. Annie stood rooted to the floor, at a loss for words. She and Brody hadn't stolen the house from anyone. Sure, she'd felt bad for the couple who'd lost the house, but that's what happened in real estate, right? And no, they'd never been told the name of the couple whose mortgage had fallen through, leaving the sellers in a panic because they'd already moved down south and bought a new house.

And now Serena sat here, in Annie's living room in Kauai, telling her she and her ex were that couple who had lost the house?

"Yes," Serena said softly. "I'm the one you took the house away from. I would have figured something out. I hadn't told Danny about the trust fund my father had left me, so it wasn't included in our financial package. Our combined incomes were enough, so I hadn't thought to mention it. But I didn't know I was going to get fired right after we offered on the house. I worked the front desk for a doctor and he suddenly let me go. Said I was 'unreliable.' What the heck does that mean? I showed up. I did my job. I was good at it."

Serena paused for breath and Annie caught hers. "I don't know what to say—" Annie started to say, but Serena held up a hand and cut her off.

"And then our real estate agent called and told me another couple had come in and offered higher. The sellers were so panicked that they took it. I tried to get them to change their mind, told them if they could wait a couple weeks or so, I'd have the money."

Serena stood and began pacing the length of the ohana, causing Marley to stand and follow her every move with his eyes. "My father had set up the trust fund so that I got a stipend every year. I wouldn't get the full amount until I was thirty. I wasn't thirty yet then, but there was a clause that in case of a dire situation, which would be determined by the trustee of the trust, I could have access to the money. I knew losing my dream house would count as an emergency. All I had to do was convince the trustee and get him to release the money. But that would have taken time. Time I didn't have because the perfect couple had come in and taken my house away from me."

Serena stopped in front of Annie so suddenly that Annie pulled back.

"I don't understand." Annie barely recognized her own voice. "What are you doing here? You knew who I was the whole time?"

"Yes. I've known you for many years. Ever since you stole my house from me." She let out a peal of laughter. "But no hard feelings! Really, I'm not mad at all."

Serena gave her a pleasant look, and sweat suddenly broke out along Annie's hairline. Her heart rate picked up speed as her brain tried to process what was happening. "I don't understand. What are you doing here?" She shook her head, trying to clear it. Was this a bad dream? Would she wake up soon?

Serena started pacing again and ignored Annie's question. "I didn't think I'd like you so much. I was prepared to hate you. But you know what? We really are more similar than I would have thought." She stopped and turned toward Annie again. "I really like you. I think we're going to be good friends."

Serena said this in a friendly tone, but the feverish look in her eyes made Annie's blood run cold. Oh god. She'd let a crazy woman into her home, gotten close to her, and actually liked her. If Annie were watching this on TV, she would have yelled at oblivious Annie on the screen: *Look what you did! You let her into your house! She duped you into thinking she's your friend, but she's about to kill you and take over your life! You're so stupid!*

Annie groped around on the couch with her fingers for her phone, never taking her eyes from Serena. She needed to get a hold of Brody, but he hadn't answered before. Should she try Sam now, in front of Serena? But this was crazy. She liked this woman. She couldn't be dangerous. But then how the heck had she found Annie? And why was she playing this game, not telling her who she really was until now? Part of her was screaming, *You dumbass! You walked into her trap. You're going to die! Get out of the house!* Yet the part who had found such common ground with Serena just couldn't completely wrap her head around the thought that the woman might not be here for good reasons.

Serena perched on the arm of the couch, seemingly at ease even while Annie felt like she was sprinting for the finish line at the end of a marathon. "I'm so glad we finally meet, Annie."

The smile she gave Annie was so genuine and friendly that it took Annie off guard, before she remembered that Serena was probably as friendly as a cobra. Her instincts on overdrive, Annie knew she needed to let Brody or Sam know. She picked up her phone and started typing, not looking at the keyboard.

"Who're you texting?" Why did Serena sound so normal? This wasn't normal! There was something weird going on, and Annie knew she was missing a part of the puzzle.

"Just Brody. Seeing how he's doing." Did he have service? Did she? Was Brody on his way home right now? Maybe he would walk in the door at any moment. She needed him here.

"Are you going to tell him about me?" Serena stood and came by Annie's side, peering over Annie's shoulder at her phone.

"I already told him about you." Annie snatched the phone away, not wanting Serena to see that she'd typed, **Psycho alert! Help! Come home now!**

"But did you tell him who I really am?" Serena pulled back and smiled again. Annie's stomach dropped at the mania behind the friendly smile. "Did you tell him how the two of you took my house and life away from me? That was my house."

Serena's voice was still mild, but her eyes shone like a fire as it overtook a forest. "You took everything from me."

29

Goddammit. Why wasn't anyone answering her? Had they even gotten her message? A sick dread started in her belly as she realized she was on her own. She had to get out of here. She needed to make a run for the main house with Marley.

"Why are you here?" Annie backed away from Serena with Marley at her side. She aimed for the direction of the front door. "Why are you really here?"

"I told you, my car broke down." Serena swiveled, her eyes following Annie's progress.

Marley stood in front of Annie, as if providing a shield. "But you didn't pick this street by accident, did you?"

"No." Serena shook her head. "I knew you lived here. I wanted to meet you in person finally. And I'm so glad I did." She offered a tentative smile, and Annie blinked at her in disbelief.

"Why? How?" Annie was having trouble keeping up. She wondered whether Serena had mental issues. Could she have schizophrenia? Bipolar? Annie didn't know the proper terms or what the symptoms were, but this wasn't the woman she'd bonded with over the past few hours.

"Don't be scared, Annie." Once again, Serena read her mind. "I'm not here to hurt you. I mean, not the way you're probably imagining right now." She smiled dead into Annie's eyes, which only made Annie more apprehensive.

Cold fear poured through Annie, even as she struggled to remember the connection they'd made today. How could things have turned around like this so quickly? This was bad. Really bad. "Tell me right now how you know who I am." She had backed up almost to the front door. "I know they didn't give you our names when we made the offer on the house. How the hell did you find me here on Kauai?"

"Annie, Annie." Serena stood and started pacing again, causing Marley's ears to prick up in alert. "I thought you were so smart. We didn't know your names, but I knew where you lived. Remember? That was supposed to be my address."

Annie's eyes widened as something finally dawned on her. "You've been watching us. Back in New York. You've been stalking us, haven't you?" Her feelings of eyes following her when they'd first moved to the lake house had been correct. It wasn't paranoia. It was Serena.

Serena stopped and turned. "No, Annie. I wasn't stalking you. I'd never do that." There was a beseeching look in her eyes. "At first I only went back to the house because I was so sad to lose it. Do you have any idea what it's like to lose all your dreams just like that?"

She snapped her fingers, the loud crack making Annie jump.

"I do, Serena. Remember?" Despite her resolve to leave earlier, Annie now wanted to hear what Serena had to say.

"I was so sad. I couldn't believe that my dream life was gone. So I went back and parked across the street. I only wanted to see the house again, to say goodbye to it and to the life I thought I would live. But then you walked out of the house with Lili. In her pink harness and leash. She was so sweet and exactly the kind of dog I would have gotten if I lived there."

"That's how you know about the pink harness." It was all making a terrible kind of sense now. Annie's instincts hadn't been wrong—someone *had* been watching them this whole time.

Serena continued as if she hadn't spoken. "I couldn't stop watching you two. You were living the life I wanted. I got out of the car and pretended to be a neighbor taking a walk. I waited until you were coming back to the house to walk toward you, and I even said hi to you." Her mouth turned up in a small smile as her eyes got a faraway look, as if picturing the scene in her mind. "It was winter, so I was all wrapped up in a scarf and hat. Lili barked at me once, but she quieted down as soon as you told her to relax."

Annie couldn't take her eyes off Serena. "That was four years ago. I don't understand. What . . ." She sputtered, as a memory came to her. "Did you drive a white car?"

"Yes." Serena's eyebrows rose in pleasant surprise.

"You used to park across the street and just sit there for a while. Brody and I wondered who it was. We even made a joke that someone was casing our house." Annie brought her hands to her face.

"I would never steal from you. What do you think I am, a burglar?" Serena's lower lip pouted. "I only wanted to see the house at first, but then I got hooked on watching you. I'd go back every week. Sometimes I'd park in the beach parking lot. Sometimes I'd park farther away and walk back. I tried to go when there were people around: after school when the buses let the kids out, weekends. I blended in with the neighbors."

"I've seen you before." Annie stared hard at Serena and realized why she'd looked so familiar. Not because she'd seen her at Lydgate Park Beach here in Kauai. But because she'd seen her around the neighborhood at their lake house. She'd thought she was one of the neighbors, someone she never really paid attention to.

"Yes." Serena's face lit up, as if she were glad Annie remembered her.

"How long?" Annie wanted to ask how long she'd been doing this but couldn't get the rest of the words out.

"How long what?" Serena tilted her head, as if contemplating the question. "How long have I been watching you?"

Annie nodded, still not able to form coherent thoughts. This couldn't be happening.

"I guess four years." Serena shrugged carelessly, as if discussing how long they'd been friends rather than how long she'd been stalking Annie. "I didn't mean to. But every time I went to the house and saw you, I'd think, *That's my life*. When I saw you working in the flower garden in front, I'd think, *That was supposed to be my garden*. I wouldn't have put roses in. I would have made it a butterfly garden with native plants for the butterflies and bees. Only echinacea, blazing stars, black-eyed Susans. I'd sit in my car and plan what the garden should look like. You don't know what restraint it took for me not to tell you to pull out those roses."

"You've been watching me garden?" Annie shook her head in disbelief. This was getting weirder and weirder. She suddenly felt horribly exposed, as if all her clothes had fallen off and she had nothing to cover herself with.

"Garden and walk Lili before she passed away. One day, only months after you moved in, she was gone. It wasn't until later that I learned she'd passed. My heart hurt for you." Serena's mouth turned downward, and she looked genuinely sad. "I also used to watch you and Finn in the backyard. You know the woods next to your house?"

Annie nodded, her senses on overload. One side of their property was a vacant lot, overgrown with trees and bushes. "You'd watch us from there?"

Serena's eyes were clear, no shame at all in admitting that she'd been spying on them. "Yes. I'd watch you and Brody barbecuing on the back deck and think, *That should have been me and Danny and our dog*. Danny was so excited to get a grill and put it on the deck outside the kitchen, looking out over the lake as he manned it. But instead, your husband and sometimes you were the ones out there."

"Oh my god, are you crazy?" Annie blurted this out without thinking and then winced. But how else to explain what Serena was saying?

To think all this time, someone had been watching them, observing their lives, and they'd never known? Annie rubbed her hands up and down her arms, trying to warm herself.

"No, I swear. I'm not." Serena stood and took a step closer to Annie but stopped when Annie held up a hand. "I never approached you, did I? I didn't do anything crazy like leave dead animals on your doorstep. I could have. But I didn't because I'm not. Don't you see?"

"I don't see. All I know is you've been watching us without our knowing. Do you hear how creepy that is?"

"I swear I wasn't trying tó be creepy. I just couldn't let go of my dreams." Serena stopped and swiped a hand over her eyes. "When you had your baby, I really felt like you were living my parallel life. That was my canoe that I was supposed to take out on the lake with my husband and son. That was *my* backyard, where I was supposed to watch my son take his first steps and play. That was *my* family that was supposed to walk to the beach together, pushing a beach buggy filled with sand toys, towels, beach chairs, and an umbrella. *My* house. *My* life. And you were living it, *not me!*"

Serena's voice had risen with each word so that she nearly screamed "not me." Annie backed up against the front door, fear coursing through her veins. Marley was now glued to her side, the hair on his back standing up. She took a deep breath, trying to gather her wits. She couldn't process everything Serena was saying, but she knew she had to do something. Serena looked on the brink of losing it, and Annie kicked herself again for letting her into the ohana.

"You need to go. Now." Annie's breath came in shallow gasps, and she was having a hard time getting air into her lungs. She'd invited a stalker into her home. She turned the knob of the front door and swung it open. But a strong gust of wind slapped the door back toward Annie, hitting her before it slammed shut. She slumped against the door, catching her breath as she watched Serena stop in front of her. The storm apparently didn't want them to leave. Hysterical laughter bubbled up inside Annie, and she swallowed hard, trying to tamp it down. This wasn't funny. At all.

"I'm sorry." Serena now had a sorrowful look on her face, reaching her hands out as if asking for forgiveness. "I didn't mean any harm. That's why I took so long to reach out to you. I wasn't going to ever, but then—" She broke off.

"I don't care what your reasons are. Do you see it's not normal to watch people?" Annie clutched her phone, knowing she should try Sam or Brody again.

"I just wanted . . . I don't know." Serena tittered, and the mania Annie had glimpsed before was loud and clear this time. "And then when we met, and I was so surprised how much I like you . . . I thought we could be friends."

Her voice trailed off and Annie could see she was fighting tears. One eye on Serena, Annie dialed Brody's number, but it went right to voice mail. She tried her father's landline, and again, it went straight to voice mail. What was going on? Why was no one answering their phone? She decided to text Brody again, hoping he had cell service, wherever he was. She typed fast, her thumbs flying, needing him to pick up on the urgency of her message. She was so intent on punching out the letters that she didn't realize Serena had walked over to her until she felt her breath on her arm as she leaned in to peer at Annie's phone.

"Who are you texting? Brody?"

Annie hated how familiar her husband's name sounded on Serena's lips, as if she really knew him. But she guessed Serena *did* know Brody. She knew them all. She snatched the phone away from Serena's eyes and held it against her chest. "None of your business. Please, just go and we can forget all this. I'm sure the storm will stop soon."

As if to say differently, a loud gust of wind howled, making the windows shake, sounding like they were in the midst of a hurricane.

"I'm not a stalker. Why would you write that?" Serena pointed at Annie's phone, where Annie had written in all capitals: COME HOME

NOW. THIS WOMAN HAS BEEN STALKING US. She must have seen what Annie wrote before Annie pulled the phone away.

"Yes, you are, and I want you out now!" Annie's voice rose to a feverish pitch.

"No. I'm not going to leave like this. You need to listen to me. I need your help." Serena gestured out the window. "And look, the flooding is getting worse. I can't go out in that."

Her eyes pleaded even as her voice took on a desperate tone. She wrung her hands together and started pacing again, muttering under her breath, "This wasn't how this was supposed to happen. This wasn't how it was going to be. What do I do? How can I fix it? I need to fix this."

Annie stared, fixated, until Serena looked up, the fire in her eyes still burning like embers.

"You stole my house, my life, from me. You can't kick me out now. You're the only person who can give me what I need. You have to help me."

"No, I don't." Annie glanced at her phone, but Brody still hadn't answered.

"Yes, you do." Serena's tone changed and she was suddenly pleading. She brought her hands together in front of her, as if praying. "You owe me."

30

They stared at each other for a moment, and then Annie came to life and grabbed Serena by the upper arm. She pulled her to the front door, but Serena resisted and a tug of war ensued.

"Annie, stop. You have to listen to me," Serena pleaded as she tried to dig her heels into the ground.

Annie fought with the front door as lightning flashed, and for a moment, she wondered whether she'd somehow entered a horror movie. She finally twisted the knob open. A crack of thunder boomed as she yanked open the door, and then they both stopped, staring out at the storm. The water had definitely risen. It was now up to the underside of the cars in the driveway, and in the backyard, the water was already coming up over the canal, and onto the bottom of the three steep steps that led from the canal up to their backyard. Before Annie could react, Serena tore herself out of Annie's grip and ran into the ohana. Marley reacted and sprinted after her as Serena went screaming into the bathroom and slammed the door.

The wind whistled and rain blew into the ohana, soaking Annie. She quickly shut the door and looked toward where Serena had barricaded herself in the bathroom. Marley stood outside the door, barking at it. Annie couldn't decide what to do. Should she take Marley and leave now? But did she really want to leave Serena in their home by herself?

Annie's phone dinged and she looked down.

B: Finally got a signal. What's going on? Who's been stalking us? What are you talking about?

A: Serena! She's been watching us.

B: What? You're not making sense. Watching us where?

A: In New York! At our lake house. She thinks we stole her house away from her.

B: Wait. What? We stole whose house? Are you okay?

Growling in frustration, Annie dialed Brody's cell and he picked up immediately.

"Are you okay?" Brody's voice came through, broken up by static and dead air.

"I'm fine. But the house. Our house. The lake." The words rushed from Annie as she struggled to make sense. "The people who asked for a third extension. It was her. Her and her fiancé, who left before the wedding."

"What? Who's getting married?"

"Oh my god, Brody. Pay attention. Serena."

"Serena's getting married?" Brody shouted over the static.

"No! She was. But he left her. She thinks we stole her house."

"We didn't steal a house. What're you talking about?"

"You're breaking up. I can barely hear you." Annie was trying not to shout because she didn't want Serena to know, but it was hard to hear Brody over the roar of the storm and the bad connection. She needed him to understand and to tell her what to do. "She thinks we stole their house. They were the buyers who lost the house when we bid on it."

There was silence, and when Brody spoke again, Annie knew he'd finally made the connection. "What the fuck? How did she even find us? What's she doing in Kauai? How did she end up with you?"

"I don't know! I don't know what's going on. You need to come home. Now. She's barricaded herself in the bathroom and she won't leave. She says she needs me to understand something." Annie ran a hand through her hair, which was wet from the brief time she'd had the door open. "Oh, and her baby died."

"What? What baby?" Brody yelled.

"Just come home! I'll explain when you get here." Annie threw a look at the bathroom door, where Marley was sitting still, staring at it and growling. She should have listened to Marley when Serena had first stepped foot in the ohana. He knew Annie shouldn't have let her in.

"I'm . . . in the car. But Kuhio Highway . . . not moving. I think . . . tree fell . . . Stuck for . . ." Annie got the gist of what Brody was saying even with the bad connection.

"Oh no. I need you. I don't know what to do. Marley is guarding the door outside the bathroom."

"Do you think . . . danger? Should I call . . . police?"

"Yes! I don't like this. Something's not right."

"I don't like this either." There was fuzz, and then Brody came in, loud and clear. "I'm calling the cops."

Annie had wanted Brody to take control, but his words made her pause. What had Serena really done to threaten her? Nothing. Well, except admit to stalking her. But she hadn't harmed her in any way, hadn't threatened her. And she'd had a good reason for watching Annie and the house. At that thought, Annie slapped herself across the forehead. She was now defending the actions of a woman who may not be in her right mind? Was there something wrong with Annie?

"Hello? Annie, you there?"

"I'm here. I . . ." She hesitated. "I think she wants something from me. From us."

"I don't like this," Brody said again. He cursed under his breath. "I'm boxed in. There's nowhere for me to go. I'm going to try the cops."

Annie gulped, wondering what was wrong with her. Why she was feeling sorry for Serena, of all people. She'd been terrified just moments before, but now she couldn't help but think of the woman she'd bonded with. She was in there somewhere, underneath the erratic behavior.

Taking a breath, she said, "Let me see if I can find out what she wants."

"Annie, I . . ." His cell cut out just then.

"Brody? Can you hear me?"

"Call . . ."

"I . . ." She opened her mouth to respond, but just then, a loud crash came from the bathroom. "Oh god." What was that? What had Serena done? Had she killed herself in there? The blood pounded through Annie's body, and alarm set in. Marley was barking his head off, which didn't help.

"Annie. What . . . on?"

Another crash came from the bathroom, this one so loud that Annie jumped and dropped her phone, ending the call by accident. She walked to the bathroom, her steps slow, afraid of what she would find.

31

Annie stopped in front of the bathroom door, one hand restraining Marley. "Relax," she said to him. He settled down but continued to growl.

"Serena?"

Silence.

"Serena, what happened?"

Why wasn't she answering? Was she dead?

Just when Annie was screwing up her courage to try the door, it flew open, framing Serena in the doorway. "The towel rack fell off the wall. I tried to put it back up, but it slipped and knocked over the cabinet in there."

"Oh." They stared at each other for a moment, a million things running through Annie's mind. "It's been loose for a while. It's not your fault." Why was she trying to reassure a stalker? Maybe because Annie saw more than a little of herself in the other woman and it scared her. Serena obviously needed help. Did Annie?

She looked into the bathroom and saw that the small, narrow cabinet they'd been using to hold toiletries had been knocked to its side, with the towel rack on top of it. It had detached from the wall, the screws still sticking out.

"I'm sorry."

Annie wasn't sure if Serena was apologizing for the towel rack, or for everything she'd revealed. It really was too bad that Serena had turned out to be unstable. She hadn't felt so comfortable with anyone in so long, and just her luck, she'd turned out to be a stalker. What did that say about Annie's own judgment?

"What do you want?" Annie wanted desperately to believe there was something innocent about Serena's actions. Something that made sense, because otherwise, was Annie just as delusional? She steeled herself, forced her voice to be firm, as if that would guard her heart against Serena. As much as she craved the closeness of their imagined friendship, the facts were, the woman had lied to her.

"I just need to talk to you. I swear." Serena's eyes pleaded with Annie to understand.

Annie eyed her suspiciously. "You came all the way from New York just to talk to me? Why didn't you talk to me while we still lived at the lake?"

"I never got up the courage before." Serena's fingers knotted together, a gesture Annie had come to know she did a lot when she was nervous. "At first I was angry. I admit it. I was angry that you stole my life. I was angry that life was so unfair and I'd lost everything while you . . ." She stopped and gestured to Annie. "You had everything. You're beautiful, with a wonderful husband, who adores you; a sweet boy; your loyal dachshund . . ." Serena stopped to throw a look in Marley's direction. "And now you have another dog. I did blame you. But then you guys looked so happy that I just wanted to meet you. To get to know you."

"Then why didn't you introduce yourself all those times you were in the neighborhood? You could have told me who you were." Annie watched as Serena walked away from the bathroom toward the breakfast bar.

"Because that would have been creepy." Serena stopped next to the stools, as if unsure if she should sit, since Annie had been so intent on throwing her out.

Annie raised her eyebrows. "And *this* isn't creepy? You coming all the way to Kauai and finding me in my house, befriending me like this, isn't creepy?" If she needed proof that something was not right with Serena's mind, this was it. "Wait. Have you been stalking me here too?" All those times when she'd felt as if someone were watching her. At the beach, at Walmart, in the parking lot of the humane society, and even at Hamura's one day. Had Serena been following her this whole time? "That's how you know where I live, isn't it? You've been following me!"

Serena opened her mouth and then closed it. She took a breath and said, "I didn't know how to approach you. Every time I got up the courage to tell you who I was, there'd either be too many people around or something would happen and I would lose my chance. So I started leaving you little gifts from your house on the lake. I thought that could be a way to ease into telling you who I am."

"You're the one who's been leaving me all those things I lost years ago?" Annie walked to her. She hadn't thought this woman could shock her further, but she'd been wrong. She'd thought she was losing her mind, somehow collecting things she'd lost over the years and bringing them here to Kauai. And all along it had been Serena?

"Yes." Serena's face was so hopeful that, for a moment, Annie really wanted to believe they were an innocent gesture of friendship. But no, these were not the actions of a stable person.

"And what do you mean 'gifts'?" Annie took another step toward Serena. "Those were things you stole from me."

"I didn't steal them. You'd leave them lying around in the front yard, or dropped by your house. I wanted you to know I kept them because they meant something to me." Serena lifted her head and gazed off, as if seeing the lake house. "You kept losing your gardening gloves. One day, you put them down by the driveway and ran in to answer the phone. I waited for you to come back out, but you didn't. So I took them." She shrugged. "I guess I wanted a piece of your life. Another time, your husband and son were coming back from the beach and they dropped Finn's shirt in the road. Neither of them realized it and kept going. I picked it up, pretending that Johnny was still alive and this was his shirt. And one time, after taking Lili for a walk, you accidentally unsnapped her collar when you took off her harness. I was in the woods next to your house, and I saw the collar fall to the ground. I waited for you to come back and get it, but you never did."

"What, you waded across the creek that separated my house from the woods and took it?" Annie's face was incredulous.

"Yes." Serena's gaze landed on her. "See, we have the same mind."

"No, no we don't." Annie's brows rose as she shook her head.

"I've been leaving things for you because I wanted to remind you of our lake house. And also to thank you for—" Serena broke off and bit her lip.

Thank me for what? And "our" lake house? Annie couldn't help wondering, but Serena didn't elaborate.

"Did you like finding them?" The hopeful tone was back in Serena's voice.

"No. I thought I was losing my mind." Annie forced herself to take a careful breath. She needed to stay calm, to figure out what to do. "I can't believe you were the one who's been taking things from our house all this time. I thought I was so careless, always losing things."

"I didn't think you would notice. They were just little things, things I didn't think you'd even remember." Serena turned wide eyes on Annie, as if it were perfectly normal to go onto someone's private property to take things that didn't belong to her.

"You . . ." Annie was at a loss for words. "Wait, did you take my sunglasses?"

"Yes." Serena's face lit up, as if Annie had just complimented her, instead of accusing her of stealing her sunglasses right out of her purse. "It was so crowded at the shopping center for the Chinese New Year celebration that I was able to get up close to you. I was standing right behind you, and the sunglasses were just there in that outside pocket.

I only took them because I could. I was going to put them back. But then you walked away before I could return them."

"Then what were they doing in my bedroom?"

"I wanted to give them back to you." Serena's face was all guileless innocence, like a young child's.

"Why didn't you just hand them to me, instead of making me think I was losing my mind?" Annie's voice rose.

"I . . ." Serena looked at her helplessly. "I didn't know it was going to cause you to have a panic attack. I'm sorry."

Annie buried her face into both of her hands. This couldn't be happening. But at the same time, relief coursed through her, making her almost limp. She wasn't losing her mind. Serena had been the one who'd been taking stuff from her and then leaving it for her to find. It was such a huge load off her, such a relief, knowing she hadn't been the one doing things and not remembering them.

When she finally dropped her hands, she found Serena watching her curiously. Annie's face heated with anger. "I really thought I was losing it, and all this time, it was you."

Serena nodded. They stared at each other.

"How?" Annie finally said out loud. "How did you know we were in Kauai? And how did you even find us here?" She needed some answers.

Serena's mouth worked, opening and closing before she finally confessed. "Just after the new year, I heard two women talking one day when I was up at the lake house. They were walking by your house, and I heard one say that you guys had just moved to Kauai. I couldn't believe you were gone. That you sold the dream house and had left." Her green eyes focused on Annie. "I don't blame you, I guess, after what happened. I was shocked, though, at the time."

"But you must have guessed why we moved here, if you've been watching us." Annie's tone was accusing.

Serena nodded. "I suspected. But I guess I never thought you'd really leave. You seemed to love the house as much as Danny and I did—I couldn't imagine that you'd just go."

"Okay, but how did you know where in Kauai we were?" Annie was trying to piece the puzzle together.

"Um." Serena looked down and, for the first time, had the grace to look embarrassed. "I used to look in your mailbox."

"You used to look in our mailbox." Annie mimicked her and then stared, incredulous that this woman had violated their privacy so much and they'd had no clue. They really were that gullible couple from a true crime show who were just sitting ducks for criminals and stalkers. Annie's mouth parted slightly, and she shook her head as if that would make all this more believable.

"Yes. I did. And one day, there was a letter from a Samantha Lin from Kapaa in Hawaii. I took a picture of the envelope because I had a feeling the address would come in handy one day." Serena ran her hand through her auburn curls, pulling on the ends so hard that her hair sprang back when she let go.

"You took a picture of it." Annie was starting to feel like a parrot, but she couldn't stop herself from repeating Serena's words. Maybe if she said it out loud, the words would sink in and make sense.

"Yes." Serena's face brightened. "And that's how I found you here."

"You found us." Annie stopped and gave her own cheek a light pat, as if that would stop her from repeating everything the other woman was saying. "I can't believe this. You looked through our mailbox, took pictures of our mail, and then followed us here? Was that the only mail you took a picture of?"

"No." Serena's shoulders lifted slightly, and she pulled her lips together. "I don't know why I did it. I guess sometimes I pretended those letters were addressed to me, that I knew people in far-off places like Hawaii and Taiwan. But I'm glad I did, because otherwise, I'd never have found you." She looked at Annie, worry clouding her eyes, as if waiting to see whether Annie would believe her.

"You'd never have found us here." Annie slapped herself again. Stop. She needed to stop repeating everything Serena said. But she just couldn't wrap her mind around any of this.

"I'm glad I did because look how much we bonded. Look how much we have in common. It's like we're the same person." Serena looked more like a little girl caught doing something naughty than a potentially dangerous stalker who'd been watching her for years.

Annie couldn't deny they had bonded over shared experiences and thoughts. She'd felt close to the younger woman. Her breath hitched as a scary thought entered her mind: Did that mean she was as delusional as Serena?

32

Annie's phone dinged and they both looked at it. It was Sam.

S: The landline is dead. If you need me, you'll have to use my cell. Hope the cell towers don't die too.

A: I tried to call earlier.

S: Everything okay?

Annie looked up. No, everything was not okay. She wanted Serena out, but now, something deep inside was telling her Serena wanted something. It was as if she knew Serena's mind, knew she was leading up to something. That thought scared Annie, even as it held her hostage, unwilling to leave the ohana until Serena finally spilled out the truth.

If she told Sam she was in danger, within minutes, her sister would be here with a baseball bat, demanding that Serena get out. Sam might be her irritating younger sister who always seemed to poke at Annie's vulnerable parts, but if anyone threatened one of their family, Sam would fight that person to the death. And right now, Annie needed answers more than a dead body. She would get the truth out of Serena.

A: Yeah. All good, considering this scary storm.

S: We'll be fine. I hope. LOL

A: Haha

S: Text me if you need anything

A: Okay.

"Are you going to make me leave?" Serena's question had Annie looking up from her phone. Serena was now seated at the breakfast bar, as if staking her claim. Annie hovered by the couch close enough that she could reach out and grab Serena if she needed.

"Yes. But first you need to tell me why you followed us to Kauai. What you meant when you said that I owe you."

"But . . ." Serena twisted her fingers together. "I thought we were going to be friends. You were going to show me around Kauai. Take me to places to eat."

"Really? You think I'm going to be friends with someone who's been stalking me all these years?"

"I wasn't. I was just . . . watching you. Watching what my life should have been." Serena looked close to tears. "I thought you understood. After everything I've been through. Losing Johnny, not knowing if I'm to blame. I just want my son back."

Her eyes pleaded at Annie to understand, and despite herself, Annie could feel her heart relenting slightly. The thing was, she did understand, at least partly. She'd never stalk someone the way Serena had, but all the other things . . . Annie got it. The loneliness, self-blame, that feeling of wanting to disappear . . .

Serena's eyes filled with tears. "Danny was so mean when we broke up. He kept saying there was something wrong with me, that I needed help. I think he blamed me for Johnny's death."

Annie looked up. Was Serena now trying to play on Annie's sympathy to let her back into her life, even after everything she'd done? And what was wrong with Annie that she was contemplating how she could explain to Brody that she'd decided to be friends with their stalker? *Hey, honey, I know she's been watching us for years, and taking things from me and followed us here, but guess what? We're now best friends!* Yeah, that'd go over so well with Brody and her family. They'd be telling her she had lost it. And maybe she had.

But look at her. Annie's heart couldn't help giving a sympathetic bump when she saw the pitiful expression on Serena's face. Annie brought her hands up on either side of her own head and closed her eyes. What was wrong with her? How could she feel sorry for this woman?

"Annie, please." As if sensing that Annie was softening, Serena went in for the kill. "You promised me you'd take me to Hamura's. I really want to go with you. You said we could take Marley and Finn hiking on Sleeping Giant. This island has so much to offer, and I want to explore that with you, like we planned." She slipped off the stool and put a hand on Annie's forearm. "I need you, Annie. Please?"

Annie groaned into her hands. Serena seemed to know just how to get to her. Because all her life, she'd been brought up to keep her word. Her mom had drummed it into all three daughters not to promise to do something if they couldn't do it. And Annie had promised to show Serena Kauai.

She dropped her hands and opened her eyes. Serena was looking at her, eyes wide, making Annie's resolve to stay firm slip. Annie's mom would understand if she didn't follow through on this promise, right? After all, this woman had been lying to her the whole time.

33

Laptop ANNIE file

I know you're a dependable person like me. I see it in your actions, the way you take care of everyone around you. It's been drummed into me since I was little that if I say I'm going to do something, I have to follow through and finish whatever I committed to. Even if it's hard and I don't want to. That's one lesson I learned from my mother when I was five.

I had just started kindergarten and told my mother I wanted to take gymnastics because every girl in my class was doing it. I pestered her about it. I wouldn't stop talking about it. She didn't want to take me, said she was busy, and I didn't need gymnastics. But I wanted it so bad that she finally relented. She signed me up, bought me the black leotard, and off I went to gymnastics class.

But I hated it. I couldn't do a cartwheel to save my life, I was scared stiff of the balance beam, clinging to it and crying my eyes out. I didn't want to jump on the horse or bounce around on the trampoline like the other kids. They even made us swing from a rope and drop into a pit of foam blocks. I was so scared I spent most of the forty-five-minute class crying.

You'd think my mother would have just let me quit and gotten some money back after only one class, but no. She made me finish the semester. Every Monday, she would drag me screaming into the car to gymnastics, ignoring my cries. Because she said I wanted it and she'd spent good money getting me to the class. So I was going to stick it out and follow through on my commitment.

And ever since then, I don't back down from a challenge or take the easy way out like some people and quit. Which is why I'm not about to give up on reaching my goal because I'm scared or I don't know how to go about doing it. Especially if you won't cooperate and give me what I want. I will complete my mission even if I have to hurt you to make you give me what is mine.

34

Annie hardened her heart and stared at Serena. She was getting to the bottom of this once and for all. She wouldn't let Serena's sad story sway her until she'd heard the whole truth. "Either you tell me right now why you're here and what you want from me, or I'm throwing you out, flood and storm and all."

"I will. I came here to tell you the truth. And to ask you for help. But you need to let me tell you in my own way." Serena took a step toward Annie. "Can we please just sit on the couch again with our wine, like we were doing before? I promise to tell you everything."

Annie hesitated, then nodded. If pretending to have that same cozy camaraderie from earlier would help Serena finally tell the truth, Annie was all for it. She wondered if Brody had called the police. If at any moment, the police were going to be pounding on the door. She needed Serena to tell her everything before that happened.

Marley accompanied her back to the couch, where he kept looking back and forth between Annie and Serena. She reached out to reassure him that everything was okay. Picking up her wineglass from the coffee table, where she'd abandoned it, she took a fortifying gulp and then looked at Serena expectantly.

Serena sat on the opposite end of the couch, then turned so she was fully facing her. "When Johnny died, I spiraled. I tried to kill myself, but no one knew, not even Danny, because I couldn't go through with it. As much as I wanted to die, I just couldn't do it."

Annie steeled her heart. She would not let her emotions get in the way until she heard the whole story.

"After a while, Danny suggested that I check myself into a psych hospital. I agreed. I don't know why. I guess I just needed the rest. And surprisingly, I enjoyed being there."

Annie's brows rose. "I thought you didn't believe in therapy, like me?"

"I don't consider those hospital stays 'therapy.' It was more like a vacation from my life, where someone else could take over and I didn't have to deal with everything that makes life so hard to live." Serena smiled. "I liked being there. I liked that the doctors and staff cared. That someone cared about me and would take care of everything. When things got tough, even after Danny left, I'd check myself in. It was a nice break from my life. From all the horrible things that happened to me."

Annie closed her eyes briefly. Serena had just said she'd been hospitalized—many times, from the sound of it. She sympathized, she really did. She told herself that was all the more reason why Serena couldn't be trusted. But her traitorous heart murmured, *You understand. You wanted to disappear too.*

Before she could stop herself, Annie blurted out, "When I lost Lili, my mom, and then the business, I disappeared for a couple of weeks. I didn't plan it. I just knew I had to get away or I was going to die." She stopped, thinking about how she'd just needed to get away from her life. Needed to go somewhere where she didn't have to deal with everything. She'd left a note for Brody and then gotten into her car and just driven away. She'd ended up somewhere on the Jersey shore, and had stayed in a motel on the beach with her phone turned off, not talking to anyone until she felt like herself again. That was when things with Brody had changed. He couldn't understand why she'd had to go away, instead of letting him help her.

"Then you understand." Serena's voice was low.

There was that zing of connection again, of feeling like they understood each other. But what did that say about Annie, that she was so in tune with a stalker who'd been hospitalized many times?

The rain lashed against the windows, and Annie began to think it would never stop. They were stuck in this bubble of time together here in the ohana, sharing terrible secrets. Annie's text alert sounded, multiple times, but she didn't look at the phone. She was close to finding out the real reason Serena was here, even as a shroud of dread dropped over her. Sam, Brody, her friends—they could all wait just for a few more minutes.

"Why would you come all the way here? What do you want from me?" Annie stared into Serena's eyes.

Serena gazed back for a moment, and then she looked away.

"Tell me." Annie's voice hardened. "I want so much to believe you, but do you see how bad this all looks? Do you not see what you've done the past few years is wrong, even illegal?" Her eyes bored into the back of Serena's head. "I'm going to ask you one more time. Why are you here?"

Serena's chin wobbled, but then she squared her shoulders and met Annie's gaze head-on, without flinching. "Because Finn is my son."

35

Annie burst into hysterical laughter. It bubbled up from inside her and escaped in a loud bark. The more she tried to stop, the more she laughed, and soon she was crying and laughing at the same time. Serena watched her, confusion on her face.

When Annie could finally speak again, she said, "You've got to be kidding me. Finn is *my* son." Her text alerts continued to ding, but her attention was on Serena.

"I know this sounds preposterous, but he's my son. I have proof." Serena's face was so open and free of guile when she said this that for a moment Annie actually believed she was serious.

Annie let out another burst of laughter. "You're so funny. You almost had me convinced there for a moment." She had to laugh—the alternative was too scary to contemplate. There was no way Finn was Serena's son. He'd come out of Annie's body, for heaven's sake. Was Serena really trying to make her feel like she had never given birth, hadn't gone through all that pain and nine months of pregnancy? She was delusional; that was all there was to it.

"Annie, I'm serious. Please stop laughing. It's not funny."

Annie snorted. It *was* funny. Looking at Serena, she wondered why she'd ever thought the other woman could be dangerous. There was nothing dangerous about her. She was delusional, that was all. Right now, she looked like a little girl who'd just been told she couldn't have what she wanted.

"Listen to me." Serena reached out to grasp Annie's arm. "Finn is my son, not yours."

Annie stared at the hand on her arm, dumbfounded. What had happened to their evening? How had they gotten from forming a new, close friendship to this woman telling her Annie's son was hers?

"I know you think what I did is creepy. I know it. But I couldn't help watching you. I needed to, as much as I needed air. It was like"— Serena let go of Annie's arm and moved her hand in the air, searching for the right word—"a necessity, like if I didn't do it, I would die. At first, it was just a need to see the life that I was supposed to live. But one day, I saw Finn playing in the backyard, and I really saw him for the first time. And that's when I suspected. I went home and did my research and . . ." Serena stopped, her mouth open, like she was reliving whatever she'd found. "I couldn't believe it. I was right. And with my suspicions confirmed, I amped up my surveillance."

"Your 'surveillance.'" Annie made air quotes. "Of us. Me and Finn and Brody."

"Yes." Serena nodded vigorously, as if happy that Annie got it. "I had to be sure, one hundred percent sure, before I could do anything about what I suspected. I studied you all, this perfect family that was supposed to be mine. I admit"—here she gave Annie an embarrassed smile—"I became obsessed. I couldn't stop watching you. I came to know you so well, your routines and the ways you reacted to things, that I felt like I knew you. Like you were a friend."

"That's why you knew so much about us." Annie shook her head, unable to believe that they'd never had any idea this woman had been watching them so closely. Yes, she'd felt eyes looking at her and gotten uneasy a few times, but it never went beyond that. They had been so careless.

"I lost my job again." Serena glanced at Annie and then looked away. "But this time, I couldn't blame my bosses. I spent so much time watching you that I didn't have time for a paltry thing like work. And when I was fired, I decided I didn't need to work anymore. My father had left me well enough off that, if I was careful, I probably wouldn't need to work again. Besides, this was more important. This was my entire life."

"Did you ever stop to think that this wasn't right?" Annie kept her voice level, even though she wanted to yell and scream.

"Maybe." Serena shrugged. "Sometimes, a little voice would say, *You can't do this. Spying on someone isn't right.* But I pushed that aside because I had to find my son. It's what any good mother would do."

"This goes so far beyond being a good mother." Why was she trying to reason with a woman who obviously didn't have any reason?

Serena continued talking, as if she hadn't heard her. "And at night, when I'd think to myself, *You're obsessed with them. Your doctors wouldn't like it if they knew,* I just told my mind to shut up. The doctors don't know everything. If I told them what I suspected, they'd definitely lock me up. And I was fine now. I wasn't depressed anymore. I had a reason for living! And the fact that I'm aware it's bad to be watching you tells me right there that I don't need to be locked up. I'm not a stalker. I'm just watching a life that should have been mine. And looking after my son from afar."

"He's not your son." Annie had had enough. "Finn came out of my body. I was there. Brody was there. *Finn* was there. You weren't."

"I was—that's what I'm trying to tell you." Serena knotted her fingers together.

Annie snorted. "I think I would have remembered if you'd been at the birth of my son. You're delusional. You *do* need help."

"I know it sounds crazy. I thought I was crazy when I first realized it. But it's true. Finn is my son and—"

Annie cut her off. "No. Stop right there. This has gone on long enough. I heard you out, just like you wanted me to. I thought we were going to be friends. Then you tell me we stole your house from you, and that you've been stalking us for years and you don't see anything wrong with it. Now you're claiming my son is yours." She stood, towering over Serena. "Do you not hear how off you sound?"

Annie's phone rang, and she reached down to pick it up from the coffee table. It was Brody. As she picked up the call, she saw that she'd missed numerous texts from him and Sam.

"Annie, what's going on over there? I'm still stuck in traffic." The reception was better than before. "The news said there's flooding along the Wailua River. A lot of debris got caught at the Wailua Bridge, creating a dam. Has the flooding gotten worse at the house?"

"Hold on, let me see." Annie glanced over at Serena as she walked to the window, Marley trailing after her. She pushed the curtain aside and looked out. The canal was overflowing, already covering the three steps that led up to their backyard, and coming up over the lawn. "The water has come up over the steps from the canal." She tried to keep her voice steady. As Sam had said, the main house and ohana were built up high, not on ground level, and the backyard sloped down into the canal. It would take a lot of water for them to be flooded out.

"How high?" Brody spoke loudly to be heard over the noise of the storm on his end.

"It's just over the back steps."

"Do you feel safe? What about Serena? Did you ask her to leave?"

"I tried. But she's still here. Did you call the police?" Annie looked at Serena again, whose eyes had widened at the word "police."

Static fuzz came from the phone, and Annie looked at it. "Hello? Brody?"

And then nothing. They'd been disconnected. It was just as well. She didn't know what to tell Brody about Serena. He was going to flip when he found out that she thought their son was hers.

She turned to address Serena. "I need you to leave. I've listened to you, and I've given you the benefit of the doubt. And I'm done."

"Annie . . ." Serena pleaded.

Annie pointed to the front door. "Leave. Now. And if you don't, the police will be here any minute. I don't care how bad the storm is."

"Please, no. I'll drown if I go out in that." Serena stood and faced Annie. "You have to listen to me. I know I went about this all wrong. I wanted to find the right way to tell you, but . . ." Her face dropped in defeat. "I always fuck everything up. But I have proof."

"Right." Annie narrowed her eyes at her. "You have proof. What proof can you possibly have, when Brody and I were both there when our son was born? What, you think I dreamed up the whole giving-birth part?" She gave a dry chuckle. "Believe me, I did not dream that up."

Serena looked her dead in the eye and said, "They were switched at birth."

36

Laptop ANNIE file

I watched you and I waited. I needed a plan. And one day, I looked at your son and something clicked in my mind. He always looked familiar to me and I kept wondering why. I kept thinking of children I knew, wondering if one of them reminded me of him. But that day, I finally realized why he seemed familiar. It was because he looked so much like me when I was little. He had the same cowlick at the crown of his head, just like mine. He has a dimple identical to mine in his right cheek. And he makes the exact same expression I do when he's surprised.

I knew what people would say if I told them this. That I was grasping for straws. But I knew deep in my heart that he is my son. I didn't have any proof, so I waited and I watched you all, when I wasn't in the hospital. I found another job, but I lost it again, because I spent so much time up there. People thought I lived in the neighborhood, and I always made sure I wasn't suspicious looking. I'd hide in the woods, where I had a perfect view of your back decks and yard.

And one day, my waiting and watching paid off. You'd just come back from the beach and your husband had stripped him naked on the back deck, to hose off the sand. You went inside and as he screamed and laughed, dancing in the cold water, I saw it. The same birthmark I had on my left butt cheek that looked like a strawberry. My heart pounding with excitement, I knew then I was right. I laughed out loud, but then clapped a hand to my mouth, not wanting to attract their attention. As soon as they were done and had gone in, I ran out of the woods and to my car in the beach parking lot, and drove right home to do research. Now that I had my proof, I had to figure out how it was possible. How did my son end up in your family? And if that was my son, then who was the little boy who had died over three years ago in his crib?

37

After those words burst out of Serena's mouth, they stared at each other for a full moment. Marley whined at her side.

Annie stiffened her spine, which threatened to crumble, and took a deep breath. "Right. They were switched at birth. I don't think that happens in this day and age. Hospitals are too careful." Her phone dinged a few more times, and she knew she'd have to answer Sam soon. And Brody. But she didn't take her eyes off Serena. "Lawsuits, you know?"

"I'm serious. I don't know how it happened, but it did." Serena's voice was gaining strength, a resolute expression on her face.

"Right." Annie turned away from Serena and looked at her phone. She'd had enough of this woman's fairy tales. What had started off as a nice evening with a new friend had quickly spiraled into a nightmare. She'd answer Sam's texts and then try to call Brody again. She hoped like hell that he'd gotten through to the police and that they were on the way here. She needed to get rid of Serena.

"Johnny's birthday was February sixth."

Annie looked up. That was Finn's birthday. And when Serena said the year, her heart actually skipped a beat. That was the exact day that Finn had been born. Her breath caught for a moment. When she finally whooshed it out, it took her a moment, but she quickly recovered.

"You've been stalking us for years. It'd be easy to find out when Finn's birthday is."

"They were born at the same hospital." And Serena named the exact hospital where Finn had been born.

"Again, you could have found that out." But a fissure of unease started at the base of her spine.

"About an hour apart." Serena continued talking as if Annie hadn't answered. "Finn was born at 12:01 p.m., and Johnny was born at 1:10 p.m."

The bottom dropped out of Annie's stomach. "How . . . What?" Finn *had* been born at 12:01 p.m.

Serena took a step toward Annie, but when Annie gave her a hard stare, she halted. "I'm not making this up. They were born in the same hospital on the same day at almost the same time. Our paths were meant to cross. There's a reason why we both found the lake house. Why our lives are so similar. Why we were meant to meet."

Annie shook herself, not wanting to believe this story. "You're delusional, Serena. Finn is my son. He looks just like me and Brody, half-Asian and half-white." People were always telling them that Finn looked like the perfect combination of the two of them.

"Danny is Chinese, so Johnny was half-Asian and half-white too."

Annie sucked in a breath, digesting this fact. But she wasn't about to be pulled into Serena's delusions. "I don't believe you. I would know if Finn isn't my child. He . . ." She stopped, thinking of all the times when she'd thought there was something wrong with her for not bonding with him more. Could there be truth in what Serena was saying? But then she shook herself, refusing to buy into it. Finn was her child, hers and Brody's. "I don't believe you."

Serena's face was so mournful that Annie would have felt sorry for her if she weren't pulling this stunt. Annie steeled herself, refusing to let the other woman soften her defenses. Finn was her child, end of story. But she couldn't help thinking back to his birth, and when they'd brought him back to her later that day.

The nurse had placed Finn in her arms and she'd looked down, expecting to feel that rush of love she'd felt when they first placed him on her chest after the birth and when they'd brought him back again after cleaning him up. But instead, she'd gone cold, frozen for a moment as she stared down at her baby. He was like a stranger to her. She felt nothing. Dimly, she was aware of Brody looking over her shoulder, making cooing noises at the baby, touching him lightly on the brow. Yet Annie continued to stare at the baby, wondering why she felt so numb.

She remembered looking up and saying to the nurse in a shrill voice, "Are you sure this is Finn? He looks different."

And the nurse had turned to her with a laugh. "Of course this is your baby. We cleaned him up, that's all." He'd been covered with a white, cheesy-looking substance when he was born.

Annie had to admit he looked much cleaner. But she'd turned to Brody and asked, "Are you sure this is our baby?"

He'd gazed at her with so much love. "Yes. Yes, this is Finn. Our son." His words had calmed the panic in her chest. She'd looked back down at the baby, determined to feel that rush of love again, but felt empty. She'd pushed her doubt aside, thinking she was overwhelmed by the birth. She'd be fine, once she'd had some rest.

Now she grimaced as the first pangs of doubt filled her. Was Serena right? Could they have been switched at birth and that's why Annie hadn't recognized her own child when they brought him back to her? Alarm coursed through her as she tried to make sense of this. Was Finn really Serena's child?

"Annie?"

She started, her eyes focusing on Serena staring at her from across the room. No. No, she wouldn't believe Serena's wild story. Finn was *her* son. What had happened the day of his birth was just the insecurity of a new mother. They had *not* been switched at birth. There was no way the hospital would have let that happen.

But then her eyes widened as a thought occurred to her. Was Serena here to take Finn? Because that was not going to happen, over Annie's dead body. No matter what doubts she had about their relationship, Finn was hers. She would do anything for him, including fight a delusional woman. Fear sliced through her even as she reassured herself that Serena would not do that. Would she? Thank goodness he was at the main house with her father and Sam. Picking up her phone while keeping her eyes on Serena, she quickly fired off a text to both Sam and her father.

> Don't let Finn out of your sight. Keep him with you at all times. Will explain later.

Sam texted back right away. Wait, what? Why? What's going on?

A: I'll explain later. Can't now. But I'm serious. DO NOT let him out of your sight.

S: You're scaring me.

Annie's father responded too. What going on?

A: Will explain as soon as I can. Just keep him with you. TRUST ME.

S: Okay. I got him. Do you need me to come over?

A: No. I got this. Just take care of him.

S: Yes. Call me as soon as you can.

38

Annie let out a breath of relief that Sam wasn't going to question her strange request. Her sister knew Annie was serious because they'd always used TRUST ME, in all caps, whenever they needed the other one to do something without asking questions. It was something the three sisters had done since they were younger. Sam would keep Finn with her.

Now what to do with Serena? What *could* she do with the storm still raging outside?

"You have to leave. Leave us alone." There was no conviction in Annie's voice—she knew Serena couldn't. But maybe she'd get lucky and Serena would just disappear in front of her eyes.

"I can't." Serena jutted out her chin. "I need Finn. I have nothing left. No one in my life. No family except for Finn. I need him."

"What?" What was Serena asking of her?

"I need him. Please. I know the kind of person you are. You're so kind, and you understand me."

"I don't understand anything right now." Annie rubbed her forehead.

Serena squared her shoulders and took a deep breath. "I want you to give me Finn."

Annie's jaw dropped and she could only stare. Weak-kneed, she reached back to support herself on the wall. Serena really wasn't in her right mind. There was no denying it now.

They stared at each other, neither moving. Tensions crackled so high between them that Annie was surprised the room didn't burst into flames.

Annie's phone rang and they both jumped. She looked down and saw it was Brody. Good, this was good. Brody would know what to do. Because Annie's brain had turned to mush.

She picked up the phone without saying anything.

"Sorry about hanging up on you." Brody's tone was brusque, the connection staticky. "Cell service is really bad. I haven't been able to get through."

"Yes." Annie watched Serena watching her as she spoke to Brody. "You need to come home. Now." She was still numb, trying to process Serena's request. "I need you." Her voice broke on the last word.

"What's happening? Tell me." There was an urgency in Brody's voice that Annie rarely heard, making her realize she was scaring him.

"I can't say right now. I need you here." Annie didn't know what else to say. There was too much to explain.

"I haven't been able to get through to the cops. They must be slammed." Annie heard every other word of what Brody had just said, but she got the gist of it.

"Come home." Her voice trembled.

"I'm calling 911. Maybe the Kapaa fire department can get to you. They're on the same side of the bridge, even if the police and fire from Lihue can't get there." Brody's steady voice calmed her slightly.

"Okay." Annie took in a shuddering breath. She needed help.

"Annie." Brody's tone had her listening. "Go to the main house with your family."

"And what about . . ." Annie kept her gaze on Serena.

"Leave her. You said it yourself: we have nothing of value. Go to your father's. Call me from there when you do."

"Okay." Annie could hear the storm, so loud outside, and as much as she didn't want to go out in it, she knew she had to get away.

"I'll be there as soon as I can. Some guy has a chain saw, and he's helping them cut up the tree so traffic can start moving again."

Her phone pinged suddenly, making her jump. Looking down, she saw it was a text from her sister.

"Who's that?" Brody asked, having heard the text alert.

"It's Sam. Our father wants me to come over. He thinks we're going to lose power."

"Yes, I agree. Get out now." His words were urgent.

"Okay." Annie's breath hitched. "I'm leaving."

When Serena heard that, she suddenly flew into action. She ran for the front door and flattened herself against it, blocking the way. Annie narrowed her eyes, trying to figure out how she and Marley were going to get around Serena and out the door.

"I know things haven't been great lately, but I love you, Annie." Brody's voice was rough and low.

At his words, tears gathered in her eyes. She honestly hadn't thought he still did. Not after what a bitch she'd been to live with.

"I love you too," she whispered.

Brody sighed, and the long exhalation vibrated down the phone line. It made Annie want to run to her husband and throw her arms around him, resting her head at his sternum and finding the place where she belonged. For the first time in a long time, her heart leaped with hope; maybe they hadn't drifted as far as she'd feared. Maybe they could still find their way back to each other.

They hung up, and Annie grabbed Marley's collar, walking him to the hooks by the front door, where his leash hung. But Serena stepped in front of her.

"Get out of my way." Annie faced Serena, as if her scowl alone would make the other woman move.

Serena didn't budge. "You have to give Finn to me."

"No, I don't. Move." Annie tried to go around Serena, but the other woman blocked her again. Fine, if she wouldn't let Annie get the leash, they would just leave without it. Annie turned to the front door, which was only a few feet away.

Serena once again moved in front of Annie, blocking the way. "I have nothing left. Except him. My son. My flesh and blood."

Annie glared at Serena. "He's my son. I will never give him to you."

"Please." Serena's face was contorted, and her red curls stood up wildly, making Annie think of Medusa. "You said you never bonded. You know he's not yours. Your baby was Johnny. You can have another baby."

"You're insane." Annie's fists clenched, trying to tamp down her anger. "I'm forty-two. There's no way I'm going to have another baby."

"I tried to get him that day . . . that day in August, but then Lindsay . . ."

Annie stared, the dread spreading from her center into her extremities until her whole body was buzzing. "What . . ."

They stared at each other and all sounds receded. Annie could hear nothing but the roaring of her blood in her ears as her mind made the connections and realization dawned.

Suddenly, Serena sprang to life, taking the few steps to the front door. "I'm getting my son."

"No!" The word ripped out of Annie, and she lunged at Serena, getting her by the hair and pulling hard.

Serena's head snapped back and she turned to grab Annie's arm, fingernails digging into her flesh as she tried to get Annie to let go.

Annie rammed her body at Serena until the woman was pinned against the front door. Marley jumped at Serena, his front paws landing hard, and she screamed, the sound lost in the howling of the incessant wind.

Pressure built inside Annie until she thought she'd explode. She couldn't think, couldn't gather her thoughts. All she knew was she had to stop this woman from getting to Finn.

Serena thrashed against her, reaching out and catching Annie on the side of the face. She raked her fingernails down Annie's cheek. Marley growled, lunging at Serena again as Annie brought her free hand up to her cheek.

Blood.

Something unleashed inside her, and with a roar, she attacked Serena. She had to knock her out somehow.

"No. Stop!" Serena shrieked, raising her arms to shield her face from Annie's fists.

But Annie didn't stop. There was no form, no skill. She just struck out with her fists, wanting to inflict whatever pain she could and stop this woman. Marley snapped and lunged at her side, helping her.

"I'm sorry." Serena sobbed as blood ran from her mouth, where Annie had landed a blow. "I didn't mean to."

Annie had Serena by the throat now, crazed beyond thinking, knowing only she had to stop this woman.

"Annie, please." Serena's eyes bulged as they pleaded with Annie. "I didn't mean to kill Lindsay. I only wanted my son."

Annie froze, hands still around Serena's neck as her senses slowly returned. Oh god, what was she doing? Her hands dropped away and she took a step back. The two women gaped at each other, as the rain pounded and the roar of the storm threatened to wash them away.

39

I sat alone in my car in the parking lot of the lake beach that day in late August. I stared at all the happy families taking advantage of the last weekend of summer and wished with all my might that this was my life. I should be sitting inside that fence, at the beach with my family, lying in the sun reading a book, knowing my son was safe running around with the other children. Maybe I'd have wine or a Truly in my cooler, and watermelon and juice for my son. I can smell the suntan lotion, the coconut scent wafting off my skin, mixing with the smell of hamburgers and hot dogs being grilled, which always signifies summer to me. My skin would be warm and slightly pink, my toes buried deep in the sand until I hit a cool spot, my hand on my cold drink.

But instead, I sat in my car, an outsider with no claim to the community that you belong to. So when I saw your son—my son!—walking out of the gates by himself, I got out of the car. Why was he outside without supervision? Even I, a nonmember, knew that all the parents were always shouting for the younger kids to stay inside the fence. I walked over to my son and scanned the bodies on the beach until I found you, stretched out on your chair, eyes closed, a book in one hand dangling down, your other hand holding on to the cup in the beach chair's cup holder. It was exactly how I'd pictured myself just moments before. For a second, I thought I was watching myself on the beach. But no, I'm the one standing outside and your son, my son, had wandered away and you weren't even aware. A sense of outraged indignation coursed through me and suddenly, I wanted to teach you a lesson. Let you see how it feels for something to not go right in your world for once. I realized this was the perfect opportunity to take back my son.

I took his hand and he willingly gave it to me before looking up with a question in his eyes. I told him I'd seen a family of turtles sunning themselves on a log near the water and did he want to go see them with me? To his credit, he said he wasn't supposed to go with strangers but I could see his curiosity was piqued. I said, "They're just right there," pointing to the woods next to the beach. "We won't go far." He agreed and was about to go off with me when that girl appeared. She came out of nowhere and snatched my son's other hand and pulled him out of my grasp. "Who are you? What are you doing with him?" The questions came at me fast and furious, with no time for me to answer. My son looked at me fearfully then, and not knowing what else to do, I turned and fled.

I sat in my car, not wanting to leave until my heart calmed. I could see my son talking to the girl, pointing toward the woods, and I knew he was telling her about the turtles. (There weren't any turtles. I made that up.) I watched as the girl nodded and then they headed into the woods.

I should have left then. I should have started my car and gotten out of there. But I was still so angry that you, the one who had everything, would leave your little boy (my little boy!) to wander around without supervision. How could you be so careless with that precious little boy?

All this time, I'd been grieving for my son, and he is still alive. I grew angrier as I stared into the woods where my son had disappeared. And I was angry at the teenage girl also for getting in my way. My anger propelled me back out of my car and I followed them into the woods. I didn't have a plan. I didn't know what I was going to do once I saw them. And that was the problem. I wasn't thinking, only feeling. I'd been hurting and alone for so long and it was finally my turn to be happy. We've been living such parallel lives. (Did I mention that we have the same birthday? I found this out during my research. You and I were born on the same day, twelve years apart. How much more proof do you need that our lives are intertwined for a reason?) But it was finally time for me to claim my rightful family.

I marched in and found them deep in the woods, close to the water's edge. The girl turned at the sound of my footsteps and put the boy behind her. She asked me what I wanted. I made my voice kind, telling her that I was his mother. The girl said, "No, you're not his mother. His mother is on the beach." I told her she's wrong, he's my son. I reached out to take his hand. But she wouldn't get out of the way. She actually slapped my hand. I couldn't believe she slapped me. In shock, I looked at my son and he gazed back at me, as if he knew—he knew!— that I am his mother.

Something snapped in me. I'd had enough. No one was going to tell me I couldn't talk to my son. Especially not a teenage girl. I pushed her. Hard. She went flying backward and ended up on her butt. I could hear the rush of air as the breath was knocked out of her and my son started to cry. I knew I should have helped her up but when she caught her breath, the girl started yelling at me to get away and leave them alone. So I left. That's what she wanted, wasn't it? I would figure out a way to get my son another time.

And I swear, when I left, she was alive. She was still on the ground, but she was alive. I could hear her talking to my son, probably soothing him. That made me madder and I wished I had slapped her to shut her up. I had just gotten to the edge of the woods when I heard my son calling the girl's name. Lindsay. His voice got louder and louder, so I turned around and ran back. And found the girl on the ground, but now with a pool of blood forming around her and my son screaming her name.

I panicked. I ran back to my car as fast I could. Thinking back, I should have scooped up my son and taken him with me. I should have thought of him first. He was terrified and any good mother would have consoled him. But I ran. Maybe I was out of practice. I hadn't been a mother for three years. But my head was filled with images of the girl. And the blood. I saw the blood and I ran, leaving my son there by himself.

I'm ashamed to say I didn't even call 911. I should have. Maybe someone would have gotten to her in time and saved her. I didn't know then that she was dead, only that she was hurt. And instead of getting her help, all I thought about was myself and how I had to get out of there.

Then the next day, I found out the girl had died. That she'd been found dead in the woods, my son crying next to her. And my blood ran cold. I knew I had killed her. Maybe I'd pushed her harder than I thought. Maybe she'd hit something when she went down, something vital. All I knew was that it was my fault. And that I'd left my son there to deal with it by himself, instead of taking him away from the scene. I was a bad mother and a killer. I'd killed before but that time was justified. No one would have blamed me. This time, I hadn't meant to.

40

Annie's head swam. She swayed on her feet, suddenly dizzy. She was frozen in place, Finn's screams echoing in her head.

"Annie." Serena's voice seemed to come from far away.

"How could you?" Annie's heart galloped.

"It was an accident." Serena's voice dropped to a whisper, and she leaned back against the front door. She looked like she would crumple to the floor if the door weren't holding her up.

Annie closed her eyes, still dizzy. The room was spinning when she opened them again. She stumbled backward until she hit the couch, and dropped heavily onto it. She could feel Marley panting next to her.

Serena was talking again, but all Annie heard in her head was the echo of Finn's little voice during a nightmare. The way he screamed for Lindsay, and shouted the word "no" over and over again. Echoes of her neighbors yelling her name, rousing her from her nap on the beach. Being jolted awake, her limbs heavy from the sun and sleep, her insides freezing even before her mind could understand what her eyes were seeing. Finn, in a neighbor's arms, crying hysterically, screaming Lindsay's name. The way he'd launched himself at her, covered in something red. Blood. She'd realized it belatedly, and only because the sharp tang of it hit her nose.

She reached up now and touched her cheek, blood coming away on her fingers. Blood. Always blood.

Annie hadn't been able to get him to calm down enough to tell them what had happened. He'd just kept saying the woman, the mean woman, was there in the woods. And then collapsed in Annie's arms, a deadweight.

She didn't really remember what happened next. Somehow, they'd gotten back to their house. Someone had called Brody, who'd been working at the firehouse in the Bronx. Neighbors must have helped them home, but she couldn't for the life of her remember if they'd walked or if someone had given them a ride the short distance to their house. Someone took Finn from her and told her to take a shower. They must have bathed Finn, because the next time Annie saw him, he was in his pajamas, his body clean and hair still damp. The police had come and questioned them, but Finn had sat in her lap and not said much. He just kept saying there was a woman with them. He didn't know her. That was all he said. When they asked him what happened, he just shook his head. And asked where Lindsay was.

Annie had nothing to contribute—she hadn't been there with them. She'd failed to protect her son when he needed her most. When Brody arrived, he took Finn from her, and the sudden absence of his warm body made her shiver. This was what it would feel like if he were gone. If whatever or whoever had killed Lindsay had gotten him.

"Annie. Annie."

Serena's voice floated to her as if from a great distance. She turned her head toward the voice, but her eyes remained unfocused. They'd never been able to get Finn to tell them more about the woman who had been in the woods with them. And now Serena was sitting here in her house, telling her she was that woman? That she was the one who'd killed Lindsay?

Annie's mind refused to focus. Because all she could think was that the woman who claimed she was Finn's real mother had killed Lindsay. And then left her son there all by himself.

41

Serena's voice drifted into Annie's consciousness.

"I just wanted my son. To finally take him home, where he belongs."

With those words, Annie finally snapped out of her stupor. Her eyes widened so much that she was afraid they would pop out. "Do you hear yourself? Do you hear how bad this all sounds? You were just going to take Finn? To kidnap him?"

"No! Of course not." Serena's brows came together in consternation. "It's not kidnapping if he's my son."

"He's not your son!" Annie yelled, shaking her hands next to her head. She couldn't believe she was having this conversation. "You are insane to think you could just kidnap *my* son. You're a criminal. I'm calling the police." Maybe if both she and Brody called, they would realize the urgency of the situation.

"Annie, please don't." Serena put her hands up together in front of her, her eyes pleading. "I didn't mean for that day to happen. I would give anything to take it back. I've suffered enough since it happened." Her shoulders lifted a bit, then settled down.

"You're not . . ." Annie struggled for the right words. "You're not right in the head."

"I'm not like this all the time. Only when something really bad happens. But I'm okay now. I have a reason to live again."

How many other "really bad" things had this woman done in her life? When Serena had told her about Johnny's death, Annie had believed her. But now she was beginning to wonder whether Serena had had a hand in what happened to her son after all. And killing a teenager, no matter whether it was accidental, was pretty bad in Annie's book.

Serena hung her head. "Danny left me because he thinks I killed Johnny. He said there's something wrong with me. That's why he wanted me to go to the hospital." She swiped the back of one hand across her face. "I know I would never hurt my son. But sometimes, I do things without knowing I did them. I have these blackouts and I don't remember anything I did while I was having them. Do you want to know my deepest, darkest secret?"

Serena's green eyes flashed at her from across the room. Annie shook her head. She didn't want to hear any more. Serena was a murderer. She reached down to rub Marley's side, telegraphing to him to stay with her. They were getting out of here. But just as she was about to bolt for the front door, Serena spoke.

"I think I killed Johnny during one of those blackouts. I think Danny was right."

"What?" Annie halted, swinging her attention back to Serena. She wanted to leave, she really did, but some sick fascination rooted her there. This was so much worse than anything she could have imagined when she opened the door to this woman.

"I've put Johnny's life in danger more than once," Serena continued, while Annie was in a half squat, about to get up from the couch. "But none of it was my fault. I didn't leave the stove burning on purpose that one time. I could have sworn I shut it off."

"What happened?" Annie dropped back onto the couch. Why, oh why, was she still here, listening to the words of a woman who had been stalking them all these years? Why wasn't she running screaming from the house? *Because maybe there's some kernel of truth to what Serena said, and Johnny was my son. If so, I have to know what happened to him.* "No," she said out loud. "No, no, no."

Serena didn't even look at Annie as she answered her earlier question. "I only ran downstairs to get the mail while the soup warmed up. It wasn't my fault that I ran into a neighbor in the mailroom. We started talking and . . . I lost track of time. The next thing I knew, the fire department was there because our apartment was on fire, and one of the firemen came out with Johnny in his arms."

Annie gasped, her quick inhalation catching in her throat. "Was Johnny okay?"

"He had to go to the hospital for smoke inhalation. But it wasn't my fault."

"Um . . ." Her mouth flopped open.

"And also, Danny told them that I fed Johnny poison. I didn't. It was an accident—a mistake. I would never feed him poison." Serena was agitated, her body twitching as her words came faster. "Johnny liked these Japanese rice crackers, and I bought a new brand we'd never tried before. There was this round container inside it, and I thought it was extra crackers or something. How was I supposed to know it was the preservatives? It looked like a cracker box, or like a dip."

"Oh, Serena." Annie was beginning to get the picture. And it wasn't a good one.

"He threw it up and everything was fine. I would never have done anything to hurt him. Not intentionally. I loved him, even though I found out after he died that he wasn't my son."

Annie stayed quiet. She had no words.

"I need to make things right." Serena's words made Annie look at her again. "You have to believe me. I'm telling the truth. But I . . ." She broke off eye contact and hugged her arms around herself, looking down at the floor.

Annie sat frozen, staring at the top of Serena's head. There had been something in her gaze just then that was eerily familiar. It was like looking into her own mind, seeing the guilt, the shame, the uncertainty that Annie herself had been living with. Only a moment before, she had been positive there was something wrong with Serena's mind. But now Annie felt as if she'd looked into the depths of her own soul, mirrored in Serena's eyes, and it scared her. Was she as delusional as Serena? Was that why they felt such a bond with each other? Why couldn't she make herself leave?

Neither spoke for a moment, and the sounds of the wind howling outside and the rain pelting down punctuated the silence between them. Marley whined at Annie's side, and she reached a hand out to soothe him.

Why weren't the police here yet? Had Brody even been able to get through if cell service wasn't good? "You have to go to the police, tell them what happened, that it was an accident," Annie finally said.

"I . . ." Serena looked up. "I can't. I can't go to jail. I need my son. He's the only thing I have left to live for. I'll die without him."

"Serena . . ." Annie took a careful breath as a sense of doom washed over her. She had to leave. Now, before Serena sucked her back into her delusions. Annie reached out a hand to grab Marley's collar, and taking another breath, she got ready to ram her way past Serena and out the front door. But before she could, the lights went off, plunging them into darkness. They'd lost power, just like her father had predicted.

42

Annie let go of Marley's collar and tapped her cell phone, which sent an eerie glow out into the darkened ohana. She had no bars. Whenever they lost power, the Wi-Fi went down, but she'd always had cell service before. Were the cell towers out too? Brody was out in this storm in his car, stuck on Kuhio Highway. All she wanted at that moment was to hold Finn close and to have Brody come home to them in one piece.

She suddenly realized that the ohana was quiet. Too quiet. Where was Serena? She turned on the flashlight on her phone and shone it around her. When the beam swung to where Serena had been standing before the lights went out, Annie's heart jumped into her throat. Serena wasn't there. Marley growled deep in his throat, causing Annie to sweep the light across the ohana. Goose bumps broke out all over her arms. There were eyes watching her. She could feel them. Feel them following her every move. Her breath hitched, and then she held it, straining her ears for any sound, any movement.

"Serena?" Annie's voice drifted out into the darkness. "Where are you?"

Silence met her and she swallowed. A whisper ran down her spine, and then Marley barked, a warning sound. Annie's body reacted before her mind. She jumped to the left off the couch, sensing a sudden motion to her right. Catching herself, she swung her light in that direction and found Serena standing there, her eyes burning and a bottle of wine in her hands.

"Oh my god, did you just try to hit me with that?" Disbelief tinged Annie's words. Her mind scrambled to catch up with what her body already knew.

Serena didn't say anything, only bore down on Annie again. She raised the bottle, her face twisted so that Annie barely recognized her. With a scream, Annie scrambled out of the way, her cell phone falling from her hands. Marley launched himself at Serena, and they fell to the ground. The wine bottle shattered as it hit the tile floor, sounding like a gun going off. Annie's leg stung, and the smell of red wine permeated the ohana. She rasped for breath, watching with horror from the dim light of the phone flashlight as Serena tried to push Marley off, kicking her legs.

With a scream, Annie ran forward. "Don't you kick him."

She focused all her attention on Serena, trying to pin her down. But Serena thrashed as Marley snarled, lunging for her with bared teeth whenever Serena tried to get up. Annie threw herself on top of the woman. Instinct took over and she fought the other woman, but Serena got the upper hand and grabbed Annie's head with both hands. Annie gasped for air as she tried to stop Serena from slamming her head into the ground.

With a growl, Marley clamped his mouth around one of Serena's arms, forcing her to release Annie. Serena shrieked.

Annie scrambled up and swung her fist. It connected with Serena's face, the loud smack stinging her hand and making her wince. Brody had taught her how to punch once, and now Annie was so glad she'd paid attention. Serena gave a cry of pain and crumpled to the ground, as limp as a jellyfish. Annie grabbed Marley's collar and hauled him off Serena.

Harsh breathing filled the ohana, and then Serena started weeping. Annie ran for her phone, scooped it up off the floor, and aimed it in

Serena's direction. Serena squinted in the sudden glare, throwing up an arm to shield her eyes. Blood ran down her face from her nose, and her tears mingled with it, making her look gruesome. Annie fought the urge to offer her a tissue, reminding herself that this woman had just tried to kill her—or at the very least, knock her out. Before she could figure out what to do, Serena started talking. But her voice was different, robotic, emotionless.

"I couldn't take it when Johnny cried. It was like a knife to my heart, and the more he cried, the more frantic I was to make him shut up. If Danny was home, he'd take him and leave the house so that I got some peace. But the morning my son died, Danny had an early meeting. Johnny had been fussing all night and neither of us got any sleep. Danny tried to soothe him before he left, but Johnny wouldn't stop screaming."

Annie's breath caught. She knew Serena was about to tell her what had really happened, and her heart wept for the infant.

"I don't remember what happened next. I told Danny that I woke up and found him so still in his crib. But I keep having this vision, as if I was watching a dream or watching someone else. And this other woman couldn't take Johnny's screams anymore. This other me picked up the pillow that was on the rocking chair in his room. This other me walked calmly to his crib and gently, oh so gently, placed the pillow over his face. He kept screaming. And I watched as this other me pressed down until there was no more screaming. There was only quiet—peaceful, glorious quiet."

Silent tears ran down Annie's cheeks. Poor Johnny. Her heart was tearing, as if Johnny were her son. Oh god, *had* Johnny been her son?

"Then the real me came back. The real me looked down at my baby in my crib, saw the way he wasn't moving, and the real me started screaming. This me called Danny, hysterical. He came home as fast as he could as I stayed by my baby's side, hoping he would wake up and start screaming again. But he didn't. He stayed quiet, so still and quiet."

Quiet weeping filled the ohana, and Annie didn't know if it was her or Serena.

"Danny left me after that. He said I killed our son and he couldn't live with me anymore. Even though everyone said it was SIDS and I was never charged. He didn't understand how much I loved our son. I was so in love with him, and I was a great mother. Most of the time. But when that other me appears . . . I can't control it. I can't control her."

Annie knew with a certainty down to her very marrow that this woman was dangerous. She was like two different people, and right now a monster was here in the ohana before Annie. She couldn't let this terrifying creature get to her son. She had to protect him.

In the dark, lit only by her cell phone, she gauged the distance from where she stood to the front door. She grabbed Marley by the collar and, with one big exhale, ran as if her life depended on it. Fumbling with the doorknob, she yanked it open, instantly confronted by the dreadful storm and the flooding, which was now at least a few inches deep in the backyard.

"Stay with me," she yelled to the dog. And with that, she plunged out into the torrential downpour, her progress slowed as she sloshed ankle-deep in the murky water. It should have taken mere seconds to run across the yard to her father's lanai but seemed to take forever. Marley splashed at her side as rain stung her face and water ran into her eyes, making it almost impossible to see. But she knew the way and trudged on through the water, until she was on her father's covered lanai, shielded a little from the rain. She sprinted up the few steps to the door and, finding it locked, pounded at it, even as she saw Serena coming out of the ohana toward her.

"Open the door," Annie screamed.

The door burst open a moment later, her father standing there.

"Let me in." Annie was about to step through the door when Serena came up the steps behind her. Annie had time to wonder how she had crossed the lawn so fast before Serena rammed into her with an elbow to

Annie's side. Annie stumbled backward, falling down the steps. She lay crumpled at the bottom, wheezing. Marley nudged her with his nose.

"Finn! Where are you?" Serena yelled. Annie watched her reach out and slap her father's arm aside when he tried to stop her from entering. She shoved him and he went down hard.

Annie scrambled to sit up. Her heart dropped when she saw Finn coming into the kitchen.

"No, Finn. Go, run!" She pushed to her feet just as Serena ran in and hugged Finn to her.

"My son. Mommy's here." Serena clasped Finn to her wet body.

Annie crawled up the stairs toward Finn, never taking her eyes off him. Her father was on the floor, groaning as he held his arm. "Sam!" she shrieked at the top of her lungs. "Help us!"

Finn was frozen in Serena's embrace as she held him by his arms, her eyes devouring him. Finn's eyes found Annie's. In the flicker from all the candles her father had placed around his kitchen, Annie could clearly see the fear in her son's eyes.

Serena's face was streaked with blood, her hair plastered to her face by the storm. Neither moved, as if locked in a universe all their own. Then Finn opened his mouth and began screaming at the top of his lungs. Annie heard Sam shout her name as she and Cam came thundering down the inside stairs toward them.

43

Finn fought to get out of Serena's grasp. He lashed out like an animal possessed and screamed, one endless, long sound that reached into the depths of Annie's heart and ripped it to shreds.

"Get your hands off my son!" she yelled. Anger swept through her body, propelling her off the ground. Within seconds, she was on top of Serena. Serena swung out an arm, connecting with Annie's cheek with a loud thwack. Annie reeled back, clutching her face.

"Don't be afraid, Finn, I'm here. It's me, your mommy." Serena was trying to console Finn, but he was fighting with all his might.

Sam finally reached the door to help Annie, yelling to Cam, "Stay back."

But Serena was like a woman possessed. She backhanded Sam across the face, sending her stumbling to the ground next to their father. Annie sprang forward to rip Serena's hands off Finn as Marley clamped his teeth around one of the woman's ankles. Serena never flinched.

"Stop screaming. It's me, Mommy." Serena shook Finn with each word.

Annie grabbed at Serena, pulling her hair, her arms, punching whatever she could reach and kicking whatever she could get. Out of the corner of her eye, she saw Sam coming at them. Marley, teeth still clamped on Serena's ankle, shook his head as if killing his prey.

Sam grabbed Finn and pulled, while Annie dug a finger into one of Serena's eyes from behind. Serena screamed and let go of Finn. Sam clasped him to her, and the momentum threw them backward in a heap to the ground.

"Get her out. Get her out!" Finn screamed. He was freaking out, big-time. "Get her away!" Sam gathered him in her arms, rocking him.

"Don't let her get him," Annie shouted to Sam, as Serena lunged for Finn.

Annie grabbed Serena's hair and pulled. Serena's head snapped back, and Annie felt a moment of satisfaction. She wanted to inflict pain on the woman who had stalked them through the years, who had made Annie feel like she was losing her mind and doing things she didn't remember. Who was now trying to steal her son. Baring her teeth, she lashed out.

To her surprise, Serena fought back, even with Marley still attached to her ankle. Blood poured down her leg. Blood. Annie stumbled at the sight and slipped on the wet ground before gaining traction again.

But Serena had already kicked out at Marley with her other foot, catching him in the side. He yelped and let go, whimpering. Fury exploded in Annie and she charged Serena, shoving her with all her might. The other woman went flying through the air, landing with a sickening crunch just inside the back door, where the rain continued to pelt in. Serena curled into a ball and Annie hovered over her.

"You will never get your hands on my son. He is my son." Annie thumped a palm on her chest, gazing ferociously at the woman at her feet.

Serena looked up at her. "No, he's mine—" She broke off, sobbing.

"Shut up," Annie screamed. "He's *mine*. He will never be yours."

For a moment, Serena seemed to wilt in front of her eyes. But then she gave an anguished cry and shot to her feet. Before Annie could guess what she'd do next, Serena yanked Finn right out of Sam's arms. She ran for the door, stumbling down the last few steps. With a speed that seemed impossible given the way the water lapped at her legs, she sloshed across the backyard to the driveway, quickly disappearing from view.

"I'm sorry. I'm sorry," Sam cried.

"Take care of Marley and Baba," Annie shouted at her.

She ran after Serena but slipped on the bottom step, landing hard. It took a moment to get her bearings. She could hear Finn's wailing, competing with the sound of the wind. Her body protesting in pain, Annie heaved herself up and fought to gain traction in the flooded yard. How was it that she, the ex-dancer, had landed like a wounded buffalo, while Serena, the self-proclaimed non-exerciser, had recovered from her fall like a ballerina? Cursing again, Annie tried to run, slogging her way to the driveway after Serena and Finn, who were already out of sight.

She struggled after them, but when she got to the end of the driveway, there was no one there. She looked down the street but didn't see them. Serena wouldn't have gone toward the river to her left, would she? Did she even know about the tunnel through the bamboo that led down to the private dock?

She had to check. Annie hurried toward the bamboo tunnel, not caring if it was dangerous to go down to the river. That woman had her son, and she would do whatever she had to, to get him back. Serena's words from earlier mocked her as she ducked under the first branches. *If Finn were in danger, would you think twice before trying to save him? At your own risk?*

Taking a breath, she ran into the small tunnel. Once inside, the roar of the storm muffled. It was as if she were in a tiny insular bubble, safe away from the storm raging outside. Only the water rising to her ankles gave any indication that Mother Nature was not happy.

Within seconds, she was out of the tunnel and standing at the grassy area above the dock, where they stored the kayaks and paddleboards. There was about a foot's drop down to the dock, which jutted out into the river. They usually jumped to the lower level, or used the gentle incline to the left almost like a ramp.

It took a moment for her eyes to adjust to the dark. The moon shining off the water as it slipped in and out of the clouds gave a faint glow, and her breath caught when she finally realized what she was looking at. The dock was underwater. She couldn't even see it.

"Oh my god," she muttered under her breath, looking at the scene before her. From her vantage point, slightly higher, Annie could make out debris and driftwood floating by in the river. But what made her gasp was the sight of Serena standing where the dock started with Finn in her arms. She was shin deep in the water, her back to Annie. Annie's heart stopped as she remembered something Serena had told her earlier: she couldn't swim.

44

"Mommy."

Finn's small voice drifted to her even above the roar of the storm. Annie's breath hitched. What was she going to do? If she made any sudden moves and scared them, they might fall into the water. Finn could swim, but barely, having only just learned recently. He'd be no match for the river. And Serena couldn't swim, which meant it would be up to Annie to save both of them if they went in.

"I'm here, darling. I'm here." Serena's voice floated back to Annie, and she watched as the other woman smoothed a hand down Finn's back. Annie couldn't understand how she could possibly hear either of them speaking. The rain splashed down hard and the wind whipped at her hair, making it nearly impossible to hear anything. Yet she could hear them, clear as a bell.

"Serena, come back. Please. Get away from the edge." Annie's words were carried away in the loud rush of pelting rain and the swirl of water. She wasn't sure if Serena had heard her. Annie took a breath and jumped down onto the lower level, where Serena and Finn were. She landed with a soft splash, and Serena turned toward her. "Please. Come back with me." Annie took a few steps forward, until she was right in front of them. "I'll help you."

She was afraid a surge could happen at any time, and then the mad, swirling river would wash everything in its path toward the ocean just beyond the bridge to their left.

"No. You don't get it, do you, Annie?" Even above the roar of the storm, Annie heard her perfectly. It was as if the two of them were connected somehow, so that the heavy rain faded and they were having an intimate conversation.

"Get what? You can tell me, once we're back inside and dry." Annie forced out a laugh. "We're all soaking wet."

"I had nothing to live for. When I was little, I was sure I was put on this earth to do something great. That's what my father always told me. But I never found that thing that I wanted to be."

"Um . . ." Annie wanted to interject, to scream at Serena to give back her son and get away from the edge. But she couldn't. She had to stand here, in one of the worst storms she'd ever seen, and listen to this woman because she held Annie's heart in her arms. She couldn't risk doing anything to make them fall into the water.

"I've always dreamed of writing a book. I can see it." Serena gazed up, as if envisioning her book in front of her. "A novel. By Serena Kent."

"You can do that," Annie said. "You can do anything you want to. But you have to get away from the river." She was desperate. She needed to get Finn back up to safety.

"I can't." Serena's tear-filled eyes turned back to her. "I tried, but I can't focus enough to write a book."

She was about to continue but stopped when they heard a voice shouting.

"Annie!" It was faint, but Annie recognized Sam's voice. Her sister was looking for her, probably worried because she hadn't come back with Serena and Finn.

Annie wanted to yell out that she was here but held her tongue, for fear of scaring Serena. With determination, she turned back to Serena. "You can get help for it, reach for your dreams. I'll help you."

Serena's face scrunched up incredulously. "You hate me."

"I don't. You need help. I need help." She took a step, now close enough she could touch them. "And maybe it's not a shameful thing to admit."

Serena made a scoffing noise and turned back to the river. For a moment, Annie's heart stopped, sure Serena was going to ignore her and jump into the water with Finn.

"I'll make you a pact. We'll do it together. We'll support each other, just like we did earlier."

Serena turned slowly around, rocking a little from the force of the water. "You would help me?"

"Yes." Annie focused on Finn, who was clinging to Serena's neck. "We have a bond. We're connected, like you said." Would that be enough to convince her?

Serena's forehead scrunched up with skepticism, but Annie could see she'd piqued her interest. Serena took a step and stumbled in the water as Finn stared down with terrified eyes.

Annie's heart stopped. Her son was balanced so precariously above the murky water. If Serena were to let go . . . Annie squeezed her eyes shut and then opened them. She had to stay strong. She had to think clearly and get her son back.

"Come back with me."

Serena didn't say anything, only turned her back on Annie. Finn peered around the woman's neck, his wide eyes signaling his terror.

Annie's hand clapped over her mouth. How was she going to get Serena away from the edge? She kept her eyes on Finn, sending him love. She would get him out of this situation. She would save him no matter what.

Sam's voice sounded again, shouting Annie's name. Annie knew she had to act now, before Sam burst onto the dock, scaring Serena. She took a deep breath and then brought a finger up to her lips, signaling to Finn to remain quiet. He gave a slight nod, and Annie reached out, her breath held.

Serena suddenly turned around. "What are you doing?" There was no mistaking the panic in her voice.

"Nothing." Annie froze, arms outstretched. "You're right, Finn is yours. I've been selfish. I . . . I'm ready to share our son now. Finn is our son."

"Our son?" Serena looked confused for a moment; then her face cleared. "No, he's mine. Johnny is yours."

"Okay, fine." Annie tried to control her breathing, to not let her panic take over. She had to hold it together. "Just get away from the edge. Please."

"No," Serena cried. "You hate me now." She looked at Finn, who was still clinging to her neck, but was staring at her with wide, terrified eyes. "And he hates me too. He's scared of me."

"Serena. Look at me. Listen to me." Annie waited until Serena turned her gaze to her. "He doesn't hate you. I don't either. Remember how we bonded back at the house? Let's go back. Please, he's scared and wet. We need to get him inside."

Slowly, Annie held up her arms, gesturing to Finn with her eyes. Her son understood and suddenly launched himself at her. She caught him in a desperate hug. Clasping him to her body, she backed up as she kept her eyes on Serena. Serena watched them, a small smile on her lips. She reached out a hand as Annie backed up even more, slogging through the water.

"Come on, Serena. Let's go inside, get dried off. We'll take a hot shower and then have a glass of wine together. Doesn't that sound good?" Annie moved to where the land sloped up and began climbing out of the flooded water. "Let's go, okay?"

Serena nodded, and just as Annie thought she was going to come back with her, a roaring sound arose from the river as water rushed toward them. Eyes wide, Annie scrambled upward until she was on the ledge above the dock. Before she could fully comprehend what was happening, a huge swell of water washed over the dock, and Serena slipped backward into the river without a sound. Annie stumbled back and grabbed a tree, anchoring herself as the current rushed at them in an angry gush, threatening to rip them away from the tree.

"Hang on, Finn," Annie screamed, her voice whipping away in the wind. She felt Finn's little arms wrapped around her neck so tight she felt as if she were choking. She focused on clinging to the branch, fighting the surging water, and struggled to get her footing. When comprehension finally hit and she saw that Serena was no longer standing on the dock below them, she let out a scream, a long, loud sound that carried above the storm as her eyes frantically searched for the other woman.

45

Annie tried to shield Finn from the storm. The night was so dark and the water murky and brown, filled with debris that surged down the river toward the ocean. She looked out across the river and thought she spotted a form, but she couldn't be sure. Was it Serena? Or a piece of driftwood? One thought kept running through Annie's mind: *Serena can't swim. She can't swim.* She took a step closer to the edge, determined to find Serena and bring her back on land.

Seconds later, Sam burst through the tunnel of bamboo. "Annie!" she screamed, grabbing her arm. "Get back. What are you doing? Give me Finn."

Annie handed Finn to her sister, then returned her eyes to the water. Should she jump in the water to look for Serena? She could swim, but the turbulent river was rushing toward the ocean. What if she got swept away? Would it be better to call for help? But how could she just stand here and watch Serena drown?

Sam pulled on her arm, dragging her up toward the tunnel. Annie struggled to get out of her sister's grasp.

"Serena is in there!" She pointed to the water. "Do you have your phone? Call 911!"

"Oh my god." Sam turned to look at the water before pulling her phone out of her back pocket. As she called for help, Annie knew she couldn't go after Serena; it was too dangerous. Tears sprang to her eyes as she stood there helplessly. As much as she'd wanted to disappear in the last four years, when faced with death, she couldn't do it. A part of her still wanted to live. She stood on the shore, one arm wrapped around both Sam and Finn, and stared into the water, praying that Serena would survive.

◆ ◆ ◆

An hour later, Annie stood out in the storm at the end of the cul-de-sac, unwilling to go inside even though there was nothing she could do. She was wet to the bone and shaking, even with the blanket she'd brought outside with her. She and Sam had taken Finn to the main house after calling 911.

Power had been restored shortly after they went in, and Annie had given Finn a hot bath. Both her father and Marley were fine, if a bit bruised, though Marley was limping slightly. Annie had wrapped Finn in a blanket, and they'd sat on the couch together, Marley next to them. Finn had snuggled into her side, not saying anything. Annie didn't speak either. She'd just held him, so thankful he hadn't gone into the river with Serena. She closed her eyes every time the image of the two of them poised at the edge of the water popped into her head. She'd been so close to losing Finn again. Her arms tightened around him and she kissed the top of his head. They were warm and safe, her son and dog.

When Annie's father said he'd made Finn his favorite soup, Finn's stomach had won out over his need to be with her. She'd reluctantly let him go. Once he was happily slurping up the chicken corn soup, surrounded by Sam, Cam, and Annie's father, Annie had grabbed a blanket and slipped outside to wait for news about Serena.

The Kapaa fire department, which was stationed only four minutes from their house, had been able to get to them. They'd called the coast guard and set up a land rescue to search the river. The fireman who spoke to Annie told her the Kapaa department didn't do night rescues by helicopter, and that one would be coming from Oahu. But it would take more than an hour to get there, given the conditions. The rain had lessened, but it was still coming down. Annie had wanted to scream, feeling so helpless. How could Serena possibly survive when she couldn't swim? When she voiced this thought out loud, the fireman explained that, with all the debris and driftwood in the water, maybe Serena would have grabbed on to something, staying afloat long enough for them to find her.

With the storm finally letting up, she knew rescue workers, along with volunteers, were on the bridge and along the shore, wherever it was safe, and using spotlights to search the river and shores for Serena. Annie shivered, rubbing her arms under the blanket. If Brody were here, she knew he'd be right there helping with the search. But he was still stuck somewhere on Kuhio Highway on the other side of the bridge. The Lihue fire department hadn't made it to them yet either. Despite what the fireman told her, with each moment that passed, Annie's hope that they'd find Serena alive diminished. How could she possibly survive in a storm like this?

She hugged her arms around herself, knowing she should go inside and see how Finn and Marley were, but she couldn't tear herself away from where she stood in the road at the end of their driveway, waiting for someone to give her news. Sam had come out a few times for updates, and to let her know Finn was okay, full after his meal and on the couch with Cam watching a movie. Annie looked back and saw Marley had parked himself by the front door, waiting for her. He seemed okay, despite having been kicked. Sam urged Annie to wait inside, but she refused, even though she was drenched from head to toe, her hair sticking to her face.

The sound of a car pulling up made Annie turn her head, and she watched as her husband parked and jumped out of his car.

"Annie!" He ran toward her, but she stood, rooted in place, until he reached her and wrapped his arms around her, wet blanket and all.

She didn't speak, just turned her face so that her cheek rested against his sternum. *Home,* she thought. Her arms were still wrapped around her chest, and she stayed like that in Brody's embrace, drawing heat from his warm body.

"You're shaking." He finally pulled away to look at her. "I'm so sorry it took me so long to get home."

"I . . . Brody. It was awful . . . I can't," Annie stuttered.

Brody rubbed his hands up and down her arms. "It's okay. Sam called and told me what happened. I couldn't get through to the police. The call kept dropping. Or it was busy. By the time I finally got through, you and Sam had already called 911." He searched her face. "They've got part of the bridge blocked off for the search—that's why it took me so long to get here. The Lihue fire department just got here too. They'll find her, if she's still . . ."

"She had our son. She grabbed him out of Sam's arms and ran down to the dock." Tears gathered in her eyes again as she pictured Finn in Serena's arms, precariously balanced at the water's edge. "I don't know what she was going to do with him. But I talked her out of it. I told her I'd help her, we'd figure it out. I grabbed Finn and I know she was coming back with me, but then the water . . ."

Grief washed over her, even as relief that her husband was here coursed through her body. He was always so good in an emergency, probably from his training as a fireman, and she knew she could lean on him. She wrapped her arms around his middle and held him tight, all her bitterness at him these last few years washing away with the rain.

"It's okay, Annie. Finn's safe. You got him in time." His body vibrated from his voice, and Annie closed her eyes for a moment, realizing she'd missed this, missed leaning on her husband when things got tough.

She picked her head up off his chest and looked up at him. "She was coming back . . ." Annie squeezed her eyes shut. "I know she was. But then the river . . . She just disappeared."

Brody held her tight, and they stood like that for a few moments, both soaking wet. The worst of the storm seemed to have passed, but it was still raining.

Annie pulled away and stared toward the bamboo tunnel, wishing Serena would just walk through there, alive. Yes, the woman had tried to kill her with a wine bottle (and how fitting if that had happened to Annie—death by wine), and tried to steal her son. But even though she knew she should be relieved that Serena was gone, Annie just couldn't rejoice in the possible death of another human being, even one who had caused such havoc in such a short amount of time.

She turned to Brody, really looked at her husband for the first time in years. She'd been so wrapped up in her own grief and misery and had taken his presence for granted. Yet he'd stood by her for this entire time while she wallowed in her misery, lashing out at him. Would she have done the same if the roles were reversed? She honestly didn't know. She wasn't as patient as Brody, and had a quicker temper. Would she have put up with all the unhappiness she'd heaped on him these last few years? It wasn't his fault her life had fallen apart. He'd been there for her, always standing by her, even when she pushed him away.

More tears flowed down her cheeks, this time for all the damage she'd done to her marriage. It was as if she had decided she didn't deserve happiness and had been trying her best to sabotage anything good. She stared into Brody's hazel eyes; saw the kindness, the compassion, the patience he'd shown while she'd wallowed in her own misery and depression; and realized he was a good man. This was her husband. And she'd been such a jerk for such a long time.

She reached out a hand and laid it against his cheek, even as her bottom lip trembled. She bit it, forcing herself to stop crying. "I love you, Brody Devlin. I'm so sorry for everything I've done and said."

Instead of answering, he lowered his mouth to hers. Annie surrendered herself to her husband's kiss, emotions clogging her heart. She'd finally found her way out of her fog. She wanted to stay like this for a long time, safe in his arms and the possibility of finding Serena alive still real.

But the next moment, the womp, womp of a helicopter drawing nearer made them both look up. The helicopter from Oahu was finally here. Maybe now they'd be able to spot Serena from above, clinging to a piece of wood, waiting to be rescued. Annie wanted so badly to believe that was possible that she squeezed her eyes shut and made a wish, as if she were a little girl. When her eyes opened, she saw a car driving down the cul-de-sac toward them. It was a police car, probably coming to update them. As the officer parked and got out, Annie tensed. She steeled herself for the worst as she watched him walk toward them, his shoulders hunched forward against the rain. Brody pulled her in against his chest, anchoring her to him as only he knew she needed right now. And together, they turned to face the policeman, who halted in front of them.

46

"Annie-ah. Drink this."

Annie looked up. She'd crawled into bed after a hot shower and after Brody had taken care of the scratches on her face, the cuts from the wine bottle on her legs, and her various bruises and scrapes from her struggle with Serena. Seeing her father at the bedroom door, she pushed herself up to a seated position. Marley was on the bed with her, clean from the bath Sam had given him. He picked up his head and looked at Annie's father. Annie was going to take him to the vet the next morning to make sure he was okay. The dog had refused to leave her side from the moment she'd come back into the ohana.

Her father walked over and passed her a steaming mug filled with who-knew-what. Annie made a face at the herbal scent emanating from it. Of course her father would be pushing herbs on her. It was always his go-to for any crisis.

"Drink it. It will help you."

Annie looked at her father, and he scowled at her. She took a tentative sip. She looked up at him in surprise and took another sip, a bigger one this time.

"See, not so bad." Her father crossed his arms over his chest in satisfaction. She was so glad he hadn't been seriously injured during the altercation with Serena.

Annie smiled, reluctant to admit he was right. It actually tasted pretty good. And the warmth sliding down her throat soothed her, bringing a calmness within her for the first time since Serena had disappeared.

"Drink whole thing."

"Okay, Ba." And she obeyed, slowly sipping the herbal concoction until most of it was gone. She leaned back against the pillows, cupping the mug in her hand. The warmth thawed her cold fingers, and she gave a sigh. "Where's Brody?"

"He's with Finn." Her father switched to Taiwanese. "They're watching a movie."

Annie pushed the comforter aside and swung her legs onto the floor. "I need to go to Finn. He's been through so much tonight."

"Wait." Her father held up a hand. "I want to talk to you."

Annie halted, about to stand up. Her father wanted to talk to her? He had never said that to her before.

Her father rubbed the side of his head. "I know we don't talk much, but that doesn't mean I . . ." He trailed off, and Annie knew whatever he wanted to say was hard for him.

She held her breath, waiting for him to continue. Marley nudged her arm with his nose, and she rubbed the top of his head.

He father turned away from her so that she couldn't see his face. "You were the one we worried about the least. Jeannie wanted to be the perfect daughter, and Chrissy and I worried she was missing out on life while trying to be perfect. And Sam . . ." Her dad shrugged and turned back to her. Annie could see the smile on his face. "You know Sam has her head in the clouds. She needed me. But you." He pointed to her. "You always knew what you wanted. You had a mind of your own. You wanted to be a dancer, and convinced your mother and me that you could make it work. You wanted to marry a white man, and convinced us it was the best for you. You didn't need us as much as your sisters. We didn't worry about you." He stopped and cleared his throat. "But maybe we should have. You've been struggling these last few years. And your mother wasn't here to help you. I didn't know what to do. So I did nothing."

Annie's mouth fell open. This was the most her father had ever said to her. And he was talking about feelings, something they didn't do in their Asian family. Who was this man? What was happening?

"I . . . Ba . . ." she stammered, then slammed her mouth shut. She had no response. It was as if he'd just told her he wasn't really her father. She wouldn't have been any more surprised if that had been what he'd said.

Her father regarded her for a moment. Silence hung between them. But for the first time since she was a little girl and used to throw herself at her father, sure he would catch her, it wasn't awkward.

"I give you herbs. And Asian remedies. Tai chi. Because that's what I know. That's what I believe in." Her father clasped his hands together. "I want to help you, but I only push you away."

"No." Annie shook her head. "I was the one who pushed you away. I didn't understand."

Her father shook his head as if disagreeing with her. "But now I have to speak up. What happened to that woman was not your fault."

Annie shrugged. She was still blaming herself, wondering whether, if she'd said or done something different, she could have gotten Serena back on land in time. There was still no sign of her. The police had come back again half an hour ago, to let them know they were still searching. If they didn't find her by morning, the Kauai fire department would take over the search. She hadn't wanted to ask when they would give up, but the policeman had read the question on her face. He'd told her they assumed someone was alive at least for the first three days.

Her father continued. "It was nature. And her own choice to go down there. You saved your son. You should hold on to that." His voice soothed the guilt.

Annie gave him a look. "I've never heard you speak so much in my life."

249

He shrugged. "The Western way, it doesn't make sense to me. That's not how I was brought up, so I don't have much to say." He turned his hands up. "Things are so different in Taiwan. But we're in America. And Sam sat me down, had a talk with me."

Annie's eyebrows rose in surprise. Sam was behind this talk with her father?

"She said to me, 'You have to reach out to Annie. You have to tell her it's okay to ask for help.'" Her father shrugged, a helpless look on his face. They stared at each other for a moment. "I'm here. You do what you need for you."

"Big Auntie won't like that." Annie looked at her father and was gratified when a hint of a smile played around his mouth.

"No, she won't." He shook his head, the smile getting bigger. "But what does she know? She still uses her dishwasher as a drying rack, no matter how many times I've told her it's for washing dishes."

Annie laughed, and tension eased out of her shoulders. Serena was still gone, but her father had just made a joke and basically thumbed his nose at his oldest sister.

They fell silent again, and now Annie could hear the sounds of an animated movie coming from the living room. She listened for a moment, gathering her thoughts.

"Thank you, Ba," she finally said.

"Okay." He turned to go, but then stopped at the door and turned back to her. "This means you will take all my herbs now, right?"

Annie laughed again, realizing she liked this side of him. He never joked with her, only with Sam and Cam. And as she watched him return to the living room, she wrapped her arms around Marley. Faithful Marley, who had fought Serena with her and tried to protect Finn. She felt a tiny bit better, which she suspected was why Sam had sent their father in to talk to her. Her sister knew Annie would be blaming herself for Serena falling into the river.

47

It was late, way past Finn's bedtime. Annie had come out of the bedroom after her talk with her father and joined them on the couch, watching the rest of the movie while holding Finn close to her. Annie and Brody had been so grateful their son was safe that they'd let him stay up. But it was finally time to put him to bed.

Tucking the comforter around Finn's chin, she leaned down to hug him, inhaling his sweet little-boy scent. Finn wrapped his arms around her neck. "Mommy?"

Annie pulled away so she could see his face. His forehead was furrowed. "I'm here," she said, reaching a hand to try to smooth the lines away.

"Where did that woman go?" He looked so worried. Annie leaned down and kissed his cheek, willing him to understand that she would always protect him, even though she'd done a bad job of it these past few years.

Annie looked her son in the eyes. "I don't know. But you don't have to be afraid of her anymore. Daddy and I aren't going to let anything happen to you."

She paused as Finn's eyes searched hers. "I'm sorry I haven't been a very good mommy to you. I'm sorry that I wasn't there for you when

Lindsay was hurt, and I'm sorry the woman grabbed you tonight. But I'm going to try harder now. You're the most important person in my life, and I'm sorry for not protecting you better."

Finn stared back at her, and she almost wept at his innocent expression. Then he surprised her by reaching out a hand to touch her face. "You haven't been a bad mommy." He took her face in between both hands and patted her cheeks before letting go.

Tears gathered in her eyes and she smiled down at him. "I'm going to do better though, okay, Finnie?"

He nodded, then let out a big yawn. She kissed him again and he closed his eyes. Smoothing a hand over his forehead, she watched him until his face relaxed and his breathing deepened. "I love you," she whispered to him.

"Annie."

She turned at the sound of her name.

Brody stood next to the mattress, holding out her cell. "It's Izzy and Julia," he said in a whisper. "You want me to pick it up?"

Annie nodded. While Brody walked back toward the bedroom and picked up the FaceTime call, she looked at Finn one last time. He was just starting to get over what had happened to Lindsay. Now he would be even more traumatized. She vowed again to do everything she could to be there for him fully.

She walked into the bedroom and took the phone from Brody. "Hello?" she said into the phone. The sight of her best friends brought a smile to her face.

"Any news?" Izzy's voice was rushed. They had called earlier while Annie was outside, and Sam had updated them. "They haven't found her yet, have they?"

"No. They're still searching. I think they hoped to find her under the bridge, where it was dammed up from all the debris and driftwood. But so far nothing. If she was swept out into the ocean . . ." Annie trailed off, not wanting to imagine the worst. "They told me they hoped she'd grabbed on to something in the water to stay afloat. Even a strong swimmer would have had trouble swimming back to land in that storm. And she can't swim."

"Oh, Annie." Izzy brought the phone close to his face, earning a frown from Julia.

Annie stifled a laugh. Her friends could still make her smile, even in this dark time. "They told me they won't give up, at least for the first three days. We have to hold on to that thought."

She closed her eyes as she said that. Because she couldn't imagine what Serena was going through if she really was still alive. The terror of being in the water when she couldn't swim. How long could she possibly hold on, if she really had grabbed on to something?

"We're here for you, okay?" Julia spoke quietly.

Annie opened her eyes to find both of them looking at her with concern. She missed her friends. Real friends, who'd been through the best and worst parts of her life for more than twenty years.

"Thank you."

They spoke for a few more minutes and then said goodbye. She stood there in the bedroom for a moment looking around. It was hard to believe that just a few hours ago, Serena had been standing here with her as she'd packed a bag. She remembered the panic attack she'd almost had when Serena stood in front of her holding the sunglasses Annie had lost. Her gaze swung to the dresser, where she'd left the glasses. They weren't there. That was funny. She clearly remembered putting them back down on the dresser, right next to the basket where she kept all her barrettes. She walked to the dresser and searched under it, thinking maybe they'd fallen off.

Nothing.

She stood still, her mind turning. But she was too tired to try and figure it out. She walked into the living room and curled up next to

Brody on the couch. Laying her head on his shoulder, she sighed when he put an arm around her. They stayed like that for a long time, neither of them moving or speaking, as they gazed at their son, safe and asleep across the room.

◆ ◆ ◆

The next morning, Annie opened her eyes to find Brody gone from the bed. Marley lifted his head off his bed on the floor by Annie's side and got up when she did. She hadn't slept much, but was wide awake. She walked out of the bedroom with Marley following with a slight limp, and checked on Finn, relieved that he was sleeping peacefully. It was too early to call the vet, but she would as soon as they opened.

She grabbed her phone off the breakfast bar, where it was charging, and then paused when she saw Serena's phone next to hers. Someone must have found it on the couch, where Annie remembered seeing it last. She picked it up and looked at the picture on the lock screen. And now, knowing what she knew, she realized it was the lake in New York. That was why it had looked familiar. She dropped Serena's phone back on the counter. She'd have to give it to the police.

Marley followed her as she went to the hook by the door and took down the towel that she'd hung there yesterday. She stopped when she caught sight of Serena's windbreaker. The woman was gone, but she'd left pieces of herself all over the ohana. With a sigh, Annie opened the front door and slipped out quietly with Marley. She used the towel to dry one of the chairs on the lanai, then sat down, pulling her legs up and wrapping her arms around them. It was so peaceful this morning, the first hints of sunlight highlighting the damage the storm had done last night. Fallen palm leaves were everywhere, debris and dirt washed up against buildings and the street and driveway littered with branches and leaves. Their lawn and driveway were still flooded, but the water had receded a lot, only about ankle deep. The air was calm and the chickens roamed about again, the roosters crowing as they chased the hens.

How was it only yesterday that Serena had knocked on her door? How had she not known the woman even twenty-four hours ago, yet now, she knew so much about her and her life? They were still searching for her, and Annie wondered at the optimism. She didn't believe Serena was still alive. She was almost sure she was gone.

Annie picked up her phone and scrolled to the selfie she'd taken of herself and Serena yesterday. She studied it, noting how happy they'd looked, how she'd been so sure they were going to be fast friends. She sighed and closed out the picture, putting the phone down on the table next to the chair.

She looked up when Brody's car rolled through the water into the driveway. Where had he gone so early in the morning?

Brody got out of the car holding several small white paper bags. She knew what they were: croissants from Haole Girl Island Sweets, her favorite pastry shop. When he reached her, he held one out.

"Is this the Havarti-and-mushroom croissant?" Annie asked, her voice shaky.

"You know it." He pointed at the bag. "And there's a passionfruit curd with cream cheese in there too."

Her heart swelled with love for her husband. He'd gotten up early and bought her two favorite croissants. He remembered how much she loved them. How had he put up with her all these years? She stood and wrapped her arms around him, pulling him close. She hoped she could convey what getting these treats meant to her, especially this morning. Because right now, she couldn't find the words to express to him how much he meant to her.

"I got the ham-and-cheese one for me and Finn, whenever he wakes up."

Annie pulled away and smiled at him. "Thank you."

"You want to stay out here? You look like you could use some alone time to have an orgy with them." He smirked at her, and she reached out and slapped his butt.

"Yeah. Leave me to my love affair."

He pulled her close and, after a deep kiss, went into the ohana.

Annie looked at Marley. "You know I have the best husband, right? I've been such an idiot. I almost lost him."

Marley dipped his head down as if nodding in agreement.

Annie laughed. "Don't agree with me, Marley. You're supposed to be on my side."

She sat back down and took out a croissant. Taking a bite, she savored the tang of the cheese and the deep mushroom flavor in her mouth. She broke off a piece of the croissant and gave it to Marley, who took it politely.

Grief welled inside her, catching her by surprise as she flashed on the moment when Serena fell into the river. She'd been ready to come back; Annie was sure of it. But now she was missing, and Annie couldn't shake the feeling she'd failed her somehow. At the same time, she was having a hard time reconciling the woman who'd tried to bash her over the head with a wine bottle with the woman she'd genuinely liked and thought would become a good friend. She wished Serena's car had never broken down on the street, that Serena had never knocked on her door.

Thinking of the car, Annie jolted up, putting the pastry down on the small table next to the chairs. In the chaos last night, she'd never told the police why Serena had been at her house. She hadn't told them about Serena's dead car. It must still be stuck on their cul-de-sac. She slipped her feet into flip-flops and told Marley to stay. She splashed down the driveway, wading through the water, but Marley followed her anyway. Great, now he'd be all dirty again, after the bath Sam had given him last night. She stopped, uncertain what to do. She wanted to go back and put Marley in the house, but he was all wet and she'd have to stop and wipe him off. Her urgency to get to Serena's car won out.

"Fine, Marley. You can come."

With the dog following closely at her side, she half walked, half waded down the street, and there it was. An unfamiliar white car. Picking up the pace, she stopped at the car and tried the door, surprised when it opened. She let Marley into the back seat, and closed the door behind him. Rather than wade around to the driver's side, Annie got in on the passenger side. She closed the door and, when she turned, saw that the keys were in the ignition.

Tilting her head to the side, she contemplated the keys, her hand reaching out toward them, almost as if they had a mind of their own. She hesitated a moment and then turned the ignition, wondering why she was so surprised when the car started right away. She knew for sure now the broken-down car had been a ruse.

Shutting the engine off, Annie sat back against the seat and stretched her legs to get more comfortable. Her foot connected with something on the floor. Looking down, she saw a brown tote bag. She stared at it for a moment, then reached down to pick it up. She'd have to tell the police about the car, have someone come get it. But before she did, curiosity about Serena swept through her, a puzzle that Annie had to figure out.

She opened the tote and rummaged inside. There was a change of clothes, a hat and a wallet, along with the usual things found in a woman's bag—tissues, wipes, ChapStick, and a bottle of water. There was also a laptop. Annie took it out and rested it in her lap for a moment, knowing it was too much to hope that there'd be a clue in there somewhere. She opened it, expecting to be asked for a password, since Serena's phone had been password protected, but to her surprise, it opened right to the desktop. It was pretty sparse, only a few files on the outer edges. It took her a moment, but then her eyes focused on a file stored right in the middle of the screen. The file was named "ANNIE."

The breath whooshed out of her as she stared at it. Then she clicked on it with Marley breathing behind her. There was only one document in the folder, and it was entitled "For Annie."

Annie opened it, her heart pounding, and began to read. She skimmed through the entries, a bit from this one, some from another. And with each entry, her mouth dropped open a little more with shock.

48

Laptop ANNIE file

When he was about six months old, he started to push himself up into a crawling position. I was so proud. Our son was so ahead of schedule, and I knew he'd grow up to be something really smart, like a scientist who finds cures for cancer. Or even the president of the United States. He'd be the first half-Asian president of the US! And I'd be his proud mother, finally knowing my place in his life. How do they refer to the mother of the president? The First Mother? I'd be down for being called that. I'd rather be the first mother than the second mother. Or the wrong mother.

After he was gone, I was fine for a while. At least I thought I was. I rented a small apartment and continued to go to work, living my life as if I hadn't just lost my son and him. And I kept going through life like nothing had happened for a couple of weeks until one day, I just couldn't. I couldn't get out of bed. I couldn't get dressed. I couldn't do anything. I stayed in bed and when my cell rang with work asking where I was, I just stared at it without picking up. I don't know how long I stayed that way, until I woke one morning and knew I needed help. I wasn't depressed. I just needed help, needed someone to care enough about me to tell me what to do, even if I was paying them to do that.

I thought with longing of my stays at the hospital when he'd forced me to go, and how relieved I was when I actually got there. I needed someone to tell me what to do again. I needed my days to be regimented. I couldn't be left to myself, drifting through life without an anchor and no one to care if I floated away or didn't show up for work.

I dragged myself out of bed and found the card for the facility and I called. For once, I did something right for myself. I was in and out of there for the next year or so. And in between, when I was home, I watched you.

I did some research and it shocked me how surprisingly easy it is to travel with a child within the United States. You don't have to provide any form of ID. You just buy the child a ticket in any name and they let him through. No questions asked. No photos to compare to, like they do with adults and their IDs. If I wasn't using it for my own gain, I'd be terrified at how easy it is to take a child and just travel anywhere with them. I'm surprised more children haven't disappeared, given the ease with which you can take a child to another state with no ID whatsoever.

Maybe one day, we'll even come back here to Kauai, when he can look back on this time and say, "Remember when you came to get me? Thank you, Mommy. I was waiting for you. I always knew you'd come find me, your real son."

Oh. My. God. Annie looked up in shock as she clicked on another entry. Reading about how Serena had planned on taking Finn and leaving with him . . . Annie's heart pounded at the thought. What would she and Brody have done if Serena had carried out her plan? It was obvious she had some kind of mental disorder. Annie made a note to look it up later. But right now, there was more to the file that Serena had left for her. Despite the dread filling her body, she kept reading, unable to look away.

I've changed my mind. After watching you for weeks, I realized, just like in New York after what happened, you never let him out of your sight. And now there's your father and sister. And neighbors. My son is never left alone, not even at home. So I need to change tactics.

I think the best way to do this is to just tell you that he is my son. My father always taught me honesty is the best policy and I think he may be right in this case. If I steal my son, people will be looking for me. But if I ask you for my son back, perhaps you'd just give him to me. Watching you all these years, I know you're a kindhearted person. You will understand the pain I've been in, losing everything. I need to befriend you, make you like me, and then I'm sure you'll understand and want to make things right.

Annie looked up, gazing out the window. Serena had planned this. She'd befriended Annie with a motive. All so Annie would just hand Finn over when she asked. A spark of anger and sorrow lit within her, that she'd been so easily duped.

She looked down and kept reading.

I'm happy. For the first time in a long time, I didn't wake up burdened, feeling as if the world was pressing down on me, trying to choke me and drown me. I didn't feel as if my limbs were so heavy that it was all I could do to swing my legs out of the bed. For the first time in a long time, my body felt light, like I could drift away. If I'd known finally having a plan to get my little boy back would free me like this, I would have done it earlier.

It's like I'm watching a video of another me, some- one who looks like me but that I don't feel is me. And this other me does things that I would never do in real life. This other me forgets things, like putting the car seat with my son in it on the driveway while I unloaded the groceries, and only realizing hours later that he wasn't in the house with me. This other me would go into the kitchen to warm up his formula, and then hours later, find myself at the grocery store, wondering how I got there and why my infant son wasn't with me. And this other me watches as I replay a familiar reel in my head from long ago, when I was ten.

It was a week after the judge had given my father full custody of me. My mother had picked me up, along with the social worker that had to be there for all our visits. She took us to her favorite national park and we hiked to our favorite hidden spot, at the side of a lake. Before I realized my mother hated me, I had adored her. I would have done anything for her, including go to this isolated spot, away from everyone, that used to scare me because we were in the middle of nowhere. It's funny that my mother liked it here, because she couldn't swim. But she said being out in nature calmed her, especially when the rest of the world was so chaotic.

That day, I could smell the alcohol on her breath. I knew she was drunk. The social worker that was supposed to monitor us had fallen behind, out of shape and out of breath. So it was only the two of us standing on a ledge next to the water. She started walking out onto the rocks in the water, humming a song under her breath and goading me to balance with her on the slippery rocks.

Despite my fear of her, a part of me still loved her, craved her attention. I wanted her to want me, to feel sad that she would no longer be a part of my everyday life. So I walked out with her, hoping this was going to be a bonding moment. But she turned to me and said, "I'm so glad to be rid of you. You've been nothing but a burden since you came into this world. Now my life can finally begin." She gave me this self-satisfied smile, and my grief overflowed. The mother that I loved and feared really didn't want me. A fury took over my ten-year-old self and I was consumed by the hatred I could feel coming out of her for me.

My love for her turned into pure anger and betrayal in that moment. When she turned away from me, as if I was nothing more than a speck of dirt in that park, I couldn't take it anymore. I rushed at her, wanting to inflict as much pain on her as she had on me. But I slipped on the rocks and I crashed into her with so much force that she went flying into the water. I sprawled there on the rocks not moving, watching the spot where she'd gone in. She hadn't even tried to save herself. She'd just sunk like a stone, probably because she'd been so drunk and the fall had taken her by surprise. When she didn't come back up, I stood and carefully picked my way back to shore. I waited there until the social worker finally caught up to me, puffing as she came into view.

When she asked where my mother was, I burst into tears and threw myself at her, sobbing that she'd left me again. That my mother had told me she hated me and was so glad to be rid of me, and then ran off, leaving me by myself. The social worker was a motherly type, plump and kind, just like what I always thought a real mother should be like. And she gathered me into her arms and shushed me, told me I would be okay, that my father loves me and I wasn't to pay any mind to what my mother said. That she did love me, deep down, but she has issues she needed to work on before she could be my mother again.

As she crushed me to her, I let myself smile, knowing that my mother would never again say anything mean to me or hit me again. Because she was gone forever.

And that is the reel that plays over and over in my head when I least expect it, until I wonder if it really happened, or if I made the whole thing up in order to justify why I haven't heard from my mother in all these years.

But it doesn't matter anymore if that actually happened or not. Because my life is about to begin again. Today is the day I will finally meet you and convince you to give me back my son.

49

Annie slammed the laptop shut, her thoughts in turmoil. Serena had killed her mother? Annie gave an involuntary shiver and looked around. Her ears perked up when she suddenly felt that familiar sensation of being watched. She listened, eyes scanning the cul-de-sac for any movement. But she was alone. Was she only imagining it, or were there eyes on her?

She could hear the helicopter above, as the rescue mission for Serena continued. Behind her, Marley yawned and Annie reached a hand back to rub his head. She had to be imagining it. Because all those other times she'd thought someone was watching her, it had been Serena. But Serena was still missing, somewhere in the water. Even though they'd been told that the victim was assumed alive for at least three days, Annie was sure Serena had drowned. Just like her mother.

Blowing out a breath, Annie got out of the passenger side, clutching the laptop to her chest. Without consciously realizing it, she'd decided to take it before letting the police know about Serena's car. She tightened her grip on it, let Marley out of the back seat, and waded back to their property. She placed the laptop on one of the chairs on the lanai before opening the door.

"There you are," Brody said, from where he was playing cars with Finn on the floor. "We were just going to look for you."

She smiled at them. "Can you get me a dry towel?" The one she'd used earlier was crumpled on the floor of the lanai.

She waited outside until Brody brought one over, and then she wiped off her legs and feet before toweling Marley off. Carefully, she wrapped the laptop in the towel and went inside.

Marley walked over to Brody and flopped down, turning his belly up. Brody scratched his belly and Finn giggled. He flipped over too, stomach up.

"Me too, Daddy," Finn said. "Rub my belly too."

Brody reached out and tickled Finn on the stomach, causing him to break out in peals of giggles. Brody looked up and met Annie's eyes. They smiled at each other, even as she wondered at the resilience of children. Finn didn't appear troubled by the previous night's events. He was laughing and playing. She hoped that meant his nightmares wouldn't intensify.

She took the laptop into the bedroom and buried it at the bottom of one of her drawers. For some reason, she didn't want to tell Brody about it yet. Maybe she never would. She had to think about it, decide what to do with the information in the laptop.

As much havoc as Serena had wreaked in their lives, she'd also made Annie see how blessed she was. She would do anything for Finn. He was her world, even if she'd been too mired in depression the last few years to see it. She pushed aside that small nugget of doubt that had been planted when Serena said Finn wasn't Annie's son. She was Finn's mother, and now she would do everything she could to help him get over the trauma of Lindsay's death and what had happened last night.

And if that nugget kept pushing through, whispering that if Finn was really Serena's child, he'd have inherited her DNA too, Annie would push it away. She looked out into the living room at her son's smiling face. He was just an innocent little boy.

◆ ◆ ◆

A few nights after the storm, Brody and Annie walked by the water at Kalapaki Beach, holding hands. They'd just had dinner at Duke's, where Sam had comped them drinks. It'd been so nice to have dinner out, just the two of them. Annie had missed that. The familiarity of splitting their meals because they both loved food and wanted to try everything and being able to just relax and talk without worrying about Finn. Annie had vowed to stop drinking so much and mixing wine with sleeping pills, but she'd let herself have just one glass with dinner.

"I've missed this." Brody's deep voice made Annie look up at him. He stopped in the sand and she halted next to him.

"I was just thinking the same thing." She smiled at him. "I'm so sorry for how I've been acting."

Brody held up a hand. "No more apologizing. I'm just glad you and Finn are okay. And Marley too." They'd taken Marley to the vet the day after Serena disappeared and been relieved that he had no serious injuries. "Let's just move forward, okay?"

Annie nodded. The police had told them yesterday they were no longer searching for a live person. They'd still look, hoping to find her body, but too many days had gone by. The news had hit Annie like a punch in the stomach. She'd known Serena was most likely gone, but she hadn't realized that, in the back of her mind, she'd been still holding out hope. Serena had been sick, but there was a woman in there that Annie had really connected with.

As soon as she'd gotten off the phone with the police, she'd driven up to Kealia Beach with Marley, just the two of them. They'd sat in the sand for most of the day, gazing out at the ocean and the surfers bobbing in the waves. Brody had let her go, and his trust in her that she'd come back was what finally pushed Annie to realize she wanted help in feeling better.

She'd made an appointment to see a therapist for next week, and had even taken Finn to his appointment yesterday after her solitary day on the beach. She'd come back calmer. What had happened with Serena had scared her. She was ready to start living again, to be Brody's wife and Finn's mother. This was her family. She would do anything for them, fight anyone for them.

Determined to do just that, she squeezed Brody's hand. "Let's put in an offer for the house in the Wailua Homesteads by Sleeping Giant."

Brody's eyes lit up. "Really? You liked it?"

"Yes." Annie squeezed his hand again. "This is our new beginning. The one thing Serena made me realize was how much you and Finn and my family mean to me."

Brody's face darkened for a moment. "My heart still stops every time I think about that night and what she'd been doing to our family all these years."

"We don't have to worry about her anymore." *Or her crazy idea that Finn is her son.* "She's gone. Finn loves going to preschool with Leila, and I'm going to start looking for a job. I don't know what I'm going to do yet, but I'm going to look."

"That's great." He smiled at her.

"And someone told me about an adult ballet class down in Kalaheo. I think it might be good for me to dance again." Annie stared out at the ocean, watching the waves crash gently at the shore. "Just for myself. I don't think I want to teach, but I miss dancing. Moving." She turned back to him. "You know?"

He nodded. "I do. It was such a big part of your life. It was your outlet. And then you just stopped. It might make you feel better to dance again."

"I'm going to figure myself out, Brody. For you, and for Finn." She took a deep breath. "And for myself."

Brody slung an arm around her shoulder and pulled her close. Dropping a kiss on top of her head, he said, "Welcome back, Annie. I've missed you."

"I've missed me too. And you, of course." She smiled softly as Brody leaned down to kiss her, so thankful he was willing to give them another chance.

50

A week later, on Sunday, Annie took Finn to Poipu Beach, just the two of them. Brody was playing golf with some of the guys he'd met on the island, and Annie wanted to spend more time with Finn. He talked the whole way down in the car, something he'd rarely done in the past when they were by themselves. Hot Chocolate sat next to him, but Annie had noticed her son hadn't been clutching him tight the way he used to, ever since he started going to preschool with Leila. He seemed completely unaffected by the night with Serena, and if that made Annie wonder, she pushed the thought aside. She was happy Finn wasn't as traumatized as he'd been with Lindsay.

They stopped at Da Crack, a Mexican takeout spot in Koloa, for burrito bowls to take to the beach. Once they got to Poipu, Annie staked out an area for them by the big palm tree at the kiddie area. They were far enough away not to disturb the honu sunning itself in the sand, but close enough that they could watch the giant turtle if it started moving.

Annie stretched out on her stomach facing the ocean and dug her toes into the white sand. It was a glorious Kauai day, the sun shining and the water sparkling. The warm sun beating down felt good. Finn was in the shallow water splashing around with a group of kids, and her heart warmed every time she heard his happy laugh. She closed her eyes briefly, knowing there were at least a dozen parents around watching all the kids. Besides, she could hear Finn's chatter over the crash of the waves.

"Mommy, Mommy. Look!"

Finn's cries had her sitting up, as her heart jumped into her throat. But then she saw he was pointing to another turtle, who was lumbering its way up the sand toward the one sunning itself. The two turtles started playing, batting their flippers at each other and lifting their heads off the sand. A crowd gathered around, staying well back from the markers warning people to keep their distance.

Finn sat down in Annie's lap and pointed and laughed at the turtles. She put her arms around him, loving the feel of him against her. They watched the turtles together until Finn turned to her.

"I'm hungry." He got off her lap and tried to unzip the soft-sided cooler.

"Let's eat, then." She helped him with the zipper and pulled out their burrito bowls. She handed him the chicken one, and he dug in. They ate in silence, watching the snorkelers out beyond the kiddie section, the water sparkling and glittering in the sun. They glanced at the turtles from time to time to see if they'd moved. When they were full, Annie cleaned up, putting the leftovers back in the cooler. She handed Finn his water bottle and he took a big gulp.

"Mommy." He didn't look at her when he said this.

"Yes?" Annie paused, her hand still on the zipper of the cooler.

"I have to tell you something." Finn put his water bottle down and finally turned to look at her, his little face twisted up in concern.

"You can tell me anything." Annie finished zipping the cooler and tried to appear nonchalant, when inside, her heart was hammering wildly.

Finn didn't speak. He stared at her, his lower lip sticking out.

"What is it, Finn? I'm here. You can tell me anything."

"Anything?" His eyes found hers.

"Yes." She reached out and pulled him against her, so that his side touched hers. "Okay?"

"I won't get in trouble?"

"No. You won't." She kissed him on the top of his head. "You're my Finnie boy."

There was a pause, and then he said, "It's about Lindsay."

Annie's heart pounded so loud she was surprised Finn couldn't hear. "It's okay. Tell me about Lindsay."

"I . . . She . . ." Finn's face went blank, and Annie tightened her arms around him.

"It's okay, really. Mommy's here."

"Lindsay fell." He turned his face away, no longer looking at her. "I tried to help her up . . . after that woman was so mean. I pulled as hard as I could . . ." He stared out at the ocean as Annie searched his face.

"It's okay," she said softly. "Whatever it is, it's going to be okay."

"I didn't mean to. I . . ." He leaned sideways until his head rested against Annie's arm. "I let go. I thought she was playing. I laughed. It was slippery—" He broke off.

Annie turned him so that she could console him, hold him close. But when she caught sight of his eyes, the bottom dropped out of her stomach. He looked so . . . detached. His face was blank. Exactly the way the therapist in New York had told them Finn was at every session. Annie stared at him, barely breathing, until he spoke again.

"She fell back. Hard." He looked out over the ocean again. "Her head . . . It hit a rock."

Annie closed her eyes and pulled Finn tight against her. All around them, kids played happily, splashing in the water as their parents watched. Tourists and locals alike enjoyed the warm day, taking advantage of the rays and cooling off in the ocean. Yet here on their blanket, Annie and Finn were wrapped in a cocoon, just the two of them, as she tried to make sense of his words. The doubt that she'd pushed away when Serena died started to creep its way back in. She squeezed her eyes shut, not wanting to give it credence.

"It was my fault, right?" Finn asked.

"Oh . . ." Annie may have had doubts, but she was not going to let Finn think he was responsible. "No, it's not." Her voice was firm. "It was an accident, okay? You didn't cause Lindsay's death."

"But . . . if I hadn't let go?" He turned to face her. "Am I a bad boy?"

"No, Finn. No. It was an accident." Annie would not doubt him.

"Bad boys get punished." He gazed at her steadily. "They get punished like Hot Chocolate."

"What?" A chill went up Annie's spine. "What did Hot Chocolate do?"

"He was a bad boy, so I punished him." Finn's eyes were clear, his little face innocent. "Over there by the rocks." He pointed to one of the rock walls that kept the waves from the shallow kiddie area.

"What do you mean?" Annie searched his face as prickles broke out on the back of her neck.

"Then I buried him, just like they do for dead people." Finn's voice was matter-of-fact, as if relaying what he'd just eaten. "Like for Lindsay."

Annie sucked in a breath. They hadn't taken Finn to Lindsay's wake or funeral. He'd stayed with Brody's sister's family. "How do you know what happens to dead people?"

"My cousins told me."

Ah. Brody's sister's kids.

"I miss Lindsay. I loved her." Finn's voice was so soft it got carried away in the breeze, but Annie heard him.

"I know, buddy. I know." She rocked him, but she didn't know if the gesture was to soothe him or her. That prickle in her neck was spreading throughout her body. "She was so good to you. She always played games with you."

"I'm sorry, Mommy. Am I going to be punished now?" Annie heard his words, but it was the way he said them, something in his tone, that felt off.

Blood roaring in her ears, Annie pulled away so she could look into Finn's eyes. And when all she saw was her sweet little boy and not a miniature sociopath in the making, she made a decision. "You did nothing wrong. Okay? It was an accident. What happened to Lindsay was an accident."

She would help him through this, tell his therapist what he'd just confessed to her, and they would all help him get past this. He was just an innocent little boy. When he finally nodded and wrapped his little arms around her, she pulled him close, feeling his heart beat against her. And if that seed of doubt had planted itself into the very back of her mind that he was Serena's child and taking after her, she steeled herself and willed it away, not wanting to let it take over her thoughts. She would defeat it.

When Finn ran back into the water, Annie slowly stood. She looked at the rock wall and walked in the direction Finn had pointed. As she drew closer to the large black rocks, she saw a fresh mound of sand. Using her foot, she brushed at it and found Hot Chocolate, facedown and soaking wet, buried in the sand. Her breath caught and her heart tripped when she saw all the small rocks Finn must have piled on top of Hot Chocolate, as if weighing him down. Finn had "drowned" Hot Chocolate, just like Serena and her mother had drowned.

Annie tried to return to her normal life. She'd left Hot Chocolate at the beach, and Finn hadn't mentioned the bear again. She'd told Finn's therapist about it, and he'd reassured her that it could be a way for Finn to process his guilt over what had happened with Lindsay. But he suggested they keep an eye on him, watch for any warning signs. Annie hadn't been able to speak. She'd gone home and googled the list the therapist had given her. And found a whole new world to obsess over as she thought back to the lies Finn had told so easily in the past. She hadn't told Brody about the Hot Chocolate incident. She would watch him closely herself.

But as much as she tried to forget about Serena and her delusions, she just couldn't get everything that had happened lately out of her mind. When she and Finn took Marley on walks, she'd find herself staring at him, looking for any resemblance to Serena. When she picked him up from preschool, she'd watch the way he interacted with the other children. (Was he detached? Was it normal to not react when all the other kids were clapping and singing?) And when someone at Safeway remarked how much he looked like her while they were grocery shopping, she'd smiled, but then studied his face, wondering if he really was her son.

Had Serena been delusional? Or was she right, and Finn wasn't Annie's? Was that why Annie had always had trouble bonding with him? Had Annie's real child died when he was almost one, possibly killed by Serena? She grew frustrated, often admonishing herself out loud to stop it. Stop letting Serena's words worm their way into her mind.

Pollie had come across Annie berating herself one day at the shelter and laughed. "You yelling at yourself now?" Annie had clamped her lips together, embarrassed. Even though Serena was gone, she continued to haunt Annie's days and nights until Annie couldn't take it anymore. She had to know for sure if Finn was hers.

While Finn was in preschool one day, Annie googled maternity tests. She could do the test at home and send it off in the mail, getting the results in one to two business days after the company received the samples. She ordered a kit without telling Brody. She'd simply do the test, prove Serena wrong and that Finn was hers, and then she could put this chapter of her life behind her and never think about Serena and her delusional stories again. She refused to contemplate what she would do if the test proved Serena right. It just wasn't a possibility.

The day after she ordered the kit, Annie and Brody took Finn out on the Wailua River on two paddleboards, at the therapist's suggestion. The river was calm, all the debris from the storm gone. It was hard to believe this was the same river that had taken Serena's life. Annie didn't want Finn to be afraid to go out on the river after that night—hence this trip. She knew he would feel safe on Brody's board with him. They paddled out away from their dock and around the bend with nothing but the mountains surrounding them. The river was quiet, only a couple of kayakers off in the distance. She pushed the paddle into the water hard, needing the physical activity to keep the slight tremor in her hands at bay. Finn wasn't the only one who needed to get over his fear of the river after that night.

Brody put his paddle down once they were in the middle of the ocean and dived into the river, making Finn squeal. He jumped in after Brody, bobbing up from his life vest. Annie studied her little boy from her board, squinting in the sunlight. He'd gone in with no fear or hesitation. Was that normal after what had happened on the river that stormy night?

Annie watched as Brody swam back to the paddleboard so they wouldn't lose it. She put her own paddle down sideways across the board, sliding one end under the bungee cord. She stood again and gazed across the river. It was so peaceful here, much like the lake in New York.

While Brody and Finn frolicked in the water, she itched to move, to stop the thoughts in her mind. She wanted to dance again, like she'd once done every day. Shifting her body weight until it was mostly in her right leg, she extended her left leg behind her. Pointing her toes, she lifted her arms up, taking a tendu back position on the board. When she was dancing professionally, she'd had the best balance of anyone in the ballet company. She wasn't the best dancer, oh no. She was too short, or too fat, not talented enough, according to the artistic director. But even he couldn't fault the "little Asian girl" who could balance on one foot in arabesque en pointe for what seemed like forever.

Slowly, testing her balance, she lifted her back leg in an arabesque, humming the tune to "Dance of the Sugar Plum Fairy" from *The Nutcracker*. As her back leg rose to hip level, her confidence returned, fingers poised, chin up. For one glorious, perfect moment, she was balanced in arabesque on the paddleboard, imagining she could hear the applause from the audience.

But then Finn shouted to her and she jerked in reaction. Arms flailing, she tried to regain her balance, but she wasn't on a sturdy dance floor. She was on a rocky paddleboard that swayed with each flail, and she knew she was going over. She let out a scream as she tried to launch herself away from the board so that she wouldn't hit her head on it. Her last image before she splashed into the river was of Finn and Brody just a few feet away, watching as she plunged into the water.

Annie came up sputtering, pushing her hair out of her eyes.

"Are you okay?"

Brody's voice was laced with laughter, and she could hear Finn hooting at her. Water stung her eyes, and her hair was plastered to her face. She groped out and one hand connected with her board. Pulling herself forward so that her arms and upper body were draped over the board, she finally blinked enough to be able to peer out through the strands of her black hair. She turned and saw her husband grinning widely at her.

"I'm fine." Her voice came out like a croak.

"You want a hand back up?"

"No, no." Annie waved a hand, as if brushing away flies. "I've got this." She turned her back on them and heaved herself up on the paddleboard. This was not her most graceful performance, sprawled half-on, half-off the board, her bikini bottom bunched up in her ass crack so that she knew she was giving Brody a more than generous glimpse of her backside. But that was okay, right? She was keeping their relationship spicy. She finally flopped onto the board and pushed herself up into a kneeling position.

"That was beautiful, Mommy," Finn yelled. "Before you fell in."

He broke out in laughter, and Brody joined him. Annie glowered at them, but then she started laughing, until all three of them were hooting, their laughter echoing on the river.

51

The kit arrived two days later. She managed to get a mouth swab from Finn by playing doctor with him, so she wouldn't scare him. She did the same for herself and then, following the directions on the DNA maternity kit, sent both of their samples back to the company. And then she waited. The instructions had said the results would be sent to her by email, so she tried to put the test out of her mind. She and Brody put in an offer on the house, which was accepted, and they celebrated by taking Finn up to Hanalei for an afternoon.

She was doing better. She had coffee with Kalani one morning and was surprised when she enjoyed her neighbor's company. Maybe they would be friends after all. She took Marley for long walks on the Kapaa bike trail, running sometimes, feeling her body come back to its former strong self. She took a ballet class for the first time in four years, her muscles trembling from exertion but elation building in her heart. She talked to Julia and Izzy on FaceTime, reassuring them she was okay, and made plans for them to come visit her in Kauai soon.

On Saturday, she went to the Puhi Grove Farm Market in Lihue with Brody and Finn, where they picked up fresh vegetables and fruits from the various stands. Finn got the pancit noodles he loved from the Manna on Wheels Filipino food stand there, while Annie got the kalbi beef plate from the Kauai Kim Chee stand that she dreamed about all week. They went to Shipwreck Beach with Sam and Cam on Sunday, and on Monday, Annie volunteered at the shelter, where she fell in love with a little chiweenie with big ears standing straight up that the shelter had named Ho'o Hui. She knew the little dog would get adopted quickly, so she spent most of the afternoon with her, holding her and giving the scared little thing as much love as she could.

And when, after dinner that night, she checked her email and saw she had a message from the company where she'd sent their DNA, she ignored the beating of her heart and tried to put it out of her mind until she'd gotten Finn ready for bed and Brody was in the bedroom watching TV. Only then did she allow herself to stop and settle on the couch. Her hand reached slowly for her laptop, and she pulled up her email. Taking a big breath, she opened it, ready to finally put this nightmare behind her.

Annie stared at her computer screen. For a second, she actually stopped breathing. Her mind wasn't comprehending what her eyes were seeing. She sat there, frozen in shock. This couldn't be happening.

Finn was not her biological son. They were 100 percent certain. The words swam in front of her. She was going to be sick. How was that possible? Had Serena been right, and her son and Annie's had been switched at the hospital? How could that possibly happen in this day and age?

But in the next moment, Annie remembered how she'd felt that first rush of love for Finn when they placed him on her chest right after his birth. And then she never felt it again. She'd had trouble bonding with him, but had blamed it on everything that had happened to her that year. She'd been so sure Serena was wrong, and that she was as delusional as that file she'd left Annie had shown. But the proof was right there in front of her. Finn was not her biological son.

Slowly, Annie placed the computer next to her on the couch and rose. She crept over to where Finn was sleeping and stared down at him. Her little boy. Who wasn't hers. If Serena's story was correct, Annie's baby had died before he turned one. This was Serena's child. Tears stinging in her eyes, Annie turned away, putting a hand over her mouth to muffle her sob. What was she going to do? Should she tell Brody that this wasn't their child? Or should she keep this to herself?

They loved Finn, and Serena was gone. What good would it do if they both knew Finn wasn't theirs? They couldn't give him back. They couldn't get their real son back either. Finn *was* their real son. They'd raised him, been his parents his whole life, and a DNA test wasn't going to make that go away. There was no reason to disrupt the fragile bond they'd formed ever since the night of the storm. He was theirs.

Needing air, Annie swept up her cell phone from the coffee table and went to the front door. She signaled to Marley, who had been lying on the floor next to the couch, and they slipped outside quietly. She needed to get out of the ohana, needed some space. Walking over to one of the two chairs on the lanai, Annie sank down, her shoulders slumped. Her mind spun out of control and adrenaline coursed through her body. Deep down, she knew what she had to do. The thought made her sick, but she had no choice. She had to protect her family.

Heaving out a breath, she made her decision. She wouldn't tell Brody, but it was a burden she wished she didn't have to carry alone. Shifting her weight, Annie realized she'd sat on something in the chair.

Rising up, she used the flashlight on her phone to see what it was. Her breath caught. It was her sunglasses. The pair Serena had admitted to taking out of her purse and that she'd found in her bedroom but that had then disappeared again. They sat in front of her now, next to a small square envelope. Goose bumps broke out all over Annie's skin as she looked around with apprehension. She picked up the envelope and took out a card, which had only one sentence written in all capital letters on it: *HE'S MY SON.*

Dropping the card so that it fluttered to the ground, Annie scanned the yard. Her heart pounded when the door behind her opened.

"Mommy?"

It was Finn, standing in the doorway in his Snoopy pj's.

"Finn." She placed a hand over her heart. "What are you doing out of bed?"

"I saw you come out here." He looked up at her, his head tilted in question. He scanned the yard like Annie had just done. "Is that woman back?"

She went to him and drew him near, kneeling down so that she could look into his eyes. Serena's green eyes stared back at her. How had she never noticed that Finn had Serena's eyes? Ice, sharp and jagged, ran through her veins. But this was Finn, her little boy.

"Why are you out here?" His little voice was so sweet, so precious to her.

"I'm . . ." She stopped, hugging him close. But then the back of her neck tingled.

Annie rubbed her head as her heart rate raced and her breath came in short gasps. Someone was watching them. She could feel it, feel those eyes that had watched her so often over the years trained on her now. But how was that possible? Serena was dead, swept out to sea. Annie's breath caught, and she forced herself to calm down so she wouldn't scare Finn as she focused on getting air into her lungs. When she could breathe normally again, she stood and sank down onto the chair, pulling him into her lap.

Had Serena survived the storm somehow? Was she out there somewhere, watching Annie again? Had she lied and been able to swim? Was she back to claim her child? A shudder of fear ran down her spine, and she hugged Finn closer. They'd never found Serena's body. The woman who had killed her mother, her son, and Lindsay. No, not Lindsay. That had been an accident. Unless the little boy in her arms had . . . She wouldn't think of that. Was Serena really out there right now? Or was Annie finally losing her mind?

"No." Annie whispered the word. "No," she said again, stronger this time.

"Mommy?" Finn turned his head to look at her.

"Yes. Yes. I'm your mommy. I love you. All of you, no matter who you are." She stared fiercely down at him.

He was her son. It didn't matter what the DNA test said, or that he might have parts of Serena in him. It didn't matter that he might end up being a sociopath with delusional disorder like Serena in the future and carry on whatever mental illness ran in their blood. He was her son, hers and Brody's, and she'd never abandon him. She would do anything for him, would help him, no matter what. They'd figure it out. Her heart contracted with this fierce love for him, and she realized all her doubts since he'd been born were gone. She would not tell Brody. He never needed to know the truth and doubt Finn. They would be a happy family.

Breathing deeply, she willed her heart to slow down and for her mind to clear. She was not losing her mind. She was getting better, going to therapy. She wasn't mixing drugs and alcohol anymore. As her breath finally slowed, Annie raised her head. She wasn't going to allow Serena, if she was really out there, to fuck with her mind anymore. This was her life, not Serena's. She was not going to doubt her own sanity anymore. That woman had played with Annie's mind for the last time.

Annie rose from the chair, putting Finn on her hip. Serena had manipulated them all long enough. It was time to put a stop to it, right here and now. She would hide Serena's laptop, keep it safe with proof of all the things the other woman had done. If Serena had the gall to come back, rising from the dead to take Finn, Annie would use it if she needed to. She would fight for her family, no matter what it took.

Squaring her shoulders, she stared out into the darkness, daring Serena to show herself. She stood there for a long time, Finn in her arms, her ears pricked for any unusual movement or sound. But all she heard was Marley's quiet pant next to her, Finn's breath tickling her ear, and the occasional clucking of chickens and a rooster crowing in the distance. When she finally spoke, her voice was strong, and it echoed into the night. "He's *my* son."

She lifted her chin and waited one more minute, daring Serena to come fight her. When nothing happened, she hitched Finn higher on her hip, and he wrapped his arms around her neck. With Marley following them, she carried her son back inside, shutting the door firmly behind her.

ACKNOWLEDGMENTS

I must first thank my amazing agent, Rachel Brooks—without her, I wouldn't be writing acknowledgments. Thank you for hearing me out when I said I'd accidentally written a thriller (and a YA and a rom-com, on top of women's fiction), all before my debut even came out. I am forever grateful for your brilliant mind and that you never use the word "soon."

Thank you to my editor Jessica Tribble Wells for being excited about this project. It is such an honor to get to work with you. To my developmental editor, Andrea Hurst: I know you won't admit how worried you were when you got the first draft, but I know you were horrified! LOL. I'm so glad I was able to put your fears to rest, and your edits were spot-on. Thank you also to the rest of the team at Thomas and Mercer: Rachael Herbert, Sarah Shaw, Kellie Osborne, Jill Schoenhaut, Jarrod Taylor, and Ploy Siripant.

My love of animals led me to volunteer at the Kauai Humane Society when I lived in Kauai for two months researching this book. Special thanks to Kim Foster, who became not only a volunteer buddy but a friend, always willing to answer my questions about Kauai. Thank you also to Jason Bartlett, Becky Oishi, Ally Kirk, Alyssa Friedberg, Daniel Madeira, Bridgette Semana, Malyssa Jardin, and Dida Kim for many memorable moments at KHS.

I was fortunate to have had the help of some amazing and generous people on Kauai who were willing to answer my questions, even the creepy ones where I asked how someone can die on the Wailua River. Thank you to Jaben Schalk, Farren Higley, Richard Duarte, Kurt Javinar, and Cameron Ventura. Special thanks to Pollie Donahue, the amazing person who got me out of Kauai when my own Lili was dying back in New York, and to Captain Reid Tanita of the Lihue Fire Department for answering all my questions about what happens when someone falls into the Wailua River and the rescue mission. Any mistakes are my own.

Thank you to my friend Lisa Hauptner, LMHC, a licensed psychotherapist who shared her expertise in mental health with me. And to my Eggplant Writers—Robin Facer, Bradeigh Godfrey, and Alison Hammer—who were the first people to realize this book was in fact a thriller.

Many thanks to my mother and father for all their help and watching our son when I am writing. To Jim: thank you for thinking my harebrained idea of living in Kauai during the pandemic was a great one. And to Lakon, who happily went along on the adventure and helped me find places where accidents can happen. To our dogs, Lokie, Mochi, Cash, and Pinot (in heaven): you are my true writing companions.

And to the readers who have read my books: I couldn't have this dream career without you. Thank you for reading, posting, and talking about my books. Your support means everything to me.

ABOUT THE AUTHOR

Photo © 2020 Dave Cross Photography

Lyn Liao Butler was born in Taiwan and moved to the States when she was seven. Before becoming an author, she was a professional ballet and modern dancer, and is still a personal trainer and fitness and yoga instructor. She is an avid animal lover who fosters dogs and volunteers with rescues. When she is not torturing clients or talking to imaginary characters, Lyn enjoys spending time with her FDNY husband, their son (the happiest little boy in the world), and their three stubborn dachshunds; sewing for her Etsy shop; and trying complicated yoga poses on a stand-up paddleboard. So far, she has not fallen into the water. For more information visit www.lynliaobutler.com.